From the romantic to the sensual . . .
From the first kiss to the grand passion . . .
Nothing does the heart more good than
love . . .

From the humorous to the hilarious . . .
From the amusing to the whimsical . . .
Nothing does the soul more good than
laughter . . .

love
and
laughter

Stories to tickle your funny bone . . .
men to fuel your fantasies!

About the Authors

Elise Title
One of Harlequin's most versatile and prolific authors, Elise Title has written for every contemporary series and is a regular on bestseller lists. Her forte is wildly funny, wildly romantic comedies. Before she began writing full-time, Elise had established a career as a clinical psychologist.

Barbara Bretton
With their wit, emotion and passion, Barbara's thirty-plus books have all become Harlequin reader favorites. She is the recipient of numerous writing awards, is a perennial bestseller, and is listed in *The Foremost Women in the Twentieth Century.* Barbara has written historical and contemporary fiction, with over eight million copies of her books in print worldwide.

Lass Small
This award-winning author has over fifty romances to her credit—thirty published in Silhouette Desire alone—and is published in over fifteen countries worldwide. Lass was distinguished with a lifetime achievement award for writing books of Love and Laughter in 1989 by *Romantic Times.*

love and laughter

Elise Title
Barbara Bretton
Lass Small

Harlequin Books

TORONTO • NEW YORK • LONDON
AMSTERDAM • PARIS • SYDNEY • HAMBURG
STOCKHOLM • ATHENS • TOKYO • MILAN
MADRID • WARSAW • BUDAPEST • AUCKLAND

HARLEQUIN BOOKS

LOVE AND LAUGHTER

Copyright © 1994 by Harlequin Enterprises B.V.

ISBN 0-373-83298-2

The publisher acknowledges the copyright holders of the individual works as follows:
ONE WAY TICKET
Copyright © 1994 by Elise Title
THE MARRYING MAN
Copyright © 1994 by Barbara Bretton
GUS IS BACK
Copyright © 1994 by Lass Small

CONTENTS

ONE WAY TICKET

Elise Title

Chapter One

Port Authority Bus Terminal
New York City
Saturday evening, April 12

MARIA D'AMATO tucked her dark brown hair behind her ears and gave the dreary, airless Port Authority Bus Terminal an anxious look. It was hard to tell the passengers from the street people who used the bus station as a shelter. A drunk weaved by her, the stench of booze emanating from him turning her stomach. Maybe this idea of hers to save a few bucks—well, a lot of bucks—by traveling by bus wasn't such a good idea, after all. A little taste of adventure was just what she needed, she'd told herself when she'd impulsively made the decision the day before. The problem was, she wasn't exactly the adventurous type.

Her disquiet began to mount as she glanced around the vast, seedy terminal trying to spot her sister, Angela, who was suppose to come to see her off.

Angela not showing up was a bad sign. The bus being late was another bad sign. Okay, so she was superstitious. It was in her blood. The whole D'Amato family was superstitious.

"Maria."

Maria spun around, recognizing her sister's voice. "Angela! Over here!" she shouted, telling herself she had to stop being so quick to think the worst.

Angela, dark and small-boned like her older sister, shook her head as she approached, breathless and disheveled. "Maria, Maria. What are you doing? Why the big hurry? What do you think? If you don't show up on Thursday your Prince Charming's gonna vanish?"

Maria certainly wouldn't admit it, but that was exactly what she thought. When you're thirty-two years old, the oldest of five sisters, all of whom are happily married, and your first serious marriage proposal finally comes along, you're not going to take the chance of screwing it up. Michael Harding was coming back from a week of meetings in Palm Springs on Wednesday and he was heading for another ten days of overseas meetings on Friday. If she didn't show up on Thursday to seal the deal, with her luck he'd fall head over heels for the British Air stewardess on his flight to London on Friday.

"I still don't understand why you didn't just fly out to L.A.," Angela said, scowling as she looked around the shabby terminal.

"I told you. There were no seats available on the flights out next Thursday. And there's a train strike. Plenty of perfectly decent people ride the bus," Maria declared, although she wasn't exactly thrilled with the group of misfits and eccentrics boarding her bus at the moment.

"I hope you're doing the right thing," Angela said with concern.

Maria gave her kid sister a defiant look. "Of course, I'm sure."

Angela frowned. "You get a letter from the guy on Friday after not hearing from him for six months and you're sure?"

Maria, her dark brown hair falling about her face despite her efforts to contain it, clutched her carry-on case in a tightfisted grip. "Well, I'll have six days on the bus to give it further careful consideration," she said, not quite meeting her sister's gaze.

So what if she had some niggling doubts. Michael's letter proposing marriage hadn't exactly swept her off her feet. Then again, there had been guys in the past who had made her feel like she was floating on cloud nine only to go on and pull the cloud right out from under her. Michael might not be the romantic type, but he was stable, successful, charming, hardworking. And then there was Cassie, his four-year-old daughter. A ready-made family. Not that she didn't plan to add to it. She wanted at least three children. For a long while, half presuming she might end up one of those dried-up old spinster aunts, she hadn't allowed herself to fantasize about being a mother. Now, all her dreams were about to come true.

A small boy, who was passing by with his mother, reached out and gave Maria's gray wool skirt a little tug. Maria smiled down at him—until her gaze fell on her skirt and she saw the sticky splotches of bubble gum stuck to it. Her best skirt. Another bad omen? Nonsense, she told herself dismissively. A trip to the dry cleaners would set it right.

"I just wish..." Angela started to say when the bus driver, a burly fellow with a ruddy face and a receding hairline, tapped Maria on the shoulder. "This all you got to stow?" he asked, pointing to the one worn brown leather suitcase at her feet.

"Yes," Maria said. "And please be careful with it. The catches are a little...tricky." Her concern was especially justified since inside that suitcase she'd carefully and lovingly folded her wedding "trousseau." Yesterday, after getting that marriage proposal from Michael and leaving a message for him at his Palm Springs hotel that she'd be arriving on Thursday, she'd raced around the city like a madwoman, buying some sexy lingerie and a dynamite black jersey cocktail dress that the saleswoman had insisted showed off her slender but curvy body to perfection. Perfection was definitely necessary; Michael was a man with impeccable taste.

Maria was hugging her sister goodbye as the bus driver lifted her suitcase up and was about to deposit it into the storage bin on the side of the bus when it collided with an equally battered-looking suitcase being hoisted into the compartment by Sean

MacNeil, a tall, lean passenger in his mid-thirties, with light brown hair and badly in need of a shave. He was wearing a jeans jacket, navy T-shirt and black cord slacks, all of which had seen better days.

"Hey, watch—" Before the bus driver could finish his warning, the damage was done. The catches on Maria's suitcase gave way and the lid flew open, her neatly folded clothes spilling out onto the grimy terminal floor. Thanks to a gusty wind, the garments started flying all around the depot area.

Maria let out a squeal of alarm as she and her sister scrambled around to collect everything. Most of the other passengers were already aboard the bus, but the sisters were joined in the chase by a couple of latecomers, including the man responsible for the calamity, who apologized profusely as he gathered up a lacy black bra, matching bikini panties and a white silk nightgown from the curb.

He smiled as he held them out to her. "Snazzy duds."

Maria, red-faced with fury and embarrassment, snatched the lingerie items from his grasp. Great. This was all she needed. A fellow passenger with a lingerie fetish. The bad omens were really starting to mount. And so was Maria's anxiety.

"Really," Angela muttered, eyeing the fellow with wary derision." The characters that ride the buses these days."

"Hey, look, I'm really sorry," Sean MacNeil said earnestly, continuing to help gather up Maria's clothes. He even tried to put them back in her suitcase for her, but he'd never been much of a packer.

"Will you please stop," Maria entreated. "You're making it even worse."

As if the situation weren't bad enough, in the midst of the chaos of trying to shake the grime off her clothes and neatly refold them, out of the corner of her eye, Maria caught sight of a teenager fleeing the scene with her newly purchased black jersey cocktail dress.

"Do something!" she cried, shoving the man responsible for the catastrophe and pointing to the runaway thief.

It took Sean MacNeil a moment to figure out what he was supposed to be doing something about, but the instant he caught on, he gallantly went charging after the youth only to trip over Maria's overnight case, which was lying on the pavement a few feet away. He landed with a loud thud.

The dress disappeared around the corner. Maria, who was staring after it, hadn't seen Sean trip and fall. "Forget it. It's too late," she said, her voice ringing with despair.

Sean MacNeil started to rise, dusting himself off and glancing at Maria. "Don't worry," he said dryly. "I don't think anything's broken."

Only then did Maria realize he'd tripped over her bag. "I'm sorry you fell," she said, "but maybe, if you occasionally looked where you were going and paid more attention to what you were doing..."

The bus driver rolled his eyes. "I can see this is going to be one of those trips," he grumbled, checking his watch. They were already ten minutes behind schedule. He snatched up Maria's repacked suitcase, this time managing to get it stowed away without further catastrophe, then announced that the bus was ready to pull out.

Maria kissed her sister goodbye.

"If you change your mind along the way..." Angela began.

"I won't," Maria said firmly.

"It's been six months," Angela cautioned as Maria started to get on the bus. "A lot can change in six months."

"Sometimes for the better," she replied with determined optimism. She wasn't going to have the dream of her lifetime spoiled by doubts or superstitions.

"All aboard for Washington, Chicago, and points west," the bus driver, already in the driver's seat, called out for the second time. Maria was the only one left on the platform.

She hurried up the steps of the bus, waving to Angela. "Don't worry. Everything's going to be... great," she most sincerely prayed.

As the door of the bus shut with a whoosh behind her, Maria felt a rush of panic. This was it. She was really going through with this. Her sister's warnings echoed in her head even as she tried to dismiss them.

She lurched down the aisle looking for a seat as the bus pulled out. Most of the seats were occupied, although she did spy a vacant one beside a balding middle-aged man in a sadly out-of-date polyester suit. He winked at her as she started to sit down and she immediately thought better of it. Every other seat was occupied as she made her way toward the back of the bus.

She got to the last row. There was one seat—and only one seat—left.

Sean MacNeil smiled as she stared dubiously at the vacant space beside him.

Good thing she was determined not to keep tallying up the bad omens. And she hadn't even cleared New York City yet.

"I always prefer the back of the bus, myself," Sean MacNeil said cheerily.

"You ride buses often?" she asked warily, still on her feet.

He grinned. "Around Manhattan."

He had a nice grin, she noted. Bordering on downright attractive. Maybe she'd overreacted a little about that lingerie fetish. Still, this was the last person she'd have chosen for a seatmate. She could always go back and sit down beside the polyester guy. On second thought—

The bus driver made the decision for her when the bus took a sharp curve onto the highway and she literally fell into the seat. Well, half into the seat—and half *onto* Sean MacNeil.

Maria quickly righted herself, moved as far from her seatmate as possible. She started to lean forward to wedge her overnight case under her seat at the very same moment Sean leaned forward to assist her. Their heads collided.

"I was just trying..." he began.

Maria gave him a pleading look. "Will you please not try," she begged, rubbing the side of her head.

"Are you okay?"

"Fine, " she lied. Not that the collision with her traveling companion's head was the real problem. It was just that too many things were going wrong and they were strongly interfering with her determined efforts to be confident and optimistic.

While Maria hated to admit it, Angela had been right. She hadn't thought through her decision to accept Michael's proposal—not even in the twenty-four hours she'd had to think it through. She'd been afraid if she thought too much, she might think herself out of it. Instead, she'd spent the past twenty-four hours convincing herself that everything would work out fine once she and Michael were together again. After all, before this six-month hiatus in their relationship, they had dated exclusively for close to seven months. So their courtship hadn't been the stuff of romance novels, but Maria had long ago learned that fiction and reality were worlds apart.

Suddenly Maria became aware that her seatmate was sizing her up. When she felt his eyes on her, she gave him a wary look, deciding that if he winked at her, she would get up that instant and stand all the way to D.C., which was their first stop.

"Interesting how we keep colliding," he said with a teasing smile.

Well, at least he didn't wink.

"You know," he added. "When worlds collide?"

He saw that she was not amused. "Look, I'm sorry. About your suitcase and your head," he said, holding out his hand. "The name's Sean. Sean MacNeil."

She pretended not to notice his outstretched hand. Nor did she introduce herself, having absolutely no intention of getting chummy with the scruffy-looking chatty fellow beside her. As soon as they got to D.C. and another seat became vacant, she intended to move.

"Your sister looked a little worried about you, back there," he said conversationally, dropping his hand to his lap.

"I beg your pardon," Maria said coolly, taken aback by his comment.

"Like maybe you were ill or something."

"I'm perfectly healthy," she said dismissively, reaching into her purse for a paperback novel. She opened to the middle of the book, even though the truth was she hadn't yet started it. This way, she figured, Mr. Sean MacNeil would assume she was already deeply engrossed in the story and wouldn't keep trying to get her life story out of her.

It didn't work.

" I'm an only child myself," he said. "Grew up in upstate New York. Winston. You ever hear of it? Probably not. The only thing Winston can hold claim to is being the home of Oscar Armstrong. You never heard of Oscar Armstrong, am I right? I'm not surprised. You see, he was..."

Maria gave her garrulous companion a sideway glance. "You aren't a traveling salesman, are you?"

He laughed. "Oh, you mean because I talk so much? Yeah."

"You are a traveling salesman?"

"No, I meant, 'Yeah, I do talk a lot,' not 'Yeah, I'm a traveling salesman.' I'm something much worse," he said conspiratorially, his hazel eyes glinting with amusement.

Maria wasn't amused. "Worse?"

"A teacher. English lit. Middlebrook Prep School for Boys in lower Manhattan. How about you?"

Maria regarded him dubiously. He certainly didn't look or behave like a prep-school English teacher. He was too unkempt, although she admitted that his look was more arty-bohemian than strictly derelict.

Sean smiled. "You don't believe me, right? Right," he said before she could reply. Not that she'd intended to reply.

He reached into his pocket. For an instant Maria felt a flurry of alarm. What if he pulled out a knife or a gun? You never knew. The papers were full of such stories. Even though this guy didn't look dangerous. In that way.

She breathed a little easier when she saw the billfold. He flipped it open so that she could see his school ID.

"The photo's lousy. I needed a haircut badly."

Maria was tempted to tell him he still did, noting that his light brown hair edged well over the collar of his denim jacket. She immediately flashed on Michael. Michael, with his refined good looks, his close-cropped blond hair, his impeccably tailored clothes. The contrast between the two men was astounding. And yet, for it all, Maria was vaguely aware that Sean MacNeil did have a certain rough-hewn appeal.

"How'd you know she was my sister, anyway?" she asked him.

He tapped the side of his head. "Simple deduction, Watson. She looked like you. The dark brown wavy hair, thick eyebrows, full lips, aquiline noses, similar builds, distinct ethnic bone structure . . . Italian, right? Definitely. Italian, for sure."

"Greek," she said, deadpan.

"No," he countered, astonished.

She had to smile at his reaction. "Okay, Italian."

"From Brooklyn, right?"

"Why don't you just tell me my life story?" she countered facetiously.

He studied her thoughtfully. "I could tell you a few things about yourself. If you really wanted to hear them."

Maria felt a little pulse of anxiety. "Not really," she muttered.

"Fine," he said, studying her thoughtfully.

"Why are you looking at me like that?" she asked self-consciously.

"You look a lot like Eleanor."

"Your wife?" She saw he wasn't wearing a wedding ring. "Girlfriend?" She hoped she didn't remind him of his mother.

"Eleanor's the heroine in the short story, 'A Life Adrift.' Actually, it's a *long* short story. Almost a novella. Anyway, Eleanor has the same dark brown eyes— You're not wearing contacts, are you?" he asked.

Taken aback, Maria informed him that she had twenty-twenty vision.

Shucking off his jacket, accidentally elbowing her in the process, he quickly apologized and went on with his description of "Eleanor."

"At first glance, she looks kind of ordinary."

"Gee, thanks," she muttered. Granted, she'd never thought of herself as stunning, but she had always regarded herself as reasonably attractive. Decent figure, good skin, pleasant features, no glaring peculiarities.

"In a nice, wholesome sort of way," Sean added with a smile. Then the smile faded. "Until you spot her eyes. It's those deep, magnetic, emotion-laden eyes that set her apart. That draw you in, even though you try to fight it." As he spoke, his voice became impassioned and his hazel eyes were riveted on her dark brown ones.

Self-consciously, Maria lowered her lids as Sean turned fully in his seat to face her.

"Eleanor's at a crossroads. She's torn between two men—Julian, a charismatic, eccentric artist, and Mark, a staid, very successful businessman." He mimicked the voice of a soap-opera announcer.

"And who does she end up with?" Maria couldn't stop herself from asking.

"Andy."

"Andy?"

"A brash and breezy writer." He flashed that dynamite grin again.

Maria found the grin unsettling and looked back down at her book, turning a page. "'A Life Adrift,' huh? Never read it."

"Well, I can take care of that easily enough," he said cheerily, digging into the worn, battered briefcase he'd grabbed out from beneath his seat. Opening the flap, he retrieved a dog-eared copy of *Horizons,* a classy-looking literary magazine.

"Maybe I'll read it later," she murmured, pretending avid interest in the novel she *wasn't* reading.

"Page 32," he said, blithely depositing the magazine over her paperback.

Maria scowled. If only she'd gotten Michael's letter a day sooner, she would have been on yesterday's bus to L.A. and she might have spent the trip sitting beside a nice, quiet grandmother who slept a lot. Not to mention that she'd still be the proud owner of that sultry black cocktail dress that was probably now hanging in a secondhand-clothes shop window.

Sean opened to page 32. Maria gave the page a cursory glance. Then a second closer glance as she caught the name of the author of "A Life Adrift." *Sean MacNeil.*

Slowly, she raised her eyes and looked over at him, the light dawning. "The brash and breezy writer that Eleanor ended up choosing?"

He was smiling. "I guess I did sort of model the character of Andy after myself, but the rest of the story is pure fiction. I never met a woman like Eleanor." He almost added *until now,* but stopped himself in time. This trip was not about finding the possible woman of his dreams. He was pursuing an altogether-different dream; a dream that he was convinced could be seriously sidetracked by letting himself get too involved with any woman—especially a living, breathing incarnation of Eleanor. And he'd dreamed too long, too hard, too desperately, to go and spoil it all now. Now, on the very brink of his life's dream coming true.

"It must be quite an...honor to get a story into a literary magazine like *Horizons,*" she said awkwardly. Expressing herself had never come easily to her—writing-wise or verbally. A few men had accused her of being withholding. Michael had called her self-contained. It was one of the things about her to which he was especially drawn. And yet, sitting there beside Sean, she found herself envying his openness, wishing she felt confident enough, trusting enough, to share more of herself.

Sean's eyes sparkled. "Getting that story published isn't the half of it."

Maria heard the excitement in his voice and found herself smiling. "Meaning?"

"Where do you think I'm going? L.A. That's where."

The way her luck had been going, it figured, she reflected.

"What about you?"

"Same," she muttered.

"Hey, great," he said, although he felt a twinge of concern. He had planned to spend the six days on the bus writing. His traveling companion was already proving distracting. How was he going to keep his attention fully focused on realizing his dream, with six days and nights beside this woman who had slipped off the pages of his story and landed practically in his lap?

Maria was too busy worrying about finding Sean too distracting to pick up on his worries about her. She decided her smartest, safest bet was to nip this "friendship" in the bud.

"Not to hurt your feelings or anything," she said, trying to be tactful, "but I was really looking forward to a nice, quiet trip. You know. A chance to read, reflect, sit *quietly*."

His hazel eyes sparkled. "So, you're not curious about why I'm heading for L.A.?"

She compressed her lips. Damn it, she was a little bit curious, despite herself. And she could see by the look in Sean MacNeil's eyes that he was just itching to share the reason with her. His excitement was infectious. And enviable.

"Okay," she said with a faint smile. "I'll bite. Why are you going to L.A.?"

"To make a dream come true."

"No, don't tell me. You want to be an actor?"

"No," he said laughing. "Have you ever heard of Lou Harcourt? No, probably not."

"Do you always do that?" she asked.

"Do what?"

"Ask a question and then answer it yourself before the person you're asking has a chance to answer?"

"You *do* know Harcourt?"

"No, but that's not the point."

Sean smiled. "He's a Hollywood producer." He tapped the magazine, which was still open to his story. "A Hollywood producer who plans to turn 'A Life Adrift' into a movie. He sent me a ticket."

"A bus ticket?" Maria actually felt a twinge of pity for the writer who'd obviously been duped by some Hollywood hustler.

Sean laughed. "No. A plane ticket. First-class, but—"

ing for in a man? Handsome, charming, successful. And then there was Cassie.

Admittedly, Michael had some drawbacks, but then no one was perfect. She could make a list of shortcomings for Sean MacNeil that ran a mile long. He talked too much, thought he knew too much, took too much for granted. He obviously gave little thought to his personal appearance and grooming. He probably hadn't been in a barber's chair in months. And he was intrusive, clumsy, and a tease to boot.

Out of the corner of her eye, she saw Sean start writing in a broad, sprawling script across the legal pad. What was he writing? Was it about her? No, that was ridiculous. He'd already "done" her!

She started to read her book again. After a few minutes she dozed off to the sounds of the bus's engine and Sean MacNeil's scratchy pen.

Chapter Two

MARIA AWOKE WITH A start just as the sun was beginning to rise, mortified to discover her head on Sean's shoulder. She sat up abruptly, relieved to see that her seatmate's eyes were closed. She hoped he'd fallen asleep before her head had landed on his shoulder. Angling her overhead light away from him, she picked up her mystery novel. A chance to start at the beginning. But as she opened to the first page, her eyes strayed to the literary magazine still tucked in between the two seats.

A little curious, she took up the magazine and began quietly riffling through the pages, taking care not to wake the author.

"Page 32," Sean murmured to her with a smile, his eyes still closed.

Maria flushed. Really, the man was impossible. She almost flung the magazine at him, but in the end her curiosity won out and she turned to page 32.

Within five minutes she was wholly engrossed. By the time she finished, she was close to tears. She bit down on her bottom lip. Sean MacNeil might be brash, outspoken and obnoxious, but his writing... His writing was something else altogether. Sensitive, perceptive, tender, honest, smart. 'A Life Adrift' went straight to the heart of a woman's search for true love. What was so unsettling was that she not only fit the physical character of Eleanor, but so many of the character's fears, thoughts and struggles were ones she identified with all too easily.

Sean set aside the legal pad on which he'd been writing while she read and stuck his pen behind his ear. "So, what do you think?" He kept his voice low so as not to disturb the busful of sleeping passengers.

"It's...good," Maria whispered back. "But...to be honest, I don't see it as a movie." That wasn't at all what she really wanted to say, but she didn't feel at all comfortable telling him how much his story moved her. Touched her. He might take it the wrong way. Or the right way, which would be even worse. Not even twenty-four hours into her journey and she was already feeling hopelessly confused.

He shrugged, glancing out at the flat, seemingly endless highway. "To be honest," he echoed, "I don't see 'A Life Adrift' as a movie, either. But as long as Lou Harcourt does, I'm not going to worry about it. This movie deal is my chance of a lifetime," he said with breathless earnestness.

"So, that's what you want? Fame and fortune?" Maria was oddly disappointed. She'd pictured a man like Sean having less shallow goals. Not that she didn't think he'd get what he wanted. He was certainly talented enough. Still, she couldn't quite see a man like Sean MacNeil fitting into the flashy, phony Hollywood scene. Then again, she didn't much fit into it, either. Nor did she want to. Her goal was simply to get married and make a home for Michael and Cassie. And, with any luck, be pregnant within a year or two. She was already late getting started.

"Forget the fame," Sean said. "My only interest is in the fortune part of the equation."

Again, Maria was thrown off-kilter. Sean MacNeil didn't impress her as a man out for money.

"Hey, don't get the wrong idea," he said with a knowing smile. "I'm not into fortune for fortune's sake. Anything but. All I want is enough money so I can stop working umpteen hours a day and devote myself fully to writing my novel. I've been struggling with it for years now, but I have so little time to give to it that it just never gets off the ground."

He pressed his hand against his heart. "It's all in here, burning away inside me. It's like, if I don't pour it out soon, it's going to either explode or turn into ashes. Either way, it's a time bomb ticking away. Harcourt says I'll get big bucks for doing the script for my story. All I've got to do is iron out a few points with some studio heads and I'll be able to sign on the dotted line. I figure it'll mean maybe a month in Tinseltown, and then I'll have made enough money to take a year off from teaching and have nothing in the world to concentrate on other than my novel."

Maria's eyes fell on his legal pad. "Is that it?"

He glanced down at the page full of scrawlings. "This? I have a habit of jotting things down when something strikes me. It may fit into the novel. Then again, it may not."

"How often does something strike you?"

He shrugged. "Sometimes I go for days, weeks, without something striking me. Sometimes I get inspired and I can't write the thoughts down fast enough."

He gazed at her for several long moments without saying a word.

"Do you want to talk about him?" he asked finally.

Maria did a double take. "Who?" Of course, he meant Michael. Why had she gone and even told him she was going out to L.A. to get married?

"No," she said succinctly.

He smiled crookedly. "Well, you've got five and a half days and nights to think it over."

"There's nothing to think over," she snapped, angry and upset that he thought she felt she needed to think it over. Even if he was right.

A frumpy middle-aged woman with bright patches of rouge on her cheeks who was sitting in the aisle seat across from them, was awakened by their conversation. "Shh," she scolded.

"Sorry," Maria whispered, abashed.

Sean leaned a little closer to her. "Awfully touchy for a bride-to-be."

"I am not touchy," she retorted under her breath, moving away from him. "Anyway, brides-to-be are always...touchy."

"Do you always do that?"

"Do what?"

"Say one thing when you mean something else altogether?"

Maria narrowed her eyes at him. "Do all people find you as irritating as I do?"

"Shh," the woman across the aisle repeated more sharply.

"Sorry," Maria said again, then deliberately shut her eyes even though she was now wide-awake.

"You can rest on my shoulder again, if you'd like," Sean whispered in her ear.

Maria felt her cheeks redden, but she kept both her eyes and her mouth shut. Twenty minutes later she was still wide-awake. Sneaking a look over at Sean, she saw that his eyes were again shut, the side of his head pressed against the window. This time he really did appear to be asleep.

Maria looked out the window. The sun had come up, but there wasn't much in the way of sunshine; the mid-April morning was drab and overcast. After a few minutes, she opened her purse and pulled out the letter she'd received from Michael on Friday morning. Six months without so much as a word, and then this remarkable missive.

Dear Maria,

If only I could find the words to tell you what a jerk I was to leave you behind. I've been kicking myself ever since. And Cassie's missing you like crazy. She's been here all of two weeks and all she keeps talking about is Maria, Maria, Maria.

Things are really looking up for me. 'Tell It Like It Is' is being picked up for syndication and I've got two other shows in the works. Not to brag or anything, but I just may be the hottest game-show producer to have hit this town in years. But then, you always said I had what it takes to make it big.

The only thing missing now is you, Maria. I need you. Cassie needs you. Let's start over. Let's get married. I've got to go down to Palm Springs for a week, but all you have to do is say the word, and I'll send you a one-way plane ticket to L.A. I'll be back April 17. Call me. Say yes. As Cassie so succinctly put it, if I'd married you six months ago she wouldn't be stuck here with a prune of a nanny—my third in two weeks. No one knows better than you that Cassie can be quite a handful. You had the magic touch with her. And, of course, with me. Let's make the magic last....

The bus lurched to a sudden stop. Sean's head banged against the window and he awoke abruptly. So did most of the other passengers.

"What do you suppose is the matter?" Maria muttered, seeing that the bus driver had pulled the bus over to the breakdown lane on the highway.

The bus driver got out of his seat and faced his riders. "Sorry, folks. Seem to be having a little engine problem." A "problem" was right. The engine had gone dead silent.

No one on the bus took the news too well. The driver raised a hand for silence. "There's a road-stop restaurant just up the way about two hundred yards. You can all walk over and have yourselves some breakfast and we'll either get this bus running like new or another one will be sent to get you within the next couple of hours. We're about ninety minutes north of D.C. so you'll have to figure we'll be running about three and a half hours behind schedule. Sorry for the delay, but . . . that's life."

Grumbling and muttering, the groggy passengers exited the bus and began their trek down the breakdown lane of the highway somewhere in the middle of Pennsylvania. The driver hadn't even bothered to name the town. If there was a town. The area looked pretty desolate.

Maria and Sean were the last ones off the bus. He was carrying his briefcase, figuring he'd do some writing while he was waiting, and Maria had her overnight case with her, figuring she'd freshen up in the rest room at the restaurant during the unplanned stopover.

Pausing as she stood in the breakdown lane of the four-lane highway, she set her overnight case down so that she could zip up her windbreaker. There was a real bite in the air. It felt more like mid-March than mid-April. Before she could retrieve her overnight case, Sean had picked it up.

"Really," she argued, "that isn't necessary." Superstitious or not, she figured she was better off keeping him a good arm's length away from her luggage.

"No one said it was," he remarked lightly, taking long strides down the road, his briefcase in one hand, the strap of her overnight case over his shoulder.

Catching up with him, she grabbed hold of the strap. "If you don't mind, I'd just as soon—" she tugged "—carry my own bag."

The next instant the bag dropped to the ground with a loud thud. Maria stood there holding the strap that had come undone from it.

"Is it my luggage in particular," she grumbled acerbically, "or do you put a hex on luggage in general?"

"You're blaming me? You're the one—"

"Did I ask you...?"

"You try to offer a helping hand—"

"A helping hand? I'd hate to be around you when you weren't trying to help."

"Are you always this crabby in the morning?"

"I am never crabby."

"Does your fiancé know how crabby—?"

"If anyone's crabby around here, it's not—"

Before she could finish the sentence he grabbed her arm and yanked her. Not knowing what hit her, Maria went flying with Sean onto the grassy embankment at the side of the breakdown lane.

"Are you...?" The *crazy* got drowned out by a huge eighteen-wheeler that went whizzing by, half in the breakdown lane.

Shaken, Maria lay there speechless. Then her eyes fell on her overnight case. Or what had been her overnight case before a good eight wheels of that truck had run over it.

Sean's gaze also rested on the crushed suitcase. "Phew. That could have been us."

She turned to him, her expression a mix of gratitude, frustration and despair. "Don't you think, for both our sakes, we should just...keep our distance from now on? I mean, it's clear to me—really clear—that if we stick around each other, we're just asking for trouble." Maria didn't even want to think about the full range of "troubles" they could get into.

Resolutely brushing herself off, she got to her feet and, without another word, strode over to her battered case, gathered it up in her arms, gritted her teeth and started walking down the road.

Something was dripping down her leg. She stopped, looked down at the stream of pink liquid running from her overnight case onto her skirt, then her leg, leaving a foamy pink trail along the side of the road.

Her shampoo.

"Tell me this isn't happening," she mumbled to herself as she set the crushed case down and tried in vain to force open the jammed lid.

Sean came up behind her. "Can I help?"

"What's the point? Everything in there is ruined."

He bent down and managed, after some effort, to get the lid open. He looked inside. Not only had the shampoo container ruptured and spilt out over everything, but so had Maria's tube of toothpaste. Then there was the pricey little bottle of Rapture perfume that had broken. The combination of scents was quite potent.

He looked up over his shoulder at her.

She merely turned and started down the road, abandoning the overnight case.

"Look, it isn't the end of the world," Sean said, catching up with her. "After we've had some coffee and something to eat at the restaurant, we'll see if there's a convenience store nearby where you could pick up some stuff—"

She stopped short and gave him a look of sheer desperation. "Would you just do me one favor?"

"Leave you alone?" he asked with a sheepish smile.

"Exactly."

FORTY-FIVE MINUTES LATER the disgruntled bus driver arrived at the road-stop restaurant to report that it was going to take half the day to get the engine on the bus repaired, so a new bus would be picking them up in an hour.

Maria, who'd deliberately joined three other passengers—a retired plumber and his sister, and a "sanitation engineer"—at a four-seater booth to avoid any further interactions with Sean MacNeil, hurried over to the driver as he sat down at the counter for a cup of coffee.

"What about our luggage?" she asked.

"We'll switch everything over before the bus gets here for all of you," he told her.

"You said, an hour. Does that give me time to run down the road to a convenience store if I'm back here in, say, thirty minutes?" One of the waitresses had told her there was a place called Wilmott General Store, a ten-minute walk at the most from the restaurant.

"Like I said, it'll be an hour, maybe a few minutes more than that, before it gets here," the driver said, opening a menu.

Maria nodded and backed away, surreptitiously glancing around the restaurant to see if she spotted Sean MacNeil. Just her luck, he'd decide he, too, needed something at the store, and tag along with her. If that happened, she might not make it there in one piece. The man was a walking disaster area.

No sign of him. She figured he must be in the men's room and, with a sigh of relief, dashed out of the restaurant without being spotted.

IT WAS A LONGER WALK to Wilmott's General Store than the waitress had estimated—fifteen minutes, the last five of which Maria had done at a jog. Not an easy feat in inch-heeled pumps. She made a mental list in her mind of the items she needed, anxious about making it back to the restaurant with time to spare.

Come hell or high water, she wasn't going to miss that bus.

Breathlessly, she hurried up the drive to the store, putting the blame on Sean for all of her misadventures so far. The ruined overnight case topped her list. If only Sean had just left her case alone, she wouldn't need a whole new supply of toiletries. Nor would the clothes she was wearing now reek of honeysuckle shampoo and Rapture perfume, both of which had oozed out of her crushed case onto her skirt, mingling with the sticky smudges of bubble gum.

As she approached the isolated little way station, which was well off the highway, she saw one solitary car parked outside. A long-haired woman with oversize sunglasses was sitting in the driver's seat, tapping her fingers on the steering wheel, the engine running. If the driver hadn't looked like she was in such a hurry, Maria might have stopped to ask her if she could wait a couple of minutes for her to pick up her toiletries and give her a lift back to the restaurant. As it was, the woman honked impatiently just as Maria started into the store.

The minute she walked in she spotted Sean MacNeil at the counter. She couldn't believe it. The man kept turning up like a bad penny.

"What are you doing here?" she demanded.

Both Sean and the man on the other side of the counter facing him—an even scruffier fellow with greased-back hair and sunglasses—spun their heads in her direction.

Sean began shaking his head rapidly, his lips pressed tightly together.

Maria was too irritated to notice.

"What am I doing here?" the young greaser behind the counter asked warily.

Maria started to explain that she wasn't talking to him, but she stopped with a loud gulp after the word, "I . . ." That's when she saw the gun in his hand.

"You. Over here," the gunman ordered her, moving out from behind the counter.

Sean sighed. "I tried to warn you."

Maria went white. Sourness rose in her throat. Her knees were like jelly, but her feet were frozen to the spot.

"I said move it, sweetheart."

Sean could see that Maria was in shock. Hell, he wasn't exactly emotionally prepared for having walked in on a robbery in progress himself.

"Just do what he says, Maria," he said in a soothing, even voice. "It's going to be okay."

The gunman grinned. "That's right, Maria. Just do what I say and it's gonna be okay," he parroted.

Maria couldn't lift her eyes off that gun. *Okay?* The sky was falling down on her and she was supposed to believe everything was going to be okay?

"I'm waiting, Maria," the gunman said sardonically.

"All I wanted was some shampoo and a...tube of toothpaste," she muttered, her heart racing. She pointed a trembling finger at Sean. "It's all...his fault."

The gunman grinned. "Women. They're all alike. They're always blaming the guy for everything."

"Look," Sean said to the gunman. "She's right. It was my fault. You see, our bus broke down and—"

"What do you think? I've got time to kill listening to your sob story?"

"Of course, you don't," Maria said hurriedly, then shot a look at Sean. "Of course, he doesn't. Don't you ever know when to...to shut up?"

"Hey, hey, hey," the gunman cut in. "Don't go giving your boyfriend such a hard time."

"He is not my boyfriend," Maria blurted. "We hardly know each other."

"She told me she didn't want anything to do with me," Sean said, trying to distract the gunman in hopes that at least Maria might be able to make a run for it. "Told me I was a jinx."

The gunman found that really funny and began to laugh. Sean shot Maria a quick nod and she started surreptitiously backing up to the door.

The gunman was still laughing as he nonchalantly grabbed Sean and pressed the barrel of the gun to his temple.

"Now get over here, missy, before I blow your boyfriend's brains out."

"She just told you, I'm not her boyfriend—"

"Shut up, Sean," Maria told him in a gravelly voice, her throat raw with terror. "Relax. I'm coming over. Just relax."

"Put your purse on the counter," the gunman ordered. "Dump everything out."

With a sinking feeling in her stomach, Maria did as she was bidden. The robber snatched up her wallet, which contained five hundred dollars. The sum total of her savings. If only she'd taken the time to get traveler's checks.

The horn blasted from the waiting car outside. Now Maria understood why the driver was so impatient. To think she'd almost hitched a ride with a couple of robbers. Talk about jumping from the frying pan into the fire. . . .

Chapter Three

"WILL YOU STOP wriggling," Sean pleaded.

"I am not wriggling. I am trying to loosen these damn ropes," Maria snapped as they stood bound together, face-to-face, in a small, dank storage shed about fifty yards behind the store.

"Look," the gunman had told them with a demented chuckle as he twined the ropes around them after first binding their wrists behind their backs, "I won't even gag you so you two can finish your fight, then kiss and make up."

Not that there was any point in gagging them, anyway. Even if they screamed their heads off, no one who entered the store would hear them way back there in that shed. Not that someone was likely to enter, since the gunman, who turned out to have been "minding the store" for his pal that day, had informed them with a broad smile that he was closing up shop. He and his impatient girlfriend were heading for points west. For one crazy moment back there, Maria had almost pleaded with the gunman to take her along, too, and drop her off in L.A. Anything, rather than leave her behind there with Sean MacNeil. Practically glued to him, no less.

She tried loosening the ropes around her wrists by rubbing her palms up and down. No give. She tried to pry her elbows under the ropes around her waist and Sean's. Maybe she could just slip down under....

Sean groaned. "You're digging into my rib cage."

"Can't you do anything?" she demanded, keeping her face averted from his.

"Like what?" Sean asked, his voice ringing with frustration. "Chew through the ropes with my teeth?"

Both of them were trying their utmost to ignore their intimate—however forced—embrace. Neither of them was succeeding. Sean couldn't help noticing that Maria had a decidedly voluptuous body, and now that her clothes had had a chance to air out some, the scent of her perfume wafting around him was undeniably alluring. For her part, Maria couldn't fail to take note that while Sean was lean, he *felt* more muscular than he looked. His chest was really quite broad, and hard, but not unpleasantly so....

"Please don't do that," Maria said archly, still trying to slip one hand free by squeezing her fingers close together.

"Do what?"

"Breathe...on me."

"I am not breathing on you," he said, exasperated. "I'm simply breathing and you happen to be in the way of my breaths."

"You could turn your head."

"You could try to make the best of an awkward situation," he countered, his tone faintly teasing.

"That isn't the least bit amusing, Mr. MacNeil."

"I didn't mean it that way," Sean said with a smile. "This may come as a shock to you, but I don't need to have a woman trussed to me to have my way with her. Or for her to have her way with me. Or, best put, for us to have our way with each other. What I'm trying to say is that I am not that desperate."

"You don't know how glad I am to hear that," she said dryly.

"In fact, there are some women who wouldn't mind in the least changing places with you," he informed her, his male ego bruised.

"Too bad they aren't lining up for the opportunity at the moment."

"Enough," he said, exasperated. "What is it? What do you have against me?"

"Shall I count the whats?"

"Skipping a couple of . . . unfortunate accidents."

"A couple?"

"Come on. It's more personal than that, isn't it? Sure, it is. I threaten you—"

"Threaten me? That's ridiculous."

"I make you uneasy."

"You're nuts."

"Do you know something? I still don't know your name. Come to think of it, I don't remember ever being this *close* to a woman and not even—"

"Maria."

"Maria. Maria." He rolled the name over on his tongue, liking the sound. Thinking that the name suited her.

"You're not going to break into a medley from *West Side Story*, I hope."

He grinned. "No, Maria. I'm tone-deaf. If I started singing to you, you'd really hate me."

She opened her mouth to tell him that singing wouldn't be necessary to achieve that end, but he cut her off with a light laugh.

"I know, I know. I left myself wide-open there. Let me put it another way—"

"Could we do away with the chitchat? I hope you realize that if we don't get ourselves out of here in ten minutes, tops, we're going to miss our bus for sure." Again, she tried the elbow maneuver, this time being careful to keep away from Sean's rib cage. The gunman had simply tied them together too tightly. There was no way out.

"I do realize that, Maria, and I'm no more pleased about it than you. Like I told you, I've got a deal to cut the very day we arrive in Tinseltown."

"My fiancé and his little girl are expecting me on the seventeenth," Maria said, wriggling out of one of her pumps in hopes of slipping her foot through the rope wrapped around her ankles. Unfortunately, the effort made her nearly lose her balance and she quickly scotched the idea.

"Oh, the fiancé has a kid?"

"Yes. That happens to be how I met him." She said, managing to get her shoe back on. "His daughter was at the day-care center where I worked and . . . well, that's how we met."

"Oh, I see."

"What do you see?" she asked defensively.

"Nothing. Just a phrase. 'I see. Oh, isn't that interesting?' That kind of thing."

"She's a terrific kid. I'm crazy about her."

"I'm sure you are."

"And I'm crazy about her father."

Sean didn't respond.

"Oh, so you don't think so?" she challenged.

"Did I say anything?"

"That's just the point. You always have something to say, but it's when you don't say something, that you really have something to say."

He laughed softly. "Could you say that again? I missed one of those 'somethings.' "

"Very funny."

"Okay, what do you want me to say?"

"Absolutely nothing. I don't want you to say another word."

"You're a very hard woman to please, Maria."

"That's completely untrue. If anything—" She stopped abruptly.

"Yeah," he said gently. "Eleanor tried to settle, too."

"I am not settling. I'm nothing like Eleanor. She's a fictional character. A figment of your imagination. Maybe you can't separate fantasy from reality, but that isn't my problem." There was an edge of desperation in her voice. She wasn't being honest with Sean. She had identified with his protagonist in "A Life Adrift" more than she dared openly admit to him.

"Look, I'm sorry. Honestly, I didn't mean to upset you."

"I'm not in the least bit upset." *Liar, liar.* "Do you think we could figure out something to do about our... immediate predicament?" The situation of being bound to him was starting to slowly unhinge her.

"We could try hopping toward the door. Maybe we can 'shoulder' it open."

Maria stared into the blackness. She could see only a few inches in front of her. Which meant all she could see was Sean MacNeil's face. "Which way is the door?"

"To your right."

"I don't think so. I think it's to my left."

"Fine, we'll go to your left."

"Great. Now, all of a sudden, you're obliging."

"Meaning?"

"Meaning that if you hadn't— Oh, what's the use? Are you ready?"

"To your left. At the count of three. One... two..."

"Wait. Maybe it is my right."

"Fine. To your right. One... two... three..."

It was anything but "fine." Their timing was off by a hair, but a hair was all it took for them to lose their balance and go toppling to the dirt floor. That is, Sean landed on the floor. Maria landed on top of Sean. Their situation was becoming more awkward and unintentionally provocative by the minute.

"Now what?" Maria muttered disconsolately.

"Let's try rolling," Sean suggested.

"Oh, God, I can't believe this is happening to me."

"If I wrote about it, no one would buy it. They'd say it was too unbelievable."

"I think we should try to... get back up on our feet," Maria said. Lying on top of Sean MacNeil was proving far more unsettling than standing pressed against him.

Sean was equally disturbed. A couple more minutes of this and he might have to start thinking baseball stats....

They made a few vain attempts to get back up, but their gyrations, however well-intentioned, were serving to do nothing but frustrate them. In more ways than one.

"Maybe we should try—" Sean started.

"I feel something hard."

Sean flushed. What the hell did she expect? "Don't take it personally."

"What? Oh . . ." Maria flushed in turn, no sooner realizing what he was referring to than becoming acutely aware of what he was referring to. Her embarrassment mingled with an inexplicable tinge of pleasure. And an unbidden flash of arousal. "I didn't mean . . . I mean . . . on the ground. I can feel something with the tips of my fingers. The handle of a . . . tool."

"A . . . tool?"

"A screwdriver, maybe."

"Oh." Sean's throat was dry. "Where?"

"By your left hand. No, I mean your right hand."

Sean stretched out his fingers. "We've got to move a little to my right. . . . There . . . Got it."

The tool turned out to be a small chisel. Sweating profusely, Sean started to work away at the rope that bound his right wrist to Maria's left.

"How's it coming?" she asked anxiously. They had rolled onto their sides, which was only a slightly less provocative position than when she was lying on top of him.

"I think we're getting somewhere," Sean said, his warm breath fanning her face.

"I'm so hot," she said. "I mean . . . it's so hot in here."

He laughed softly. "Look, will you stop worrying that I'm getting the wrong idea. You wish you'd never laid eyes on me. If you had to get tied up with anyone—literally or figuratively—I'm the last man on this planet you'd choose."

"Not the last. I'd definitely pick you over that creep who stole my last five hundred bucks." She hesitated, remembering how Sean had tapped the pocket of his trousers, indicating the small bundle he had from exchanging the plane ticket for the bus. "What about you? Did he take everything?"

"Everything I had on me. I still have my bank card and a few hundred bucks I can access." He continued sawing away.

"I'm sorry," she said softly.

"Really?"

"I guess I've behaved pretty badly with you. It isn't like you did anything on purpose. And I have to admit that I'd have been a lot more frightened if I'd walked into that store and found myself alone with that gunman. He might have—" She swallowed hard. "Anyway, thinking I was your girlfriend may have kept him..."

"Honest?" Sean filled in the blank with a smile.

They both laughed. A moment later, to Maria's relief, she felt the rope give way around her wrist. She was so happy to have one arm free, she almost threw it around Sean's neck. However, she managed to curb the impulse, working instead to help him get them completely free.

The door turned out to be behind them and it took only a couple of kicks for Sean to get it open. They both winced from the glare of the light and shivered as the chill morning air rushed into the shed.

Maria checked her watch. "Ten minutes. We could still make it if we run."

"What about the police? Shouldn't we report the robbery? Everything else?"

"First thing is to get to the bus. Then we'll explain to the driver what happened and he'll have no choice but to hold the bus up for us to make our report," she reasoned.

Sean nodded, then looked down at Maria's shoes. "You can't jog in those."

Those dark brown eyes flared with determination. "I can do anything if I have to."

BLISTERS WERE POPPING up on blisters and the soles of Maria's feet literally burned by the time they rounded the bend in the road and saw the road-stop restaurant they'd left short of an hour ago just up ahead.

"I don't—see—the bus," she said, gasping for breath.

"Maybe it hasn't come yet," Sean said, not even breathing hard. Along the way, he'd informed Maria that he'd run track in college and still jogged a few miles every day.

By the time they approached the restaurant, Maria was hobbling and wincing in pain. Sean was just ahead of her, getting to the door first. He looked in, blocked her way and turned to her.

"You're not going to like this," he said solemnly.

Her heart sank. "The place is empty, right? Right. The passengers are all gone, right? Right."

He smiled. "Now you're doing it. Answering your own questions."

Maria was in no mood for levity. "I knew it. I knew it. Let's face it. It's been one disaster after another from the first. If something can go wrong, it will go wrong."

"Well, I guess we have time to make that police report now," Sean said, holding the restaurant door open for her. "Come on. I'll buy you a cup of coffee."

Frustration and despair etched in her features, Maria walked in ahead of him. "What I need is a shower and a change of—" Just inside the restaurant she stopped short and her mouth gaped open.

"What?" Sean asked, alarmed.

"Oh my God, my clothes. My suitcase. It's . . . on the bus. I don't have anything but . . . the clothes on my back."

"Well," Sean said with a shrug, "we're in the same boat."

"Through no choice of mine," she was quick to remind him.

Sean grinned. "You may not believe this now, but people often tell me I grow on them."

Maria brushed off her sooty, sticky skirt. Not that it did much good. "I don't intend to be around you long enough for that to happen," she muttered.

"FIVE FOOT EIGHT," Sean said with confidence.

Maria shook her head. "No, definitely closer to six feet."

"I'm six feet," Sean argued, raking his fingers through his mussed-up brown hair. "And that creep was a good two, three inches taller than me."

"Five foot eight would be four inches shorter than you," Maria interjected.

"I teach English lit, not math," Sean said facetiously.

"I'm five foot six and the guy was definitely more than two inches taller than me," she said dismissively, crossing her shapely legs at the knee and kicking one bare, blistered foot—she'd temporarily discarded her shoes under the restaurant table—back and forth.

Sheriff Len Burke's pale gray eyes dropped to her swinging leg for a moment. Maria instinctively smoothed her dirty, rumpled skirt well over her knees. The sheriff cleared his throat and looked down at his notepad again, rubbing his index finger up and down his hawkish nose.

"Let's see what we've got so far," Burke mused. "The gunman had either brown hair or auburn hair—"

"Brown," Sean reiterated.

"Definitely auburn. And greasy," Maria added.

"That's true," Sean conceded. "His *brown* hair was greasy."

The sheriff sighed. "You do agree he was wearing sunglasses."

"We couldn't very well disagree on that," Maria said brusquely.

"Gold wire frames," Sean said.

Maria arched a thick eyebrow. "Silver."

Burke rubbed his nose. "Let's go back to the getaway car." He focused on Maria. "Now, you're the only one who saw it, correct?"

"I caught a glimpse of it from inside the store," Sean said.

"Like I said, it was a dark blue sedan," Maria said, her gaze fixed on Sean, daring him to disagree.

"It could have been dark blue." A faint smile curved Sean's lips. "Or black."

The sheriff motioned to the waitress passing by their table. "More coffee, Flo." It was clear they were going to be at this a while.

Forty-five minutes and three cups of coffee later, the sheriff shut his notepad and rose from the booth. "Well, that about does it, I guess."

Maria blinked. "Does it? Does what? What about our money? The bus? Our suitcases? We're stranded. You're not just going to leave us . . . like this?"

The sheriff's fondest wish was to do precisely that. Never had he encountered a pair more at odds than these two. Still, he did feel sorry about their predicament.

"Well, I suppose I could give you a lift to the bus depot." He checked his watch. "'Fraid there are only local buses running until tomorrow morning."

"How local?" Maria asked, her heart sinking.

Chapter Four

Sleepy View Motor Lodge
Calhoun, West VA
Sunday evening—Monday morning

"THAT'S IMPOSSIBLE," Maria informed the sleepy desk clerk at the decrepit little motel across from the bus station where they'd disembarked at close to eleven that evening. "You couldn't possibly have only one vacancy." How many travelers could pass through this backwater town miles from the nearest city? There had to be at least a couple of vacant rooms.

The clerk, a gaunt, balding man in his early thirties, shrugged. "Regional women's bowling convention. Lucky we aren't all full up. One pair from Kingsville canceled at the last minute or I'd have that No Vacancy sign outside all lit up."

"Lucky for us," Sean deadpanned.

"Sure is," the clerk said. "So, what do you say? For thirty-nine bucks you've got yourselves one nice little double with TV, shower, and if you-all play your cards right, Millie—she's on the morning shift—will see to it you get a nice hot cup of coffee before you drive off. . . ." He rubbed the side of his face. "Oh, that's right. You're not driving a car. You come on the last bus into Calhoun—"

"And I'm leaving on the first bus out of Calhoun in the morning," Maria said sharply. "Are you sure there isn't another motel or bed-and-breakfast place in this whole town?"

The clerk grinned, revealing several missing teeth. "No real call for more."

"Except when the bowling convention's in town," Sean said dryly.

The clerk chuckled. "Big doings for Calhoun, all righty."

Maria shot Sean a hostile look. She didn't find his quips in the least way amusing. Nor did she find the idea of sharing a room with him for the night cause for laughs. To think, twenty-four hours or so ago, she'd been reluctant to even sit beside him on the bus.

"We'll take the room," Sean said, plucking down two twenties on the counter. Fortunately, using his bank card, he'd been able to access a couple of hundred dollars from his fast-dwindling account. He didn't want to think about the six hundred and fifty bucks he'd had on him before walking into that general store. That's what he got for trying to play Sir Galahad. The only reason he'd hiked over to that store was to replace the toiletries Maria had lost after her overnight case had gotten run over. Why had he been trying to get in her good graces, anyway, he wondered? The woman obviously couldn't stand him, wanted nothing to do with him, wished she'd never laid eyes on him.

And now they were about to share a room in a sleazy motel in the middle of nowhere. With a little start, he remembered a scene in "A Life Adrift" where Eleanor and Andy meet one final time in an intimate little inn by the seashore and have an incredible night of passionate sex. This wasn't exactly an inn and the babbling brook wasn't exactly the Atlantic Ocean. And then there was the more crucial reality. Eleanor and Andy were products of his imagination. He and Maria were flesh and blood, and while his imagination could run riot, he had no control over his "heroine's" thoughts or feelings. This was going to be interesting.

Interesting was not the word Maria would have chosen. *Dumb, awkward, disquieting.* Any or all of those suited her viewpoint a lot better. For all her ranting and raving about how all her misadventures had been Sean's fault, she was having trouble feeling strictly angry at him, much less coolly indifferent. Try as she might, she kept thinking about his broad chest, his dynamite smile, the way he could make her laugh. Given half the chance, she was pretty sure Sean could make her feel plenty more than amused!

THE MOTEL ROOM WAS matchbox size, the double bed taking up most of the dark knotty-pine-walled space. There was a TV that sat on a narrow bureau across from the bed, but it was black-and-white and only the weather channel came in with any clarity. On the wall beside the TV was one of those framed paintings on velvet—a unicorn in a forest.

The minuscule bathroom had no tub, and the stall shower had more rust spots on it than an old jalopy. Repelled though she was by the sight of it, Maria breathed a sigh of relief when she turned on the taps and actual hot water came pouring out.

"Mind if I...go first?" she asked, sticking her head out of the bathroom.

"No, be my guest," Sean told her, crossing to the bed and testing it out. "Not too bad."

She stared at him, stunned. "You don't mean that you intend to...sleep on that bed?"

He stood, scratching the side of his face. "Oh...I see. You mean that you..." He glanced back at the bed.

"Well, I guess we could...draw straws...."

Sean patted his pockets. "No straws." He looked down at the marginal floor space in the room. "Not much room to stretch out."

"Meaning, since I'm smaller, that you expect me to take the floor, I suppose," she said archly.

"Meaning that I'd trust you to behave yourself if we shared the bed," he corrected.

She stared at him. And to think he'd said it with a straight face. "You'd trust me? That's a laugh. I'm going to the West Coast to get married. You're the one with...nothing to lose."

"That's not true. Anyway, not to hurt your feelings or anything, but you don't exactly..."

Maria stiffened. "Turn you on?"

"Well..."

"I don't believe it. What about Eleanor?"

"Eleanor was fiction. And for all you know, there's already a real Eleanor waiting in the wings."

"Is there?"

"No. I can't afford distractions right now. I've got to devote all my energy to my creative work."

"Distractions? So, that's how you view women?"

"Distractions. Complications. Commitment. None of which I can afford at the moment."

Maria's gaze shifted to the bed. She was exhausted. All she really wanted to do was go to sleep and hope that tomorrow would go better than today had gone. There was certainly enormous room for improvement. She covered her mouth as she yawned.

"I didn't take advantage of you back in that shed, did I? No, I didn't. And now we won't even be tied up together, so you can always kick me out of the bed if I forget myself. Which I won't." He held up his hand. "Scout's honor."

"How do I know you were ever a Boy Scout?"

"Shucks, I left my merit badges in my suitcase."

"You're a laugh a minute," she said soberly.

"So how come I can't even coax a smile out of you?"

"I guess I just don't find any of this very amusing."

"Okay, let's get back to our sleeping arrangements. What do you want to do, Maria?"

She scowled. "I don't know." Her scowl deepened. "I'm not sure." Who wasn't she sure of, though? Him or herself? There had been a moment or two back there in that foul shed when she was lying on top of him...

"I've got to take a shower," she announced, that being the only thing she felt sure of at the moment. "Maybe I'll be able to think straighter after I get all the dust and grime off me."

About five minutes later, Sean knocked on the bathroom door. "Hey, how's the hot water holding up?"

No sooner had he finished asking the question than he heard the taps shut off. "What?" she called out.

"Nothing."

A minute later, Maria cracked open the door. "I...washed my clothes while I showered to save water, but now..."

Sean grinned. "What? No nice, soft terry bathrobes hanging up in there, compliments of the establishment?"

"I guess the bowlers got them all," Maria quipped.

"Want a blanket?"

"If you don't mind."

Sean went over to the bed, pulled back the floral-print bedspread, which was made out of a stiff, scratchy polyester, and tugged off the much softer, pale blue cotton-knit thermal blanket underneath.

A plain white top sheet remained, which Maria suggested Sean could use as a makeshift robe when he got out of the shower.

"Good idea," he said, taking it into the bathroom with him after Maria exited looking like an Indian princess and smelling all fresh and soapy. Her scent had a visceral impact on him. Maybe he couldn't be trusted, after all?

Sean's shower didn't last long. After little more than two minutes, the water quickly went from hot to tepid to cold. The icy water wasn't so bad. It helped douse any lurking erotic fantasies.

Shivering as he stepped out of the shower, he dried off on a threadbare towel, trying not to let his eyes linger on Maria's delicate undergarments hanging out to dry on the towel rack. It could stir new fantasies and he'd have to duck back in under that cold water again. Using his fingers, he combed back his hair, rubbed his two-day-old growth as he inspected himself in the mirror and concluded that if he could get his hands on a razor in the morning, he'd give up his plan to grow a beard. Somehow, he'd thought he'd feel more "Hollywood" with a beard. Feel more *Hollywood*. What a notion. Nothing he could think of doing was going to make him feel less like a fish out of water. Then he started imagining that poor little fish, lying on the hot concrete, flailing around, gasping for air, slowly dying....

That was the price of having a vivid imagination. With a little shake of his head that sent wet strands of hair flying, he wrapped the sheet around his goose-bumped body, toga-style, and stepped out of the bathroom.

Maria started to smile as she looked over at him from the edge of the bed where she primly sat cocooned in her blanket.

"What? You've got something against the Romans?" he quipped.

She did smile, then. "No. Nothing at all."

He leaned against the knotty-pine wall. "So, did you dig up any straws while I was gone?"

Maria picked at a loose thread on the blanket, her eyes averted from him. "I was thinking...."

"Yes?"

Slowly, she lifted her eyes and looked directly at him. "I do think I can trust you, Sean."

He wasn't sure what surprised him more. Her making such a statement or making it so earnestly. Probably a little of both. He grinned and rubbed his scratchy jaw, his gaze fixed on those dynamite chocolate brown eyes of hers.

"What? " she asked nervously. How was it that she could feel both edgy and comfortable with this man—this practical stranger—at the same time? She couldn't figure it out. That is, she kept trying not to figure it out. Standard operating procedure. Don't think too much or you'll end up in trouble. With Michael, that had meant deciding not to go through

with marrying him. With Sean, it could be deciding
something else altogether. For it all, the man did
have some very appealing qualities.

"I was just thinking that now, even if I wanted to
be...untrustworthy, I couldn't."

Maria laughed softly.

"Do you know that's the first time I've actually
heard you laugh?" he said, crossing the room toward her. "You have a very nice laugh, Maria."

"This may come as a surprise to you, but I happen to have laughed plenty in the past." She sighed.
"Granted, I have been pretty grim since we inadver-
tently started this misadventure together. That,
coming on top of getting Michael's letter out of the
clear blue..."

"I take it Michael's your...fiancé?"

Maria nervously pressed her palms together. "We
broke up six months ago. He got this big break to go
out to L.A. to produce a game show and he felt it
would be...best not to have any..."

"Ties binding him?" Sean teased gently.

Maria smiled, but he saw sadness flicker in her
eyes. Oh, those dark, alluring eyes.

"Then, a couple of days ago, he wrote telling me
how much he missed me, how much Cassie missed
me...."

"His daughter?"

"She's just turned four. Michael and his ex-wife
have shared custody. Cassie lives with her mother in

Connecticut for six months and then she lives with Michael the other six.''

"I see.''

Maria's eyes narrowed. ''Every time you say that, you make it sound like you see much more than . . . there is to see.''

"What do you think I see?''

She wagged a finger at him. ''Oh, no, Dr. Freud. I'm not falling for that ploy. Look, a guy can have a change of heart. Absence makes the heart grow fonder. It may be a cliché, but how does something get to be a cliché if it hasn't been proved true over and over again?''

Sean sat down on the bed beside Maria. ''Why are you getting so defensive?''

"Look, if you're going to spend the whole night analyzing me,'' she said testily, ''you can sleep on the floor. Or on the roof, for all I care.''

"Hey, I'm on your side, Maria. If this is what you want . . .''

"It's exactly what I want.''

His hand moved over her hand. For some inexplicable reason she didn't move hers away. Their shoulders were barely touching, but they were both aware of the contact.

"It's just that . . . it all happened so fast,'' she admitted.

"The same for me,'' Sean said. ''One day I'm sitting in my tiny studio apartment trying to figure out which bills I absolutely have to pay this month and which ones I can hold off on, and then the doorbell rings. And there's this express-mail letter from Louis Harcourt accompanied by a first-class ticket to L.A. and a small check for the option on my story. He calls that night, tells me he wants me to adapt 'A Life Adrift' for a screenplay and then he starts throwing amounts of money at me that are making my head swim. All I have to do is get out there, sign the deal, and I'm set for life. Up until that moment, I figured I'd spend the rest of my life struggling to make ends meet, and never have either the time or the money to write my book.''

She turned to face Sean. ''How old are you, Sean?''

''Thirty-four. Why?''

''You're thirty-four and you've finally been given the chance to have what you've always wanted. I'm thirty-two years old. The oldest of five sisters. The rest are all married. I want a home, kids...''

''A husband?''

She smiled. ''Yes, a husband. And Michael will be a good husband. He's a good father. He's wonderful with Cassie.'' She hesitated. ''Of course, he's very busy. He can't give her as much time as he'd like to give her. He does tend to get caught up...in things.'' His *own* things. Okay, so he tended to be a bit self-involved. It could be worse. He didn't drink to excess. He didn't use drugs. He had no terrible habits—that she knew of....

"So we're both going off to fulfill our dreams," Sean said, but there was a touch of wistfulness in his voice. He squeezed her hand, then released it. "Well, talking about dreams, I guess we should...get some sleep."

Maria nodded tentatively. "Yes...I guess you're right."

"Right or left?"

"What?"

"Which side of the bed do you prefer, Maria?"

"Oh. Oh, right."

"Fine."

"No, I mean...right, I understand."

"Then you want the left side?"

"No."

"Wait, let's start over."

Maria giggled. "Right."

Sean grinned. "Hey, if our plans fall through, we can always go on the road doing a stand-up comedy routine."

Maria sobered up quickly. "My plans won't fall through."

"I was only kidding. Neither will mine."

They settled on sides, Maria rolled up in her blanket on the left, Sean, with the sheet wrapped around him, on the right.

He reached over and turned off the lamp on the wobbly nightstand, bathing the room in darkness.

Suddenly, there was an ungodly rumble. The wall behind their heads literally shook.

They both popped up, Maria throwing her arms around Sean in a panic. "Oh my God, do you think it's an earthquake?"

Sean held her close. "I don't know."

"Should we...do something?" she whispered, clinging to him.

"What do you want to do?" he whispered back, his breath against her ear, his arms moving around her.

This time she didn't complain about him breathing on her. In the midst of her fear, she managed to be very conscious of how disturbingly good it felt to be in Sean MacNeil's embrace. "There could be... aftershocks."

Sean was pretty sure he was feeling some of those "aftershocks" already.

Maria's head tilted up. Sean's angled down slightly. As if by radar, they found each other in the blackness. A strange little flutter danced down Maria's spine. Sean's pulse shifted into overdrive. He slipped his tongue past her teeth, exploring, as if mapping out the terrain. He found it very much to his liking. As Maria found her explorations of his mouth. Their kiss deepened. They fell together back on the bed. Maria's blanket came undone. Sean's sheet began to slip.

It's just that the world might be coming to an end, she rationalized. *And if that's the case, this is as good a way to go as any—*

A loud rap on the door sent them flying apart, scrambling to cover themselves back up.

"Maybe we have to...evacuate," Maria mumbled.

Sean flailed around for the lamp, knocking it over, bending to feel for it in the dark. When he finally found it, it wouldn't go back on.

"Say," a booming woman's voice shouted from the other side of the door. "Sorry about the racket. Got a little carried away."

Sean moved cautiously across the room in the dark, stubbing his toe and letting out a loud yelp along the way. When he opened the door, he gave the squat, buxom young woman a dazed look.

"What did you say?"

The woman smiled sheepishly. "I was just showing my pal Gert a good release. Only I didn't mean for the ball to get away from me and go crashing into the wall."

Sean, whose mind—and body—was still caught up in that passionate kiss with Maria, continued giving the woman a baffled look.

The woman frowned. "The bowling ball. Didn't you hear something slam against your wall a minute ago?"

When Sean shut the door moments later, he was laughing so hard he doubled up and had to lean against the door for support.

"It isn't that funny," Maria grumbled from the bed, too mortified by that kiss and where it might have led, to be amused. "I really thought it was an earthquake. You did, too. We both thought we were . . . done for. I thought it was all over. I wasn't thinking straight. Will you please stop laughing."

He couldn't stop.

"Well, you can go right ahead and laugh yourself silly. I'm going to sleep," she said resolutely.

Still chuckling, Sean made his way back to the bed and crawled in beside Maria.

Even as he lay beside her, a little chuckle would escape every few seconds.

"Sean."

"Okay, okay, I'll stop laughing."

Maria rolled onto her back. "I don't believe any of this is really happening to me," she mused. "First our bus breaks down, my overnight case gets trampled by a sixteen-wheeler—"

"Eighteen-wheeler."

"I walk into a robbery in progress—"

"Don't forget I was there, too."

"Have all my money stolen, get thrown into a vile, dirty shed, tied up—"

"You should feel grateful it was me in that store when you walked in. Just think, some old geezer with foul breath and a beer belly could have been in there instead of me and you could have ended up getting bound to him."

Maria continued to ignore Sean's wry, running commentary. "I miss the next bus, which now has my suitcase on it, end up riding locals for twelve hours and making hardly any headway. And now, to top off what certainly had to go down on record as being the worst day of my life, I'm in a tacky motel in the middle of no-man's-land, surrounded by women with bowling balls, lying in bed with a stranger with the sense of humor of a twelve-year-old...."

"You didn't kiss me like I was a twelve-year-old," he teased.

Maria scowled. "If you were a gentleman you wouldn't have brought that up," she said archly.

"Come on, Maria. You take life too seriously. It was only a kiss. Of course if that 'earthquake' hadn't turned out to be a runaway bowling ball—"

"Absolutely nothing would have happened," she said with more conviction than she felt. What was the matter with her? Nerves, she decided. Pre-wedding jitters. And, okay, Sean MacNeil did have a certain roguish charm. She thought about his story, remembering how warm, honest and sensitive his writing had been. Surely, someone capable of such perceptiveness and grace couldn't be all bad. Ironically, she thought she'd somehow feel a lot safer if he were.

She cleared her throat. "Since you did bring up that...kiss, Sean."

"Yes, Maria?"

"I don't want you to...get the wrong idea. It just...happened. It doesn't mean anything. It certainly doesn't change anything."

"I see."

"I mean it, Sean."

"I'm teasing you. It doesn't mean anything. Like you said, it was just a kiss." Under his breath, he added, "But what a kiss."

"What did you say?"

He smiled in the dark. "Nothing. Good night, Maria."

"Right. We should get some sleep. Our bus leaves at seven. I hope the clerk remembers to wake us."

"I wake early anyway. Don't worry about it."

She rolled onto her side, facing away from her bedmate. "I can't help it. I worry. I come from a long line of worriers." Not that she'd admit it to Sean, but right now the least of her worries was about waking for the bus tomorrow morning. Right now she was worried about the eight or nine hours she had to get through before morning came. Eight or nine hours lying naked, save for a blanket, in a motel-room bed with a practical stranger who was also naked beneath his makeshift toga.

Would something more have happened if that woman bowler hadn't knocked on their door? Maria suddenly felt a little dizzy, like she was racing toward the edge of a cliff. She shut her eyes tightly, trying desperately to conjure up Michael's image. Somehow, she couldn't manage it. No big surprise. It had been six months since she'd seen him. She was sure as soon as she laid eyes on Michael again, all the old feelings would return.

She compressed her lips. *All her old feelings.* That was the problem. Her feelings hadn't all been positive. There were qualities in Michael that disturbed her, even though she always made a concerted effort to overlook them. She'd been swept off her feet by him. He'd wined her, dined her, romanced her like she was some princess in a fairy tale. She'd admired his self-assurance, rejecting what some people—like her sister, Angela—interpreted as narcissism.

All four of her sisters had had plenty of criticizing for Michael after he'd taken off for L.A. Maria had tried to defend him. All these months, she'd kept telling herself that one day he'd wake up and realize how much he needed her. And he had. The problem was, was she starting to wake up, too?

Sean rolled onto his side, facing Maria. He could feel the restlessness and anxiety emanating from her even though she lay perfectly still. He stroked her hair lightly. "You've done enough worrying for one day. Go to sleep, Maria."

His touch was oddly soothing. She closed her eyes and smiled. "A bowling ball. It is kind of funny."

Sean smiled, too. "One for the books, all right."

"Good night, Sean."

"Good night, Maria."

She nodded, but she didn't fall asleep right away. Her worries were lurking in the stillness, springing back on her like mosquitoes. Why had she kissed Sean so passionately? Was she attracted to him? Well, obviously she was attracted to him.

But she was in love with Michael. Wasn't she? She was going to marry Michael. Wasn't that what she'd dreamed about for months? All right, so things had gotten a little out of hand with Sean. After all they'd been through together these past twenty-four hours, was it any wonder? Once they were en route to L.A. again, everything would settle down. Really, there was nothing to worry about. So why couldn't she stop?

SEAN AWOKE WITH A start from a bad dream. All he could remember of it was that he was at a Hollywood party and there was this huge swimming pool and he was in the middle of the pool surrounded by producers, directors, buxom starlets, and agents. And they were all taking turns pushing his head under the water. Every time they let him come up for air, he saw her—alone on the terrace behind the house. Maria. Watching sadly. And in his dream, he remembered thinking how ironic it was. A fish out of water. And just when the fish went and found some water, it started drowning....

Sean pushed the dream from his mind, smoothed back his hair and tried to focus on his watch. He brought his wrist closer.

No. It couldn't be. Surely his watch had stopped last night. At ten-fifteen. Because that's what time his watch said it was. And if it wasn't ten-fifteen last night, that meant it was ten-fifteen this morning. Which also meant they'd missed their bus again....

Chapter Five

On the highway
Randolph, Georgia
Monday afternoon

"SORRY, FOLKS, THIS IS as far as I go," the trucker said, pulling over to the side of the road at Exit 7. "Wish I had an umbrella to give you."

Maria wished he had one to give them, too. It was pouring rain outside.

"Sure you don't want to stop a while in Randolph until the weather clears up?" the trucker asked.

Maria shook her head. They'd been listening to the weather report on the radio and the weatherman predicted rain well into the night.

The trucker winked at Sean. "My wife's stubborn, too."

"Oh, she's not my wife," Sean said.

"Sorry, girlfriend."

"She's not—"

"Thanks for the ride," Maria told the trucker, cutting Sean off.

The pair climbed down from the eighteen-wheeler onto the side of the road. Sean pulled up the collar of his denim jacket—not that it was going to do much good. Maria was a bit better off with her windbreaker, which had a hood, but within a matter of minutes the rain had soaked through the material.

Five minutes passed without a single vehicle passing them in either direction. They were both soaked to the skin.

"Maybe we should hike into Randolph," Sean suggested, crossing his arms over his chest.

"You're welcome to go, if you like. I figure I can't get any wetter than I already am," she declared. At least it wasn't as cold as it had been up north. She could have been wet and frozen.

"I can't let you hitchhike alone."

"You're not responsible for me. You can do whatever you like."

"Is that so?"

"Yes," she said defiantly. Blinded by the rain, she missed the mischievous smile tilting the corners of his mouth.

Suddenly she found her sodden shoulders being firmly gripped by Sean's hands and he was pivoting her around to face him. Before she could demand to know exactly what he thought he was doing, his mouth was moving over hers, his fingers were caressing her rain-streaked face.

He didn't kiss her immediately. Instead, he ran his tongue across her wet lips, stroking them. To Maria's dismay, she didn't make a peep of protest. She was mesmerized. Her lips seemed to part of their own volition, and a little gasp of arousal involuntarily escaped from her throat.

Sean slipped his tongue past her lips, along her teeth. Her own tongue darted out, made contact with his. Her hands found their way around his neck. His hands moved around her waist, drawing her up against him. Mindless of the rain beating down on them, their kiss grew hot and bold.

They never even saw the car whiz by—the only car in seven minutes—until it was too late.

"Now see—what you've—done?" she stammered, slapping him on the chest.

Sean blinked the rain out of his eyes. "You told me to do what I wanted."

"I didn't mean . . . that," she countered. "I'm almost a married woman."

"Then why'd you kiss me back?" he challenged.

"I didn't." She pushed the wet strands of hair away from her face. "It was . . . instinct."

"So, what about Michael? Is he a good kisser?"

"What a ridiculous question!"

"You kiss him back the way you kiss me back?"

"Yes. No." Desperately, she stared up and down the empty highway. "Doesn't anyone drive this way?"

At that precise moment a car rounded the bend, heading in the right direction. Finally, a piece of good luck. As it drew closer, Maria began to wave her arms wildly, determined to make the driver stop for her if she had to throw herself right in the approaching car's path.

"YOU POOR DEARS. You're soaked to the bone," Emily Morton, a tiny white-haired woman whose head was just barely visible over the steering wheel, exclaimed as the sodden pair climbed into the back seat of the compact sedan.

"Thank you so much for stopping," Sean said. "We were really getting desperate," he added, winking at Maria.

Maria tossed him a dirty look, then addressed the grandmotherly lady. "How far are you going?"

"Over to Bolton."

To Maria's despair, she learned that Bolton was exactly twenty miles down the highway. At this rate, she'd be lucky to make it to L.A. before May.

As they drove the twenty miles, Maria sat glumly silent while Sean and Mrs. Morton kept up a lively stream of conversation, Sean filling the old woman in on their many misadventures since departing the Port Authority terminal in New York City. She was consolingly sympathetic, tsking countless times, interspersing the sounds with several more, "You poor dears."

Maria stiffened when Sean mentioned the Sleepy View Motel. To her relief, he gave a sketchy overview, not even mentioning that they'd shared the same room.

When they got to the Bolton exit, Maria asked Mrs. Morton to pull over and leave her at the side of the road.

"I'll do no such thing," the old woman said adamantly. "You're coming home with me."

"No, really..." Maria began to argue.

"My daughter and son-in-law live just down the street from me and we'll stop there for a minute so I can pick up some dry clothes for both of you. Lydia's about your size, Maria. Tom's on the heavy side, but he's probably still got some clothes stored away in his closet from when he went on one of those silly grapefruit diets and lost twenty pounds. Went right out to JC Penny and bought himself a slew of new clothes, then proceeded to put back the twenty pounds and then add on a good twenty more."

"Isn't that the way it is?" Sean mused.

"Don't you know it," Mrs. Morton said with a chuckle. "Anyway, as soon as we've gotten you-all into some nice dry clothes, I'll heat up my lamb stew and get some good hot food into your tummies."

"I don't suppose there's a bus or a train station in Bolton?" Maria asked as the car turned off the exit ramp onto a desolate road.

Mrs. Morton chuckled. "Not too likely. We've only got seven hundred people living in Bolton. But, never you mind. We'll figure something out." She slowed as they came to a big pothole. "So, it's L.A. you're heading for. What's out there?"

"I'm getting married," Maria said.

Mrs. Morton beamed. "Well, isn't that nice. And if you don't mind me saying, Maria, you've got yourself a nice young fellow. I can always spot the good ones. You ask anyone in Bolton. Guess you can call it a sixth sense. Your fiancé here has a good heart. It shows in his face. He's kind, generous, thoughtful. And I bet he loves children. Isn't that true, Sean?"

"Well, yes. I'm crazy about kids, as a matter of fact."

"I knew it. And you, Maria. I bet you want a houseful of little kiddies."

Maria was flushed. "Well...yes. I would."

Mrs. Morton sighed. "And I'll tell you something else. Even though you-all have been through so much heartache these past couple of days, I predict it's only going to make you feel closer, make your relationship that much stronger. Adversity does that when two people love each other."

WITH A SURPRISINGLY youthful vigor, Mrs. Morton, who had to be on the other side of seventy, ushered Maria and Sean into her dining room, a plain but homey space, the striped blue-and-white wallpapered walls covered with framed family photos. A large old oak pedestal dining table and eight chairs rested on a Persian carpet in the center of the room. In one corner was a built-in hutch whose shelves were filled with china and knickknacks. White lace curtains covered the three windows.

"Really, I wish you wouldn't go to so much trouble," Maria said, convinced it would be hours before they'd be able to gracefully make their departure.

"Are you sure you couldn't use some help in the kitchen?" Sean asked, feeling a pleasant lethargy setting in, which he didn't quite understand. After all, he had as much of a need to make it to L.A. on schedule as Maria. Harcourt had made it clear that he'd gone to great pains to arrange this meeting with a major studio exec and that it was imperative they show up right on time.

"Now, you-all just sit down and relax," Mrs. Morton insisted, nudging them toward two chairs that were side by side. "It'll only take me a few minutes to heat up that stew. Then after you've eaten, if you'd like to take a little nap..."

"No," Maria said so sharply, her face reddened. "I mean...we really have to get going."

"Ah, young love. So impatient. But I was young once, so don't think I don't understand," the old woman said with a twinkle in her eye.

Maria could feel Sean's eyes on her. She didn't have to look over at him to know he was smiling. He was enjoying this. He loved seeing her squirm.

Mrs. Morton stopped at the kitchen door, turning back to smile at the pair before she stepped inside. "You-all look worlds better in those nice, dry clothes."

Maria had to admit it certainly felt good to be out of their wet garments, even though she felt a little ridiculous in her new outfit. In the scoop-necked white blouse and full floral-print skirt that Mrs. Morton's daughter, Lydia, had insisted she keep, Maria felt like she was dressed for a country hoedown. Sean, in a starched white dress shirt and gray polyester pants that didn't quite reach his ankles—Lydia's husband, Tom was a good two inches shorter than him— looked like a country hick dressed for Sunday church. A country hick in bad need of a shave.

As soon as Mrs. Morton disappeared into the kitchen, Sean turned to Maria with a wiseacre grin. "So, why didn't you say anything to her?"

"About what?"

"You know about what, Maria. About letting her believe you and I—"

"What do you mean, why didn't *I* say anything?" Maria cut him off with a hoarse whisper. "Why didn't *you* say anything?"

"She was talking to you," Sean whispered back.

"Anyway, what difference does it make? So she thinks you're my fiancé. It I had told her the truth, she might have gotten . . . the wrong idea about us."

"Right. And we certainly wouldn't want anyone getting the wrong idea," Sean murmured.

Their eyes met and held for an overlong moment, then they both looked away at the same time. To their mutual dismay, the wrong idea was seeming less and less wrong by the minute.

AFTER THE LAMB STEW—two heaping helpings for Sean— Mrs. Morton ushered the pair into her cozy living room, sat them down together on her green floral sofa and fixed them with a pair of expressive blue eyes.

"Now the question is, how to help the two of you on your journey."

Maria brushed back a strand of still-damp hair from her face. "If I could just get to the nearest bus or train station..."

Sean put an arm around her shoulder. "Don't you mean *we*, honey?"

Mrs. Morton tittered. "Yes, you can't very well get married without the groom, Maria."

Sean hugged her to him, playing it up for all it was worth. Well, at least one of them was enjoying this charade.

"Such a handsome couple," Mrs. Morton cooed. "You'll have to send me a wedding picture. You-all promise now, you hear?"

"Oh, absolutely," Sean drawled. "A big eight-by-ten glossy, right, sweetheart?"

"Right," Maria said tightly. "Now, about that bus or train station, Mrs. Morton..."

"Would an airport do?" the elderly woman asked.

Maria sat bolt upright. "An airport?" Of course, there was the matter of paying for the flight, but she supposed she could call home and ask one of her sisters to charge the flight for her. She wouldn't call Angela, though. Angela would ask too many questions. Lucia. Yes, Lucia would do it with no questions asked. Well, maybe with a few questions, but Lucia, bless her, never pressed.

"An airport would be fantastic," Maria exclaimed. "If I...*we*...could get a flight out anytime today for L.A..."

"Oh, I don't think Gordy would be able to take you that far," Mrs. Morton said. "But he could get you as far as Texas."

"Texas?" Maria repeated, with less enthusiasm in her voice. Then again, Texas was a lot closer to L.A. than Virginia.

"You're actually in luck," Mrs. Morton said.

"That would certainly be a shift," Maria mumbled.

Mrs. Morton, who was a bit hard-of-hearing, didn't pick up Maria's remark. "You see, tomorrow's the day Gordy's got to fly to Little Springs to pick up the tamales."

Maria shot Sean a glum look. Clearly the old woman—while a complete dear—was balmy.

Sean wasn't so quick to write the elderly woman off. She reminded him a lot of his grandmother. Maybe there really was a guy named Gordy who had to fly to Texas for tamales. Stranger things had happened. All he had to do was think of his and Maria's joint misadventures over the past twenty-four hours. If he related their story to someone, he was pretty sure the person listening would think he was nuts.

Maybe he hadn't heard right. Maybe she hadn't said "tamales." So he sought confirmation.

"Did you say tamales?" he asked.

Maria leaned forward, now on the same wavelength as Sean. Maybe they had misunderstood. After all, the elderly woman did speak with a thick Southern accent.

"Oh, yes. Not just tamales, of course," Mrs. Morton said.

Maria and Sean shared a look. So much for having misunderstood.

"There's also the tortillas, salsa, and all those special spices," Mrs. Morton explained. "For Chico's."

"Really," Sean said in a humoring voice.

"No, my dears, I'm not off my rocker," the elderly woman said with a little chortle. "Gordy owns a Tex-Mex restaurant over in Dry Creek, which is all the rage down here. He also owns his own plane. Once every couple of weeks he flies on down to Little Springs, Texas, to his food supplier. Oh, the tourists can't get enough of our Southern-fried chicken and our grits and all, but we locals sometimes hanker for something different. I adore those chicken-and-cheese tortillas. Naturally, my doctor has a bird every time he catches me in Chico's. I'm supposed to be on a low-fat diet. But I say, at my age, I'd rather eat, drink, and be merry. And if I go tomorrow, at least I'll go happy. Anyway, my beloved Billy, may God rest his soul, is up there waiting for me.'' She looked heavenward, then explained that she and Billy had been joyfully married for just short of fifty years.

''I only hope the two of you will be as happy as Billy and I,'' she said softly.

Maria swallowed hard. She was feeling increasingly guilty for having led the old woman on.

Sean found his gaze straying to Maria. If things had been different—for both of them—maybe...

''So, tell me,'' Mrs. Morton asked, ''are you fond of Mexican food?''

Maria gave a halfhearted nod. Right now, food of any nationality was the last thing on her mind. Unfortunately, the first thing on her mind at the moment wasn't getting to L.A. Sean MacNeil kept on worming his way to the top of her priorities.

''I'll confess something to you,'' Sean said to his hostess.

Maria felt her stomach constrict. Was he going to ''blow their cover''?

''I'm not much on Mexican food, but I happen to be crazy about Southern-fried chicken, myself,'' Sean said.

''Then we-all will have some for dinner,'' Mrs. Morton enthused. ''I've got a nice plump chicken in the refrigerator and if I do say so myself, I make the best Southern-fried chicken in all of Randolph. Then after dinner, we'll get you both settled down for the night.''

Maria felt a rush of alarm. Another night with Sean was more than she felt ready to handle. "We don't even know if your friend, Gordy, will take us to Texas...."

Mrs. Morton smiled. "Gordy's my oldest boy. He always listens to his mother. I'll call him and let him know he'll have two passengers for his flight tomorrow morning."

The old woman eyed Sean. "I'm afraid you'll have to take the sofa, my boy. Maria, you can have the spare bedroom. Oh, I know these days couples live together in sin, but sin ends at my doorstep, so..."

"Oh, we don't sleep together," Maria blurted out, then flushed scarlet.

Sean grinned. "Certainly not in the biblical sense, Mrs. Morton. We're both old-fashioned that way."

Maria popped up from the sofa. "Surely, if there's a private airport nearby, I might be able to find someone to fly...us...to L.A. tonight. You've already been so kind to us. We don't want to put you to any more trouble, do we, Sean?"

Before he could respond, Mrs. Morton assured them it was no trouble at all. "I love having the company and people to cook for. Besides, I doubt you'd find someone to fly you anywhere at all tonight, my dear. Or any other time, for that matter. The only other plane in Randolph besides Gordy's belongs to Howard Farrell. And even if you could get him to agree to fly you clear on to Los Angeles, California, you'd have to sober him up first. Howie's a sweet boy. When he's sober.''

''When is he sober?'' Sean asked.

Mrs. Morton tapped an age-spotted finger to her lips. ''I do believe he went on the wagon for a whole week back in 1989.''

Chapter Six

SEAN RETURNED TO THE booth in the all-night diner that looked out over the bleak runway of the tiny private airport. Apart from Gordy's little Cessna, which was now taking off for the return flight to Virginia, there were only three other aircraft sitting out there.

Sean slipped in across from Maria, who was staring blankly at the list of songs on the wall-mounted jukebox beside her.

"Smile, beautiful," he said cheerily.

Maria instantly turned to Sean. It was still hard to get used to seeing him clean-shaven. Mrs. Morton had lent him her deceased husband's razor the night before. He looked so different without all that stubble. She saw now that his features were more chiseled than she'd imagined. He was, she was forced to admit, quite handsome. Especially when he smiled, which he was doing at the moment.

"What exactly am I supposed to smile about?" she asked cautiously.

"Would a flight to L.A. be reason enough?"

Maria was temporarily speechless. "You mean it? You honestly mean it?"

He grinned. "Yes, I mean it. I always try to say what I mean. When I'm meaning to be serious, that is."

"When is that?" she quipped dryly.

He tapped his index finger to his lip. "Let's see. There was a time when I was serious for a whole week. Back in 1989."

She threw a packet of sugar at him. "Did you really arrange a flight to L.A. for us or is that another one of your warped jokes?"

"And here I'd been hoping that my brand of humor would grow on you in time."

"We don't have enough time for that to happen. Thank goodness."

He grinned. "Whereas your sense of humor—admittedly a touch caustic at times—is growing on me, Maria."

"Sean."

"Okay, okay. You see that cowpoke sitting on a stool at the end of the counter?" He pointed back over his shoulder.

"The big guy wearing the snakeskin boots with the spurs and the Roy Rogers hat?"

"The very one."

"He's a pilot?"

"Nope. But he's meeting one here in about ten minutes. And the pilot he's meeting is flying down to Mexicali, California, just north of the Mexican border, and the cowpoke is pretty sure his pal wouldn't mind making a quick stop in L.A."

Maria nervously smoothed back her hair. She couldn't believe it. Now, instead of arriving in L.A. who-knew-how-many-days late, she was actually going to get there with time to spare. It was almost too much to hope for. Especially given the string of disasters that had fallen in her path so far. There had to be a catch. Why should things start going her way at this particular point?

"How much does the cowpoke think his pal will charge us?" she asked anxiously. The pilot would probably want a fortune to make an unplanned stopover. How would they pay for it? She didn't have a dime to her name and Sean had less than a hundred bucks on him and there wasn't likely to be a cash machine nearby for him to take money out of what she guessed had to be his fast-dwindling bank account.

Sean's face broke into an impish smile. "That's the best part. He says his pal doesn't enjoy flying alone. The cowpoke was supposed to fly down to Mexicali with him, but he's got some kind of horse show he has to attend. So, he says his pal will be so glad for the company, he probably won't charge us a dime." He paused for a moment, then added, "Naturally, I'll contribute on the gas."

Maria frowned. "It sounds too good to be true."

Sean reached over and took her hand. "Come on, Maria. Don't you think it's time we had a piece of good luck?"

TWENTY MINUTES LATER, Maria's expression was glummer than ever. The pilot hadn't shown up. Sean had gone down to check with the cowpoke, and she spotted the pair of them over by the phone booth. The cowpoke picked up the receiver and dialed a number.

Maria, who was convinced by now that nothing was going to go right for her on this disastrous trip, was certain the pilot wasn't going to show up. Maybe he was a drinker, too, and was passed out drunk at some Texas bar. Or maybe he got sideswiped by a bull on his way over and was laid up in traction in a hospital bed. Or maybe...

She didn't realize Sean had returned until he gave her shoulder a little shake.

"No problem. He's on his way," Sean said confidently.

"He won't make it," she said morosely. "Something will go wrong."

"He'll make it. He'll make it. His girlfriend said he left ten minutes ago and he should be walking through the door any second," Sean assured her, sliding in beside her.

"No..."

The door to the diner swung open and a short, stocky middle-aged man with a shock of red hair, wearing jeans, cowboy boots, and a bomber jacket sauntered in and waved at the cowpoke.

Sean winked at Maria. "See, I told you."

Maria watched in tense silence as the two cowpokes had a powwow at the end of the diner. Several times, the pilot cowpoke shot a look over his shoulder at them. The third time he did it, he smiled and gave a friendly little wave.

" Didn't I tell you?" Sean said, nudging her.

"Okay, okay, I'll never doubt you again." God, she couldn't believe it. She was actually going to be in L.A. before the sun set that night. And Michael wouldn't have to know a thing. Explaining this whole wild escapade to him would be pointless. Or raise some questions she didn't want raised. No, she decided. The thing to do was to go down to the bus station on Thursday just as the bus was pulling in and pretend nothing at all had happened.

"He's coming," Sean whispered.

Maria put on a bright smile as the redheaded pilot approached their table.

"My friend back there says he can vouch for the two of you. Is that right?" the man drawled.

"Oh, right," Sean said. "Absolutely."

"You know him, then?" he pressed.

"Not—" Maria started to say, but Sean nudged her in the ribs.

"Not for that long," Sean replied. "But sometimes it doesn't take all that long to get chummy, if you know what I mean?"

A slow smile appeared on the pilot's face. "Yeah, I know what you mean." His eyes fell on Maria. "You know what he means, ma'am?"

Maria gave Sean a sidelong glance. "Well, yes...I suppose."

"You two are experienced flyers, then," he said.

"Oh, yes," Sean said.

Maria nodded. "We flew down here from Virginia."

The pilot smiled. "Okay, I guess we ought to be taking off, then. Just got to go pick up a few boxes from Luke's jeep—office supplies—I'm in the office-supply business. I'll just go on and load them on board and we'll be set."

" Hey, we'll help," Sean said.

"Sure," Maria seconded. "The sooner we take off, the better."

The pilot grinned at her. "We're on the very same wavelength, ma'am."

"Maria," she said, extending her hand as she and Sean rose from the booth.

"You can call me Rusty," the pilot said, taking hold of her hand and giving it a little squeeze.

Sean introduced himself next and once everyone had shaken hands they exited the diner.

Luke, the cowpoke in the snakeskin boots, was already waiting at his jeep. There were a half-dozen medium-size cartons piled on the back seat.

Rusty handed one to Maria. She was surprised that it was so light and commented on it.

"Staples," Rusty said. "Those Mexicali folk go through staples like water," he added with a chuckle.

Sean took up a box marked Pencils and the two Texans carried the rest of the cargo, Rusty leading the way to his four-seater Piper Cub about thirty yards away.

The foursome were halfway to the plane when they heard a scream of sirens and saw two plain gray sedans and a local police cruiser come roaring onto the runway.

Rusty cursed under his breath and started to make a dash for the plane until Luke shouted to him that he wouldn't make it. Instead, cartons in hand, they went racing for Luke's truck. Burning rubber, they took off.

The two sedans took off after the jeep, but the cruiser that had Little Springs Police Department emblazoned in bold black letters across the side of the car, squealed to a stop a few yards away from Sean and Maria.

The pair stood there frozen to the spot, completely dazed, mindlessly clutching their boxes of office supplies.

"I SWEAR I THOUGHT the box was filled with staples," Maria said hoarsely for what felt like the hundredth time. A fan squeaked overhead as it spun, doing nothing but recirculating the hot air in the drab interrogation room. She was sweating profusely and terrified beyond all imagining.

"And Rusty told me I was carting a box of pencils," Sean said, wiping his damp forehead with the back of his shirtsleeve.

The sheriff of Little Springs, a lean, mean-looking Texan with a pockmarked face and two slits for eyes, and the two bland-looking blue suits from the FBI's Bureau of Narcotics stared at the pair with blank expressions. In contrast to the alleged "felons" the threesome looked cool as cucumbers.

After a long, drawn-out silence, the sheriff, who sat behind a small metal desk, folded his arms across his chest and tipped his chair back against the wall. "Rusty, huh. So you two were on a first-name basis with Altman alias Armstrong alias Andrews," he drawled, running a finger back and forth across his thin upper lip.

"He never even mentioned his last name. Any of them. He told us to call him Rusty," Maria said wanly. "We just met him maybe five minutes before you arrived on the scene. His friend Luke was the one..."

"Right, tell me about Luke, Miss D'Amato." The sheriff spoke her name like he didn't believe for a minute that it really was D'Amato. And since she had no proof of identity on her—thanks to having been robbed the day before—she couldn't very well convince them.

"We don't know any more about Luke than we do about Rusty," Sean insisted. "Like I keep telling you, we got a lift from this fellow Gordy from Randolph, Georgia, who was flying down here to Little Springs to pick up tamales."

The sheriff wore much the same expression on his face as they had when Mrs. Morton had first told them about Gordy and the tamales.

"I know what you keep telling me, Mr. MacNeil. The problem here," the sheriff said, pressing his hands together and cracking his knuckles, "is that you're not telling me and these two patient fellows from the narc squad here what we want to know."

"We don't know anything," Maria said weakly.

"We certainly didn't know those cartons were packed with cocaine or that those two cowboys were drug smugglers," Sean said.

"Won't you call Mrs. Morton in Randolph, Georgia?" Maria pleaded. "I'm sure she'll vouch for us."

The sheriff smiled. The faces of the two plainclothesmen remained blank. "Yes," the sheriff said, "but who's gonna vouch for her?"

"Oh, for heaven's sake," Maria said, exasperated. "The woman's seventy if she's a day."

"We busted a drug ring south of here a few months ago and the ringleader was this old geezer in his early eighties," the sheriff countered. "Let's face it. These are hard times for old folks on a pension. Some of them are forced to turn to crime to make ends meet. I'm an understanding fellow, Miss D'Amato, but crime's crime and we all took an oath here to uphold the law."

Maria threw up her hands. "This is insane. I have never even gotten a jaywalking ticket. I have never seen cocaine before in my life. I wouldn't know it if it hit me in the face. Why don't you find the real criminals and ask them?"

"You mean your pals, Rusty and Luke?" the sheriff said with a caustic smile. "Oh, we'll find them, all right. And let me give you a piece of sound advice. If you two was to say you were willing to turn state's evidence on those two characters, now we might be able to work out a deal with you." The sheriff glanced at the two narc boys. "Isn't that right, boys?"

"That's right," Tweedledee and Tweedledum said in unison, their expressions still as vacant as ever.

Sean leaned forward, rubbing his face, frustration and despair beginning to get the best of him. But he had to make these guys see reason, if only for Maria's sake. "Look, can we start all over again? It was like this...."

Chapter Seven

Little Springs Jail
Little Springs, Texas
Wednesday morning

"D'AMATO," A VOICE barked. "Rise and shine."

Maria, almost in a stupor, had to be shaken awake on her cot by Laureen, a voluptuous blonde in a skintight, low-cut, fuchsia sweater and black leather miniskirt. One of her two cell mates.

"Gotta get up, honey," Laureen drawled.

Maria squinted her eyes open groggily, saw the heavily made-up blonde smiling down on her and shut her eyes again. *Oh please, let this all be a bad dream.*

"D'Amato," the guard barked again. "You want to loll around this joint all day or do you want to get out of here?"

The instant Maria heard the words *get out of here,* she popped up in a flash, forgetting about the bunk bed above her upon which Sue Ellen, who was drying out, was still snoring loudly. She remembered the bunk fast enough when her head crashed into the bar running across it.

"Did you say...get out of here?" Maria asked hoarsely, rubbing the wounded spot on the top of her head.

The bars to the cell slid back. "That's what I said," the guard repeated laconically.

Laureen grinned at Maria, revealing a crooked front tooth. "See, didn't I tell you it would all work out?"

The guard rapped his knuckles against the bars. "Let's move it, D'Amato. I don't have all day."

Maria sprang out of the cot, paused briefly to give Laureen a hug. "Thanks for listening to my long, sad story."

Laureen grinned. "Thanks for not asking me to tell you mine. I mean it really gets old. How come a nice girl like you blah, blah, blah?"

Maria smiled. "You take care, Laureen."

"You too, Maria. And you be sure to give my best to your pal, Sean. Sounds like quite a fellah. Tell him if he ever comes back this way—"

"D'Amato."

Maria hurried out of the cell. "Say goodbye to Sue Ellen for me," she called back with a wave.

SEAN WAS WAITING FOR her in the sheriff's office, which was only a couple of steps up in decor and comfort from the interrogation room where they'd spent close to three hours being questioned the previous night. Sean looked disheveled, once again in need of a shave, and anxious, but the anxiety bled from his face when she smiled at him.

The sheriff actually rose from his chair as she stepped inside. "Have a seat, Miss D'Amato."

This time he spoke her name like he truly believed it.

Sean gave her a reassuring smile. She sat down beside him. He reached over and took her hand. She held on for dear life.

"You'll be pleased to know, Miss D'Amato, that we got a few things straightened out," the sheriff said, his manner and tone of voice completely different than the night before. Maria also noticed that the blue suits weren't present this time around.

"First off," the sheriff went on, "we've got Luke Cooper in custody. Rusty's still on the lam, but it's only a matter of time. Luke's gonna play ball with us and that makes me and the FBI boys real happy."

"What about . . . us?" Maria asked nervously.

"Cooper confirms your story. Says he didn't know you from Adam and neither did Rusty. They figured you'd make good dupes if they ran into trouble."

We were dupes, all right, Maria thought.

"Then I also gave a call over to the sheriff's office in Rochester, Pennsylvania. He confirms the police report on that robbery at the general store you two gave him. Oh, and you'll be happy to hear your pocketbook and Mr. MacNeil's briefcase and wallet were turned in by a motorist who spotted the items tossed in a trash barrel at one of those roadside rest spots about five miles out of town. Naturally, the money and credit cards were gone, but your driver's licenses, photos and such were intact. And the papers were still in your briefcase, Mr. MacNeil. If you leave a forwarding address I'll get word back as to where they can send your things."

"Right," Maria said, feeling the oddest sensation at the thought of leaving Michael's address. Well, that was where she would be staying from now on. She caught a glimpse of Sean out of the corner of her eye. He'd told her the hotshot Hollywood producer was putting him up at one of the posh Beverly Hills hotels temporarily, but that as soon as everything was finalized, he'd help Sean find a nice, classy, beachfront bungalow. Funny, but when Sean told her about his upscale accommodations, he hadn't sounded particularly bowled over at the thought of living in the lap of luxury. Neither one of them, she realized, was particularly impressed by material things. Money was not an end in itself for either of them. Maria simply wanted a home and family. Sean wanted enough money so he could write his novel full-time. Yet now, for different reasons, they were both being thrust into a world of glitz and glamour. She wondered how Sean would fare as a "celebrity." It would be different for her. She'd have Michael, Cassie, a home of her own....

"Well," the sheriff said, rising, "I guess you two are free to go."

Neither of them had the faintest idea where they were going, but they got out of the jailhouse in a hurry.

Once out on the street, they came to a stop and looked at each other.

"Are you okay, Maria?" Sean asked with such tender concern that tears sprang to her eyes and her bottom lip started to tremble.

Sean traced a finger down her cheek, and the next thing she knew, she was walking into the circle of his arms.

"Oh, Sean." It was all she could say.

"I know, baby. I know," he murmured, holding her close.

She sniffed. "You...smell funny."

He grinned. "Eau de clink."

She drew back and sniffed at herself. "Oh, God, I smell awful, too." Tears started to stream down her face as the whole terrible night hit her full force.

"Cheer up, Maria. How much worse can it get?"

Even with the tears flowing, she gave him a sardonic look.

"Okay, here's what we're going to do. Find ourselves a cash machine, get some dough, buy ourselves a change of clothes—even when these duds were nice and clean, let's face it, they weren't exactly us. Then we'll get ourselves a room...."

Maria pulled away fully. "Whoa."

"Relax. Just to shower and change. Sheriff Drury says there's a train out of Little Springs at four this afternoon that goes as far as Silver Falls, Arizona. From there, he's pretty sure we can hook up on a train or possibly a bus to L.A.''

"You mean we might really make it to L.A. by tomorrow, after all?" she asked incredulously.

"By tomorrow night, you'll be in Michael's arms and this will all seem like nothing more than a bad dream," he said wistfully. Only it wasn't some other guy's arms he was picturing her being wrapped in. It was his arms. He pictured it vividly, feeling an unfamiliar ache inside himself.

Maria stared at him. "It hasn't all been ... bad," she murmured. Far from it, she thought. Some of it had been altogether wonderful. Would any man ever make her get so angry or laugh so hard again? More to the point, would Michael?

Sean met her gaze. He thought if he wasn't careful he could lose himself completely in Maria's eyes. "No, it hasn't."

They were both quiet for a long moment, both of them privately wishing L.A. was a longer way off.

"Well, I guess we'd better...find that cash machine," Sean finally muttered.

Chapter Eight

Babbling Brook Motel
Little Springs, Texas
Wednesday—late morning

THE BABBLING BROOK Motel, a short walk from the Little Springs train station, was several cuts above their last motel accommodations and a veritable palace when compared to the jail cells where they'd "lodged" last night. Their room had clean, off-white walls and a queen-size bed whose cotton bedspread done in Southwestern hues had matching drapes. Nice, plush maroon carpeting covered the floor. There was a color TV, a phone in the room, a coffeemaker and even a little patio out back that faced onto a real babbling brook.

The bathroom was pure heaven. As soon as Maria spotted the sparkling-clean tub, she knew that there was nothing she wanted more in the world at that moment than a nice, long bath.

"Go for it," Sean said as he saw her eyeing the tub from the bathroom door. He was feeling altogether chipper as he took out his new pair of jeans, white cowboy shirt and fresh underwear from the shopping bag. From another sack, he removed a new denim jacket, his old one having shrunk a good two sizes after Mrs. Morton had put it in her dryer. "The train leaves at four-ten. That gives us close to six hours."

"I may spend five of them in the tub. Why don't you go first?" she suggested, unpacking the bag of toiletries. She actually hugged her brand-new tooth-brush to her chest.

"Okay," he said compatibly. "I won't be long."

Maria smiled at him. They were both in great spirits. Like two lost souls who'd been to hell and back together. Survivors. Comrades. Pals. She thought about what Mrs. Morton had said about adversity making them feel closer to each other. She did feel close to Sean. Maybe a little too close...

Getting her mind off Sean, she took out her new purchases from a sack—a plum-colored cotton-knit jersey jumper, a paler mulberry man-tailored cotton shirt and a charcoal-heather V-neck cardigan. Also in the bag was a pair of sensible, comfortable, black leather loafers. Sean had insisted he didn't want her having to walk down the aisle a cripple—which she might be if she continued wearing those pumps.

Walk down the aisle. When Sean had made that comment, it had given her this funny feeling in her stomach. Butterflies. Pre-wedding jitters. Or wasn't it the idea of walking down the aisle that had her in-sides churning? Was it who she was walking down the aisle with? Was there a small part of her that was beginning to think that she'd be a lot less anxious if it were Sean and not Michael with whom she was tying the knot? Nonsense, she told herself. And even if it wasn't utter nonsense, it was a hopeless fantasy. Sean had made it totally clear from the get-go that marriage was out of the picture for him. If he was going to be married at all, it was going to be to his art.

"Sean," she called out to him as he started for the bathroom.

He glanced back at her. "Something you forgot to buy?"

"No. I just want you to know that . . . I'll pay you back for everything you bought me today. And for half the motel room."

"That's okay. I owe you."

"What do you mean?"

"In particular, I mean that dress that got away back at the Port Authority Bus Terminal. In general, I mean . . . well, everything. Anyway," he added, "in a few days, if all goes as planned, I'll be rolling in dough, remember?"

She studied him thoughtfully. "Why aren't you smiling? Isn't that what you want more than anything? I mean, so you can be free to write your novel?"

"Money's serious business. I told you I could be serious about some things."

"Serious doesn't preclude feeling happy," she said.

He wagged a finger at her. "Now who's playing Dr. Freud?"

MARIA DIDN'T SPEND five hours in the bathtub, but she did spend close to thirty minutes, only getting out when the skin on her fingertips started to resemble raisins. Drying off on a nice fluffy towel, she brushed her hair, brushed her teeth and even put on a bit of newly purchased lip gloss. Then she slipped into her new panties, bra, shirt and jumper, and stepped barefoot into the bedroom.

"So, what do—?" She swallowed the rest of the sentence when she saw Sean, dressed in his jeans and new shirt, stretched out on the huge bed, fast asleep.

Maria yawned, finding the idea of a little shut-eye mighty tempting herself. She hadn't exactly had a great night's sleep on that foul, crummy cot in the jail cell.

As soon as she saw that the motel room did have an alarm-clock radio that she could set so there'd be no chance of sleeping past the time they needed to leave for the train station, she decided to follow Sean's example.

After setting the alarm and double-checking to make sure she'd set it properly, Maria's gaze shifted to the bed. Once again she was finding herself in the awkward situation of sharing a bed with Sean. Only now, it didn't feel so awkward. Actually, she wished she did feel a little more awkward. Instead, she felt a lot of other emotions. Breathless, disoriented, charged-up. Her gaze drifted down Sean's sleeping form. Clean-shaven again, his damp hair curling slightly, his shirt opened halfway down his chest, his jeans...

Her gaze lingered on his jeans—the way they fit him so snugly. He made a damn sexy-looking cowboy, even if he'd been born and raised in upstate New York.

Damn you, Sean MacNeil. You come catapulting into my life, spark catastrophe at every turn, and all I have to do is look at you and my heart's plummeting to my stomach. Even when she'd been convinced without question six months back that she was in love with Michael, he'd never had quite this effect on her. Then again, he'd never put her through the turmoil, aggravation, fury, and frustration that had been consuming her since Sean had first swung his suitcase into hers and all her clothes had gone tumbling out on the pavement. Now it was her heart doing the tumbling.

Gingerly, she stretched out way over on her side of the bed, being as careful as she could not to wake him. Oh, the joy of a nice, firm mattress, clean sheets, a soft pillow. She closed her eyes, thinking she'd drift off within seconds.

Only she couldn't sleep. She just lay there, flooded with confusion and all sorts of anxieties, now that L.A. really was only a day away.

"You're doing it again," Sean murmured.

She gave a little start. "I thought you were asleep."

"I was. And then the delicious smell of fresh soap and minty toothpaste started drifting past my nose and woke me up."

"Sorry."

"Don't be. It's a great smell."

She smiled. "You smell a lot better yourself."

Sean rolled onto his side to face her. "So what are you worried about now, Maria?"

"Who said I was worried? Okay, I'm worried." She sighed. "I keep thinking, why did Michael change his mind? Six whole months without a word and then..."

"And then Cassie arrives on his doorstep and you're wondering if he really wants a wife or a live-in child-care worker?"

"You're playing psychiatrist again."

" Am I wrong? I'm not wrong."

"So you've got it all figured out."

"No," he said softly. "Far from it." If he did have it all figured out, his pulse wouldn't be pounding away at his temples, his priorities wouldn't all be in a jumble, and he'd be thinking about his novel instead of obsessing over a woman who was about to get married. Well, she'd made it as plain as the nose on his face that marriage was her goal. She was completely up-front about it. Just as he had been about never wanting to make that kind of commitment. Marriage scared the hell out of him. He knew too many married would-be writers who'd ended up having to give up their dreams to support the wife and kiddies....

"He says he loves me. Well, he wrote he loves me."

The expression in her eyes was so piercing he had to look away. "And you love him."

"Yes." She shifted her gaze from him now. "I did love him six months ago. Why wouldn't I still love him?"

"You tell me, Maria," he said softly.

She shut her eyes. "Okay, I have some...reservations. Michael has his faults. But so do I. So do we all."

"Everyone except me, that is," he teased.

She gave him a friendly nudge in the arm. "Right. You're one of a kind."

"So are you." This time there wasn't a hint of teasing in his voice.

A rush of panic shot through her. Or was it desire? The two emotions were hard for her to separate at the moment. "Sean, we can't..."

He didn't pretend not to know what she was talking about. The sexual tension enveloped them like a thick blanket. He drew a little closer to her. "Does that mean you don't want to?"

"Yes."

"Yes, you do? Or yes, you don't?"

"No. I don't know. I can't think straight around you."

"What if we put off thinking until later?"

Her heart was pounding. "This is crazy."

"Name me one thing that hasn't been crazy since we met."

Maria laughed softly. "I can't."

His fingers moved to her hair, threading through the thick strands. "Neither can I," he murmured, pressing his lips to hers.

They moved against each other, their bodies fitting as smoothly as the pieces of a puzzle.

He smoothed her hair away. "We're getting our fancy new duds all wrinkled. Don't you think it would be smart to take them off?"

After a moment's hesitation, they undressed quickly, with a kind of adolescent awkwardness, at opposite sides of the big bed. Naked, they stared across at each other in a moment of mutual shyness.

"You're beautiful, Maria." Now he was drawn, not only by her incredible eyes but by her lovely body. Despite her slenderness, there was a sensual, womanly fullness to her breasts and hips. He was instantly aroused.

Maria smiled tremulously, pleased by his lean, firm body as much as how it reacted to her. They slid quickly, eagerly under the cool sheets and met in the middle. They kissed again—a wild, lawless kiss, full of passion and abandon.

They began to stroke and caress each other like long-lost soul mates. So many events had bound them together over these past few days, this event seemed inevitable.

"You know, as awful as it was in jail last night, I thought about you and... and it wasn't so unbearable," she confessed as his fingers traced an invisible line down her spine.

"I thought of you every moment, Maria. I will never be able to not think of you."

They held each other tight, clinging to each other, fighting to make sense of their crazy feelings; wanting somehow to stop time in its tracks. Tracks that would lead them tomorrow on such different paths. Tracks that they each felt they must travel on to get what they wanted. There might be passion and desire between them, but they both knew there was no future.

Maria felt such bittersweet pangs. This was a beginning and an end for them. She drew back a little, fixing her eyes on Sean, as if committing him to memory. Only it wasn't necessary. There would be no forgetting. Not even if she tried to forget. And she knew there would be moments when she would try. Try desperately. Once she and Michael were married, there would be times she would feel both guilt and unbidden passion for this man who had evoked so many contrary and confounding emotions in her.

Sean stroked her cheek with the back of his hand. "Don't worry, Maria. Not now."

She smiled tremulously. "I'm not worrying, Sean."

They began making love, taking it slow, every touch filled with tender consideration. Maria tried desperately and without success not to compare Sean with Michael. There was no denying that Michael had been an expert lover. He knew all the right moves, clearly took pride in his creativity, endurance, and expertise. Sean, on the other hand, made love to her with his heart. Sloppy, noisy, clumsy, but so ardent and so intent on pleasing her that it nearly brought Maria to tears.

She felt sensations that were completely new to her—taking, giving, sharing, conquering, surrendering—all at the same time. With Sean, she could relinquish the reserve that had been an intrinsic part of her lovemaking with Michael. Somehow, Michael had always seemed less interested in her than in the pride he took in the conquest.

Sean made her feel desirable, beautiful. No, more than that. Precious. He crooned his pleasure over every inch of her body, which he explored, stroked and tasted with boyish gusto.

She held on tight as the tiny tremors began to shake her body. Sean kissed her, caressed her—his face, even though clean-shaven, rough against her cheek, his body hard and throbbing against her body.

Sean was trembling, too. He hadn't planned this. If anything, he'd tried to keep his guard up against just such an occurrence. Yet, the whole time—even when he truly believed she hated him and he felt she was being a pain in the ass—something inside him told him this moment was inevitable. All last night in that jail cell, when he wasn't sick with worry over how she was faring in her cell, he was besieged by fantasies about her, about what she would be like in bed.

Expecting nervousness, caution, and reserve, her spontaneity, impetuosity and openness had reawakened parts of him that had lain dormant for years. Maria made him potently aware of the difference between having sex and making love. It was a difference he would never forget.

He heard her breathing coming in shallow pants, saw her luminous brown eyes speaking to him from her soul. He claimed her lips as he claimed her body, feeling, as they connected, a surge of joy that was beyond description.

Afterward, for a brief time as they lay in each other's arms, Maria's body curled into Sean's, they felt removed from real time, real space. They had created a tiny encapsulated universe and inside that world they experienced a sense of peace and well-being that neither of them had known before.

He gently stroked her hair and Maria knew she should be thinking about loyalty and morality, but all she could feel was Sean's body against hers; Sean's heart beating in rhythm with hers.

Don't think, she told herself. *For once, don't worry. Have this time. This once-in-a-lifetime time.*

She pressed her lips to his chest, right over his heart. Tears spiked his eyes as a wave of possessiveness that he knew he had no right to, swept over him. Tomorrow, she would be in another man's arms. In a matter of days, she would be another man's wife.

And yet, oddly enough, he knew that she was his in a way that she would never be Michael's.

"Maria...."

"Yes?" Even she could hear the anticipation in her voice. What if he asked her to change her plans? What if he told her she was a fool to marry Michael? What if he told her he no longer wanted to be a bachelor for the rest of his life? What if...?

The shrill ring of the alarm clock kept Sean from making his response. They stared at each other, suddenly feeling guilty and exposed.

"Well, I guess...we've got a train to catch." His voice was a bare whisper.

Maria nodded, not trusting her voice.

Swinging their legs over opposite sides of their bed, they reached for their clothes and dressed quickly and silently. They got to the front door at the same time, their hands reaching and meeting at the doorknob. For an instant, their gazes met and then they both looked back at the rumpled bed, remembering each other's responsive bodies, the plateaus of pleasure they had found, the tenderness and the passion—all fused together.

Maria dropped her hand from the doorknob and Sean opened the door. The glare of the late-afternoon Texas sun hit them full in the face as they stepped outside, but they each knew they were leaving indelible traces of themselves back in that motel room.

Chapter Nine

As THE BUS ROLLED INTO the station, both Maria and Sean did a double take. This wasn't just any bus heading for L.A. This was *their* bus. When the bus driver opened the door and stared down at them from his seat, he scratched his head.

"You two get hitched?" he asked.

"What?" Maria and Sean said in unison.

"That was the consensus when you two didn't show for the bus back in Pennsylvania."

"That's ... ridiculous," Maria said. "We'd never even set eyes on each other before we boarded your bus. Why would anyone ... think such a thing?"

The bus driver shrugged, pointing back at his busload of passengers. "Not *any*one. Just about *every*one. Oh, two or three thought you'd gotten kidnapped, but the rest figured the way you two were going at it from the time we left New York City, you were gonna end up tying the knot."

Maria flushed. So did Sean.

"For your information," Maria said, climbing aboard and addressing the passengers as well as the driver, "it just so happened we did get kidnapped."

"And that's just the half of it," Sean said, coming up behind her.

Maria reddened even more. There were a number of titters from the peanut gallery. "Sean means we were robbed, got caught in a torrential storm, got flown to Texas by the owner of a Tex-Mex restaurant, got mistaken for being part of a drug ring and ended up spending the night in jail, and..." She let the rest of the sentence hang.

"And that's not the half of it," Sean repeated with a teasing smile as they started down the aisle, looking for seats.

Maria poked him in the ribs. Seeing an empty seat beside an older woman who was busy knitting, she swung into it.

"Oh," the woman said immediately, "you two will want to sit together. I'd be happy to move...."

"No, really, it isn't necessary," Maria said firmly.

Sean sighed under his breath and continued down the aisle to a vacant seat a few rows back.

Ever since they'd left the motel in Little Springs, there'd been a constrained awkwardness between them. So much had happened between them so fast, it was impossible to digest it all. Their heads were spinning. Maria felt awash with guilt and alarm. How could she have made love with Sean and be about to marry another man? How could she become so passionately attracted to a man in a matter of little more than four days? Four insane, disastrous days. How could she start out hating Sean and wind up loving him?

Loving him. Oh, God, did she love him? Talk about jumping straight from the frying pan into the fire. At least Michael wanted to marry her. At least he'd told her he loved her. Sean had never uttered the word *love*. The last thing in the world he wanted was to get married and be tied down to a wife. Oh, sure, he'd told Mrs. Morton he loved children, but he was probably just intent on winning her favor. If he loved kids so much, why was he so opposed to having any of his own?

It was impossible, she thought. The only solution was to put Sean out of her mind altogether. In ten hours she'd be arriving in L.A. Michael and Cassie would be waiting for her, embracing her, ready to embark with her on a new life. She was doing the right thing. She was getting what she wanted. Stability, security, family. All things that Sean could never—or at least would never be willing to—offer her. Everything was going to turn out just fine.

Maria stared past the woman who was knitting, and focused on the passing landscape, watching it roll by. So, if everything was going to be so hunky-dory, why was she feeling so miserable?

Sean sat beside the same middle-aged woman who'd kept asking him and Maria to be quiet that first night on the bus. She was peeling an orange and offered him a section.

Sean shook his head. "No, thanks."

His seatmate introduced herself as Adele Fine and proceeded to give him an unabashed study. "So, you two had yourselves quite an adventure."

He smiled wistfully. "You could say that."

"I read your story."

He glanced over at her. "Excuse me?"

"'A Life Adrift.' You left it on your seat."

"How did you know I wrote it?"

"I overheard the two of you talking. So, you're going to be a big Hollywood screenwriter. My son's in the business. He's an assistant director with aspirations."

"I don't have aspirations," Sean said quietly. "As far as Hollywood, I mean. I'm negotiating a deal to write the screenplay for my story and that's the very last screenplay I intend to write. In fact, the faster I can get out of Tinseltown, the happier I'll be." Especially now. Especially knowing that Maria would be living there. Living with her husband, her stepdaughter. The thought of running into her was more than he felt he could handle.

Adele Fine gave a little snort.

"What?" he asked.

"You're a babe in the woods, Sean. Once they get their hooks into you in Hollywood, they don't let go till they're good and ready. As to when you're ready..." She waved that off as so much nonsense.

"My son's roommate is a screenwriter. Danny Chapin. Ever hear of him?"

"No," Sean said. "To be honest, I'm not much for movies. I prefer reading."

"You mean you prefer writing," Adele said with a smile. "And, even though I'm far from an expert, let me tell you that you do it damn well, pardon my French. I was crying like a baby when I finished your story. That Eleanor. She was really something." She paused, her gaze drifting up the aisle.

Sean knew exactly what she was thinking. He nodded. "Yeah, Maria reminded me of Eleanor the instant I laid eyes on her."

The woman gave him a friendly little nudge. "And Eleanor ended up with Andy, right? The writer?"

"Maria's ending up with Michael," Sean said somberly. "The hotshot game-show producer."

"Michael?"

"Michael," Sean reiterated.

Adele Fine sighed. "It's a real pity."

Sean sighed, too. "Tell me about it."

IT WAS ABOUT FIVE-THIRTY in the morning and Maria had finally managed to doze off when the bus came to a grinding halt. Her eyes sprang open. *Oh no,* she thought. *Not again.*

Several other passengers stirred, but many remained sleeping. Maria slipped out of her seat and went up the aisle to find out what was wrong.

"Look for yourself," the driver said, pointing straight ahead to the road.

Maria stared out the windshield as the sun was just peeking over the horizon and she blinked rapidly. "Turtles?"

"Yep."

Sean came up behind her. He hadn't managed to get to sleep yet. "What's up?" he asked.

"Turtles," Maria muttered.

Sean glanced out at the road. "Holy cow, you ain't whistling Dixie. There must be hundreds of them. What are they doing?"

"What does it look like they're doing?" Maria snapped. "They're crossing the highway."

"What for?"

The driver chuckled. "To get to the other side."

"Another comedian," Maria snickered.

Sean grinned at the driver. "I thought it was funny."

"You would," Maria said, turning to go back to her seat.

Sean blocked her path.

"Do you mind?" she inquired.

"I mind a lot," he answered. He glanced at the driver. "How long do you think we're going to be held up?"

The driver shrugged. "Last time I hit a turtle migration, we were stuck for close to an hour."

"Sean," Maria said tightly, "I'd like to return to my seat."

"I think what you need is a breath of fresh air," Sean countered.

"I don't think it's your place to decide what you think I need."

"Please, you two," the driver entreated. "I've got a lot of sleeping people on this bus. If you're gonna start going at it again..."

"You're right. We don't want to disturb the passengers. Could you open the door?" Sean asked him. "We'll step outside."

"Do not open that door," Maria ordered the driver. "I am going back to my seat."

Sean stood his ground, blocking her path.

Maria glared at him.

"Oh, those eyes," he murmured. "Doesn't she have great eyes, driver?"

"Sean, if you don't get out of my way this instant..." she hissed.

The door whooshed open. Sean winked at the driver, then practically dragged Maria off the bus. Several passengers had woken by this point and were looking out their windows at the two of them. Most of them were smiling.

Maria turned to Sean, steaming. "You know what's going to happen, don't you?"

"No, I haven't a clue."

"That bus driver will probably drive off without us. We'll be...stranded again."

"Naw," he said with a teasing smile. "That would be too much to hope for."

"Oh, be serious, Sean," she said, exasperated.

He reached out and caught hold of her shoulders. "Do you really want me to be serious?"

Maria's breath caught. "Yes." She pressed her lips together. "No." She shook her head. "I don't know."

"What do you want from me, Maria?"

She looked away. If she had to tell him that, then there really was nothing she wanted.

"I've never asked anything from you," she said quietly.

"I know. I've been the one who kept getting in your way. If I'd sat next to Mrs. Fine that first day, I guess...none of what happened to us...would have happened."

"I guess not," Maria said so softly Sean barely heard her.

They stood silently for a few minutes.

"Damn it, Maria. I'm not sorry. I'm not sorry any of it happened, except maybe that crummy night in jail. And I'm especially not sorry—"

She spun around and pressed her fingers to his lips. "Don't, Sean. Don't say anything more. Please."

"Just tell me one thing, Maria, and then I'll shut up."

Maria's gaze drifted toward the bus. She saw a good dozen passengers looking out at them. "We're providing the entertainment."

"Maria."

She looked back at Sean. "Okay, what is it?"

"Do you regret any of it, Maria?"

She closed her eyes and let the memories of those past five days sweep over her. That first encounter, her clothes flying everywhere, Sean tripping over her overnight case as he started in pursuit of her runaway dress; their tug-of-war over that same overnight case on the side of the road, Sean grabbing her so suddenly, falling with her onto the grassy embankment where she watched that eighteen-wheeler make a pancake out of her case. He'd saved her life, and she hadn't even thanked him. Everything else that had happened to them rolled through her mind like a videotape on fast forward—the robbery, being tied up together in that shed, feeling those first unbidden flashes of arousal, flashes that came faster and more frequently as they spent that cozy day and night with Mrs. Morton pretending to be engaged to be married. Even though that encounter had ultimately led them to spend a night in jail, it hadn't stopped her mounting desire for Sean. What had happened in that motel room afterward was something neither one of them could have stopped. Would have wanted to stop.

Slowly, she opened her eyes. "No, Sean. I don't regret any of it." She smiled winsomely. "Maybe you'll include some of it in…your novel. I never did tell you that I think you're a wonderful writer. I don't doubt for an instant that you will write the Great American Novel."

"Maria."

"You know, there's one thing you can tell me, Sean."

He looked at her expectantly. *Help me, Maria. There're so many things I want to say, but I'm scared to death.* "Anything," he said quickly.

"Who is Oscar Armstrong?"

He gave her a baffled look.

"That first day on the bus. When you told me you grew up in that little town. Winston. And you told me the only reason Winston was famous was for being the home of Oscar Armstrong. Who was he?"

"My grandfather. On my mother's side. He was famous for marrying my grandmother, who had my mother who had me." A soft smile curled his lips. "Another example of my warped sense of humor."

Maria swallowed hard. "No. No, it isn't warped. That's funny."

He touched her cheek lightly with the back of his hand. "So, how come you're not smiling?"

"I am," she whispered, close to tears. "It just doesn't always show."

He stared into her eyes. "Your eyes show everything." Everything but the one thing he needed to know: that there was no way in the world she could now go through with her marriage to Michael.

The door of the bus whooshed open. "All clear. You two get things settled?" the driver called out to them.

Settled? they both thought. *Now that was funny!*

Chapter Ten

Bus Station
Los Angeles
Thursday afternoon

"LOOK, DADDY, LOOK! There she is!" Cassie shouted excitedly, tugging on her father's suit jacket.

No sooner had Maria alighted from the bus, than the four-year-old, her blond ponytail flying, raced for her.

Maria scooped Cassie up in her arms and gave her a big hug. "Why, I almost didn't recognize you, you've grown so much. And where did all that hair come from?" she playfully asked, tugging on the little girl's ponytail.

"It grew. I'm going to let it grow forever," Cassie said emphatically.

Maria looked up at Michael, who had walked over to join them. He looked even more handsome and well-groomed than she'd remembered. His sandy-colored hair was perfectly coiffed. His three-piece blue-gray suit was impeccably cut. He looked so reassuringly conservative. So self-possessed. So sure of himself. Well, at least one of them was.

"Hi, darling," he said warmly, giving her a light kiss on the lips. "You look beat."

"No, she doesn't, Daddy. She looks beautiful," Cassie piped in.

It was at that precise moment that Sean walked past the "happy" threesome. Maria watched him go by from the corner of her eye, then spotted a limousine driver holding up a card with the name, Sean MacNeil. No more buses for Sean. It was going to be first class all the way for him from here on out.

"What's the matter, Maria?" Cassie asked, staring up into her face. "You look sad."

She forced a smile as she gently lowered the child to the ground. "Your daddy's right. I am beat."

"I still can't imagine what possessed you to come out here by bus, Maria," Michael said. "You never know what screwballs you might run into."

"No," she said with a whisper of a smile. "You never know."

Michael gave her a close look. Then he drew her into his arms. "I am glad you're here, darling. I've been counting the minutes."

"Me, too," Cassie said, taking hold of Maria's hand.

As Michael held her close, Maria's gaze fell on Sean, who was walking off with the chauffeur. Suddenly he glanced back and for a moment, their eyes met before Maria lowered her lids, afraid he'd see the pain and loss mirrored in her gaze.

"I'm really sorry about this," Michael was saying.

Maria focused back on him. "What?"

"I said I hate having to run off like this, but I was expecting you to arrive before lunch. Cassie and I were going to take you to Spago. It's almost two now and I've got a damn meeting over at Fox at three. I'll have my driver take the two of you home and I'll grab a limo."

"When will you be back?" Maria asked anxiously. She'd thought he'd at least have cleared this one day for them to spend time together.

"By dinner, I promise," Michael assured her, bussing her on the cheek. "I know. Why don't you make a reservation at Seito's. You'll love it. They've got the best sushi in town."

She hated sushi. "What time?"

"Eight. No, better make that eight-thirty."

"Isn't that . . . awfully late? I thought we could all have dinner together tonight—you, me, and Cassie."

"Oh goody," Cassie said, jumping up and down. "I get to eat sushi, too. What is sushi, Daddy?"

Michael gave Maria a faintly sharp look, then ruffled his daughter's hair. "You wouldn't like sushi at all. It's raw fish."

"Yuck ," Cassie said, scrunching up her little pug nose.

"Maria will make you some delicious spaghetti and meatballs for supper and tuck you into bed before we go out," Michael said with that note of cool authority that Maria used to define as self-assurance.

"Spaghetti and meatballs," Cassie said gleefully. "Just like when I was in your school, Maria. Remember how much I loved your spaghetti and meatballs?"

"Yes," Maria said quietly. "I remember, Cassie."

"WELL, MY BOY," Lou Harcourt said as they roared away from the studio in the producer's sleek red Ferrari coupe. "You did it. You really blitzed them."

Sean wasn't so sure. "They seem to want an awful lot of changes."

"Naturally," Harcourt said, popping a cigar into his mouth and pushing in the car lighter. "You don't mind, do you?"

"Well, actually..." Sean wasn't fond of cigar smoke in the best of circumstances. And even though he was close to signing a deal for a quarter of a million bucks for writing the screenplay for "A Life Adrift," this somehow didn't feel like anything close to the best of circumstances.

"I'm telling you, buddy, you've got them eating out of your hand," Harcourt said, lighting up.

Sean looked over at the producer. He smiled faintly. Harcourt looked so much like his stereotype of a hotshot Hollywood wheeler-dealer. The classy suit, the slicked-back hair, the gold Rolex watch, the fancy sportscar.

"I'd like to try to get the first draft in by the end of the month," Sean said. "Then, if there aren't too many revisions, I thought I'd rent a cabin up in the mountains...."

Harcourt chuckled. "Cabin, schmabin. We'll get you a swank little bungalow like you never dreamed of, right on the ocean. A hop, skip and a jump from all the action. And Sean, baby, nobody writes a first draft of their first screenplay that doesn't need a lot of revisions. So, settle in, my boy. We're gonna have ourselves a wild and woolly ride."

Sean sighed. "I've already had that, thanks," he mumbled.

"What's that?" Harcourt asked.

"Nothing."

"Well, we've got to celebrate tonight, that's for sure. I'll get us a couple of knockout starlets that are gonna make you drool, kid, and we're gonna go to this nifty sushi bar over in Little Tokyo. You'll love it. What's it called again? Oh yeah. Seito's. What do you say I make a reservation for around eight-thirty? No one who's anyone in this town eats before then. Maybe if your luck holds out, kid, you'll see some people there that'll make your eyes pop out of your head."

"Is that the only dress you brought with you?" Michael asked as he walked over to her in the small-but-elegant waiting area of the Japanese restaurant. He didn't even make an effort to conceal his displeasure at the white jersey top she'd teamed with a simple houndstooth-check skirt. Cassie had told her she looked great. So had Cassie's baby-sitter for the evening.

"I did have this fantastic black sheath, but it got away," she said dryly.

Her fiancé gave her a skewed look. "You haven't been drinking, have you?"

"No," she said. "But I'd like to start."

Michael glanced cautiously at her. "You're behaving very strangely, Maria. Ever since you stepped off that bus..."

"Don't you think we'd better let the maître d' know we're here before someone else takes our reservation?"

"Not to worry, darling. Hiramatsu wouldn't dare not hold my table, no matter how late I showed up."

My table. Not *our* table, Maria couldn't help but notice.

She grabbed his arm as he started for the maître d's desk.

"What is it?" he asked, looking back at her.

"Michael..."

"You've never eaten sushi, right?"

"Yes, but that isn't..."

"Darling, sushi is a staple in L.A."

She pressed her hands to her mouth. "A...staple." All she could think about was that box of "staples" she'd been caught red-handed with back in Little Springs. A giggle escaped her lips as she remembered how she and Sean kept trying to explain to the sheriff that they really did believe they were loading staples and pencils onto the plane.

"Maria, what are you laughing about?"

She sobered up. "Oh, it's just something that happened along the way."

"I see."

She smiled wistfully. No, unlike Sean, he didn't see. Unlike Sean, Michael would never see. Which was why she had to tell him tonight, as soon as possible, hopefully before the sushi arrived, that she couldn't go through with it. She couldn't marry him....

"ARE ALL SCREENWRITERS so quiet?" the curvy twenty-two-year-old starlet cooed as she slipped an arm through Sean's.

"I'm not really a screenwriter. I'm just a writer who's writing one screenplay," Sean muttered as he walked through the restaurant door that Harcourt was holding open for him.

"Don't let him fool you, Denise," the producer said. "I've already got a half-dozen other properties I'm gonna have this genius adapt for me."

" No way," Sean insisted.

Brenda, Harcourt's date, who looked to be eighteen or nineteen, batted her big blue eyes at the producer. "I hope there'll be a hot part for a sexy ingenue in one of them."

"What do you think of me for Eleanor in 'A Life Adrift'?" Denise asked Sean as they entered the vestibule of Seito's. "Lou says I should definitely read for the part."

Sean felt a wave of depression hit him like a punch to his solar plexus. What was he doing here? How could any human being in their right mind imagine this ditzy, bland-faced, two-dimensional starlet could ever play Eleanor's pinky finger, never mind the actual character? And it wouldn't even surprise him if Denise or someone like Denise ended up with the part. Less than seven hours in this town, and already he knew he'd made a big mistake. All of a sudden his list of gripes about teaching at the prep school and therefore never having the time or energy to write seemed like just that. Gripes.

Hell, he loved teaching comparative literature. He loved those kids in his classes. Teaching wasn't the reason he wasn't writing his Great American Novel. *He* was the reason. He was missing something inside himself and that's what kept him from putting pen to paper. He was missing passion. He was missing love. The kind of love where nothing made any sense and yet everything made sense.

Maria. If he could sing her praises, he would. Right there in that restaurant. He loved her. Why the hell had it been so hard to tell her? And now it was too late. He'd lost her. And if he didn't leave this crazy town in a hurry, he'd lose himself, too. He wished now he'd picked up a bus schedule for the trip back to New York so he'd know what time to get there in the morning.

"Okay, our table's ready," Harcourt said, interrupting Sean's ruminations.

"Lou, there's something I've got to tell you—" Sean started.

"You gotta try the raw tuna," Harcourt interrupted. "What do they call it in Japanese again?"

MARIA LET OUT A LITTLE gasp as she saw Sean and his entourage enter the restaurant. He couldn't miss her either, as the maître d' was leading his party right past her table.

Sean stopped dead in his tracks as he approached her.

"Maria." His throat was dry.

"Sean." Her heart was racing.

Harcourt started to nudge Sean past the table until he recognized Maria's dining companion. "You're Michael Harding, right?"

"In the flesh."

The two young starlets' eyes lit up.

"Michael Harding?" Denise simpered. "The game-show producer?"

Michael gave her a provocative smile. "I know, ladies. You both want to be the next Vanna White."

Maria's and Sean's eyes remained fixed on each other while the others engaged in "business" chitchat.

"Maria, we've got to talk," Sean said.

"I know," Maria agreed.

"There's so much I—" He stopped short, the man at the next table suddenly catching his eye. "I don't believe it."

Maria was baffled. Until she turned to see who had drawn his attention away. Quickly, her gaze shot back to Sean.

"Rusty," they said in stunned unison.

"Rusty who?" Brenda asked excitedly, thinking she might get an intro to another Hollywood mover and shaker.

The man with the bright red hair heard his name and looked up. It took him a second to spot Sean and Maria in the group, another second or two to figure out why they looked so familiar. Then he cursed under his breath, leaping up from his seat to make a fast exit.

"He's getting away!" Maria shouted, springing from her chair. Everyone in the elegant, sedate restaurant turned to stare at her for making such an outburst.

"Not this time!" Sean shouted back, nearly running into a waiter carrying a tray of sushi as he raced after the drug smuggler. That left Maria, only a couple of paces behind Sean, to meet both the waiter and the sushi head-on.

Her outfit was now decorated with pieces of seaweed and raw fish as she continued racing after Rusty. It was Sean who tackled him right at the arched entry and then pinned him to the ground.

Maria bopped the downed felon on the head with another platter of sushi that had been meant for her table. "Someone call the police!" she cried out.

Sean grinned at her. "You smell awful."

She laughed. "I know."

"I don't give a damn."

"You don't?"

"I love you, Maria. What do you say we get our friend Rusty here behind bars, then take a honeymoon bus ride back to New York?"

"I say there's nothing like a cross-country bus ride. Maybe we can stop in Reno and tie the knot."

"Perfect," Sean said, as two of L.A.'s finest came bursting into the restaurant.

Epilogue

"ARE YOU ASLEEP?" Sean asked.

"No," Maria said, lifting her head from his shoulder. "I'm too excited to sleep. Are we almost in Reno?"

He grinned. "That eager, are you?"

"Yes," she said without hesitation. Then her eyes met his. "What about you?"

He pressed a moist kiss on her lips. A kiss filled with love. "If there was a minister on this bus, I'd have him do the honors right this minute."

"You still didn't tell me how Harcourt took the news that you didn't want to write the screenplay."

Sean shrugged. "He gave me a pep talk for about twenty minutes, then told me that screenwriters were a dime a dozen in Hollywood and if I didn't want to make a killing, there were plenty of guys just itching to take my place."

"It was a lot of money, Sean. Enough for you to write two or three novels without having to work."

"I don't need not to work, Maria. What I needed all along was a muse," he murmured, drawing her close. "You didn't tell me how Michael took the news that you weren't going to marry him."

She grinned. "Better than he should have. Before we left the restaurant with the cops and Rusty in tow, I saw that pretty redheaded starlet you were with giving Michael her phone number."

"The man doesn't waste time."

"No. That's one thing you can say about Michael. Of course, I could say a few other things about him, but I won't. It doesn't matter now."

"What about Cassie? I hope she didn't take it too hard."

Maria touched Sean's cheek. He would think about the child's feelings. "It's okay. I told her I'd visit her a lot in Connecticut. She's there with her mom six months out of the year. She made me promise when I come to see her to make her my famous spaghetti and meatballs."

"Famous, huh."

"World-class. You happen to be marrying a great cook. I'm Italian, remember."

He laughed. "I remember."

She snuggled against him and they were both about to close their eyes when the bus jerked to a sudden stop.

"Oh, no," they muttered in unison.

"Not another breakdown," Maria prayed aloud.

"Or more turtles wanting to get to the other side of the road. Did you ever wonder why—?"

"Sean."

"What?"

"Look. That passenger standing next to the bus driver."

"What about—?" He didn't need to finish his sentence. The passenger spun around at that very instant and pointed the gun in his hand at the rest of the riders.

"Nobody move," the thin, mean-looking gunman barked. "I'm hijacking this bus to Tijuana."

The woman in the seat closest to the hijacker cried out in alarm, distracting his attention for a moment. In that moment, Sean and Maria shared a look. No way were they going through this again.

They sprang from their seats at the same time as the woman who had cried out swooned and passed out cold.

Distracted, the hijacker didn't see Sean and Maria descending on him until it was too late. Maria went for his legs, Sean for his gut. With a loud grunt, the hijacker went flying backward, landing in a heap on the floor. Sean whipped the gun from his hand and the whole bus cheered the pair. Ten minutes later, the police were dragging the hijacker off the bus.

Sean winked at Maria. "Maybe I'll write a mystery novel and the protagonists could be this married duo who met on a cross-country bus ride...."

Reno, Nevada
Friday evening

"THIS IS IT," Sean called out to the bus driver as they started by a little white wedding chapel festooned with neon lights in downtown Reno.

Maria grinned. "You're right. It's perfect."

The bus squealed to a stop and the whole bus unloaded.

The minister greeted the huge group at the door. He smiled. "I'm afraid you've made a mistake. This is a real wedding chapel, not a sight-seeing spot."

The bus driver, who looked remarkably like Ralph Kramden from the old TV show, "The Honeymooners," nudged Maria and Sean toward the minister. "We've got ourselves a couple just itching to tie the knot. And we all," he said, waving his hand, "are their witnesses."

"Well, isn't that...different," the minister said, looking a bit muddled.

The minister's wife, a diminutive woman with a mop of gray curls, came scurrying over. She took one look at the wedding couple-to-be and tsked. "Oh, this will never do," she said, ushering them both off to a room to the right of the foyer. There, on a rack running the length of the room, was an assortment of wedding gowns—everything from a white stretch minidress to a full-length satin-and-lace gown with a long train—and tuxedos. Sean winked at Maria as he pulled out an outfit that Liberace and Elvis might have fought over. Maria made a face.

A SHORT WHILE LATER, the minister's wife, Mrs. Love—or so she said—played the wedding march on the small portable organ. The doors from the foyer opened and Maria, wearing a reasonably simple ankle-length white silk dress and a lacy veil, entered on the bus driver's arm.

The passengers lined the front seats on both sides of the aisle. Minister Love stood at the pulpit and Sean stood before it. Despite his teasing about what he might wear, to Maria's relief, he'd opted for a plain gray tux. And he'd even borrowed a razor from the minister, so he was clean-shaven.

As Sean watched Maria walk down the aisle, he thought she really was his dream come true. Never had he felt more truly blessed or more truly happy.

Maria smiled as she joined hands with Sean. Who would ever have imagined, at the disastrous onset of her cross-country trek, that this would be the outcome? She couldn't imagine a better one.

Now if only they could get through the ceremony without some new disaster befalling them. Then again, they were agreeing to go through with this "for better" or "for worse." And since they'd had plenty of the "worse," they figured they were more than due for the "better." As they sealed their vows with a passionate kiss, they realized the "better" had already arrived.

After the ceremony, everyone climbed back into the bus for the trek back to New York City. As the bus pulled out, Reverend and Mrs. Love smiled impishly.

Hanging on the back of the bus was a big sign.

JUST MARRIED

THE MARRYING MAN

Barbara Bretton

Chapter One

CATHERINE O'LEARY ZASLOW knew twenty-seven ways to kill a man, and on that morning before Thanksgiving she contemplated a twenty-eighth. If looks could kill, her agent would be six feet under.

"I must be crazy," she announced as Max took her coat then handed it to his assistant. "I don't know how I let you convince me to come all the way down to Manhattan for this meeting. This is the day before Thanksgiving, Max. Normal people are home baking pies, not taking meetings."

"This was the only day Riley McKendrick could make it," Max said. "We had to grab him when we could."

Cat took a seat at the long conference table. "So who is this Riley McKendrick, the uncrowned king of England?"

"Better than that," said Max, taking a seat opposite her. "McKendrick's the best time-management expert in the country. I know how you feel about organization, Catherine, but the time has come—"

"Forget it! If you think I'm letting one of those schedule-loving lunatics into my house so he can alphabetize my spices and color-code the toilet tissue, you're crazy."

"Think how successful you'd be if you could actually find your computer in that rattrap office of yours. I've been to your house, Catherine. I'm surprised you can find your children."

"You mind your business, Max, and I'll mind mine." What difference did it make that she had the organizational abilities of the average fruit fly? Everyone was clean, fed and happy. If more was required in raising children, she couldn't imagine what it was. Besides, her kids weren't any of Max's business, her books were. And these days her mystery novels were number one on bestseller lists across the country.

"Frank Fairbairn's production has doubled since he hired a time-management specialist to whip him into shape." Frank Fairbairn was her closest competition in the murder-mystery field. Max looked downright wistful at the thought of double production.

"Frank Fairbairn is a man," Cat pointed out. "His wife keeps his world running smoothly."

"Listen, if a wife'll get you back on track, I'll find you a wife."

"Gracie and I do just fine on our own." Gracie was her housekeeper, confidante and partner in chaos.

"I know Gracie," Max reminded her. "That's not a very convincing argument. The woman can't make scrambled eggs without consulting *The Joy of Cooking.*"

"I know why you're doing this," she said, tapping her index finger against the tabletop. "Last year it was a personal trainer, this year it's a time-management consultant. You're too trendy for your own good, Max."

"Trends come and trends go," Max intoned, "but an organized life is forever."

She glanced at her watch. "What time was he supposed to be here?"

Max shifted uncomfortably. "Ten o'clock."

"It's ten-fifteen," she observed. "Sounds like the world's best time-management consultant needs to have his credentials updated."

"This is Manhattan, Cat. He probably got stuck in traffic."

Cat rose then, walked around to the other side of the table and placed a quick kiss atop Max's elegant, perfectly barbered head. "Dinner's at four o'clock tomorrow, Max. We'll pick you up at the train station at three-fifteen."

"Catherine, Catherine, Catherine! See reason, please. An hour with Riley McKendrick will change your life forever."

"Sure, Max," she said. "That and a magic lamp with a genie inside. No nearsighted weenie with an obsession for clocks and calendars is going to get close enough to—" She stopped, a frown creasing her forehead. Max's smile was incandescent. His eyes sparkled. He'd seen reason!

Her heart soared with delight until she realized Max was looking right past her toward the door.

"McKendrick!" Max said in a booming, hail-fellow-well-met voice he reserved for contract negotiations and Elite models. "We were about to send out a search party."

"Sorry," drawled a deep male voice behind her. "Flat tire on East 54th Street."

The number-crunching clock-watcher. She barely suppressed a groan. If she hadn't stopped to kiss Max on the head, she'd be safely in the elevator and on her way home.

Well, big deal. She'd turn, she'd smile politely at the poor dweeb in the doorway, then excuse herself with dispatch.

She turned. She looked. Her entire life seemed to pass before her eyes.

That was no dweeb. That was the Marlboro Man—in all of his untamed, uncivilized Wild West glory.

Her jaw dropped open, and for a moment she wondered if she'd need professional help to get it closed.

The guy wore artfully faded jeans, a cream-colored sweater and a leather jacket that looked as if it had a few stories to tell. Her gaze slid across his torso, down his long, *long* legs, to the boots. And not the kind of boots you'd find on some ersatz urban cowboy. These were the real thing—tough, worn, sexy as hell.

Same as the man who wore them. He was at least six-four—and most of that was muscle. Hard, well-developed muscles, some of them in places where she'd believed only Greek statues had muscles. Dark hair, green eyes...your basic Adonis. For a moment she considered swooning but thought better of it. These were the nineties, after all, and modern women were supposed to take things like amazing male pulchritude in stride.

He was the kind of guy you saw on the cover of a paperback historical romance, one of those perfect specimens that came complete with a bosomy blond companion clutching at his manly chest.

That couldn't be the clock-watcher. Maybe he really *was* a cover model and that was why he was looming in Max's doorway. If she could breathe at all, she'd breathe a sigh of relief. Max handled a few big-name romance authors and he probably had a say in who posed for the covers. Riley McKendrick must be standing behind the Marlboro Man, hidden behind the cowboy's broad shoulders. You could hide a redwood tree behind those shoulders.

"Cat." Max's voice broke into her reverie. "I want you to meet Riley McKendrick."

She waited for a small, plain man to peer around the cowboy's shoulder but none did. *It can't be,* she thought, heartbeat accelerating. *It's just not possible!*

The cowboy smiled down at her. *This* was the man who watched clocks for a living? Impossible. Men who looked like this guy usually spent more time watching their mirrors. His teeth were white, shiny and symmetrical. Instead of money, the tooth fairy had probably left porcelain caps under his pillow.

"C. O. Lowe," McKendrick said, as her hand was swallowed up in his. "I know your books."

She nodded, aware that he'd said he *knew* her books, not that he liked them.

"My name's Cat," she managed, wishing she had more experience dealing with cowboy Adonises, "and I'm not interested in getting organized." Blunt but true.

"That's what they all say."

"I'm sure they do," she murmured as reason made a delayed return, "but let me say it again. I don't know what Max promised you, but there's no deal. Not with me."

Max popped up between them, a referee in a Nino Cerutti suit. "Coffee," he said in an unnaturally cheerful voice. "That's what we need. Coffee." He looked toward McKendrick. "How do you take it?"

Talk about a loaded question. A voluptuous shiver rose up from the soles of her feet and she wondered if anyone would notice if she poured a pitcher of ice water over her head.

"Black," said the cowboy. "No sugar."

"Cat?" Max asked.

"With cream," Cat mumbled. "Two sugars. Decaf."

"Decaf?" asked McKendrick.

"What's wrong with decaf?" she asked.

"Most people drink coffee for the caffeine."

"I drink it for the taste."

"No taste in decaf."

"That's why the cream and sugar."

"That's illogical."

"So sue me."

Max mumbled something then vanished in search of refreshments. Cat considered the wisdom of following hard on his heels but the cowboy barred the way.

"So what exactly do you have against organization?" McKendrick asked, bracing an arm against the doorjamb.

In for a penny, in for a pound. "Organization is anathema to the creative spirit." *Anathema,* she thought with a grin. Let him chew on that for a while.

He didn't bat an eye. Was it possible—brawn and brains? Dangerous combination. "I've seen your office," he said. "Your creative spirit better come with a road map."

"What do you mean, you've seen my office?"

"Max sent me pictures."

"Max will need a road map of the intensive care ward if he doesn't stop doing things like that."

"Don't blame Max." The guy had a smile that could light up a movie screen. "I asked him for one."

"Someone should have asked *me*."

"Someone should've sent in a wrecking crew."

Max hustled back in, balancing three mugs of coffee and a plate of bagels. "Now this is what I call synergy. Two people at the tops of their fields, coming together for mutual benefit."

"Sorry, pal." McKendrick shook his head. "No deal."

Cat glared at him. "What do you mean, there's no deal? That's not for you to say." She turned to Max. "There's no deal."

"Don't be hasty," Max said, looking from Cat to McKendrick. "We can—"

"Forget it, Max," McKendrick broke in. "She doesn't want my help."

"Hold on just a minute!" Cat's voice rose in annoyance. "I don't *need* your help." A small but vital difference.

"Yes, you do," said Max, setting the coffee mugs and bagels down on the table. "You need a lot of help, Cat."

She was aware of McKendrick's eyes on her, and she had to remind herself it was professional interest on his part, not personal. Not that she wanted it to be personal, but there was something thrilling about being the focus of such undivided male attention.

Cat forced a laugh. "You're becoming very melodramatic, Max. Next thing I know you'll tell me this is a planned intervention for the hopelessly disorganized. It just so happens that I thrive on chaos."

"Your last two manuscripts were late."

"Jack had a tonsillectomy when I was finishing *The Kindergarten Caper* and we found termites right at the climax of *Dead Cowboys Never Talk*." She smiled sweetly at McKendrick. "No offense."

"None taken." His grin told her he knew otherwise.

She met Max's eyes. "A tonsillectomy is an act of God, right?"

"Only when it's *your* tonsillectomy."

"It was my son's. That's the same thing, isn't it?"

"Not to Global Publishing."

Max sighed longingly. "I know one author who finished up a book longhand in a storm cellar while a tornado ripped apart his house."

McKendrick helped himself to a mug of coffee. "I know of a writer who broke both arms and still made his deadline."

You would, she thought. "Those people need serious therapy. No one is that disciplined." *Or that demented.*

"Wrong," said McKendrick. "A hell of a lot of people are that disciplined." He paused for effect. "And that organized."

She shuddered. "What a frightening thought."

"Want to hear a really frightening thought?" Max volunteered, handing her a mug of coffee. "No more extensions on your deadline, Catherine. I know chaos, and you're heading straight for it.''

"I love you dearly, Max, but you're a bachelor. Your idea of chaos is misplacing your copy of the *Sunday Times Book Review.*" She put down the coffee mug and gathered up her belongings. "Thanksgiving's tomorrow and I have a million things to do. Stuffing, turnips, the pies . . .''

"Tomorrow's Thanksgiving?" asked McKendrick.

"Didn't those cardboard pilgrims in the lobby tell you something?" Cat turned to Max. *This guy manages time?* her look said. *Doesn't even know tomorrow's a national holiday.*

Max cleared his throat. "Riley's been in Tokyo the last few months," he said, as if that could explain away McKendrick's appalling lapse of memory.

"Pleasure?" asked Cat.

"Business," said McKendrick.

Max lowered his voice conspiratorially. "The Japanese government," he said. "This guy taught the Japanese something about organization.''

"Wow," said Cat, who wasn't the slightest bit impressed.

She could almost see the lightbulb flash on over Max's head as he turned to McKendrick. "You'll be on your own tomorrow, Riley?"

"Looks like," said McKendrick.

Oh, no, Cat thought. *Don't do this, Max. Not with him. . . .*

"How long's it been since you had a homemade Thanksgiving dinner?" Max continued.

Was it her imagination or did a look of sadness flicker across McKendrick's movie-star face? "Couldn't tell you, Max."

"That long?" Max asked.

"That long," said McKendrick.

Don't pay any attention to them. McKendrick's a grown man. This is a big city. Somewhere out there is a turkey with his name on it, and he's smart enough to find it.

Max was a rat and a traitor. He knew she was a sucker for strays, especially around the holidays, and he was doing his best to manipulate her into issuing an invitation.

Not this time, Max. I'm smarter than that. She'd choke before she uttered anything that even remotely resembled a dinner invitation.

"Flannery's on East 47th has a pretty good spread," Max went on, "or you might want to try Stein's Deli near Rock Center. They have a restaurant in the back and the best turkey in the city."

"Thought I might drive on up to Boston," the cowboy drawled. "Celebrate Thanksgiving where it started."

"It started in Plymouth," Max said. "Why don't you—"

"—come to my house." It sounded like her voice but she had the insane urge to look over her shoulder for her evil twin. *Have you lost your mind, Cat?*

Consorting with the enemy is dangerous business.
Especially at her own dining room table.

Max beamed at her. Why not? She'd played right
into his hands like the lily-livered, softhearted dope
she was. Could she take it back? She struggled to
find a way to erase her foolhardy words.

She needn't have bothered. McKendrick wasn't
interested.

"Thanks for the invitation," he said. He probably practiced that sexy drawl into a tape recorder
every night. "But I'm not much for family celebrations."

"You'll be alone." *So what, Cat? That's his
problem.* He didn't want to come to her house. She
didn't want him there. She should be relieved. But
no. The words were out before she could stop them.
"Nobody should be alone on Thanksgiving."

Max's smile widened. "Cat has this thing about
strays during the holidays, Riley. She'll hound you
until you say yes."

"Been alone most of my life," said McKendrick.
"It's the way I like it."

If Cat had a nickel for every time she'd heard macho statements like that, she could single-handedly
pay off the national debt. But it was different this
time. *He means it,* she thought, and it struck her as
a terrible shame. There was something shadowy in
his gaze, something bittersweet and lonely, and despite her better judgment, Cat felt herself melting.

"Mr. McKendrick?" She sounded cool and collected, amazing when you considered the strange rush of emotion that filled her heart. "You'll come for Thanksgiving dinner, won't you?"

He nodded.

She smiled.

He met her eyes and for an instant she thought she saw them years from now, looking back at this moment as the one that changed their lives. She drew in a deep breath, trying to regain her equilibrium in a world that was shifting more rapidly than she could handle. She'd never understood the concept of love-at-first-sight. Everyone knew love grew slowly, cautiously, built on a foundation of friendship and respect. This was lust. Nothing more than lust. She had to remember that.

"So it's on?" Max asked.

McKendrick held her gaze. "It's on."

Max barely restrained a whoop of excitement. So did Cat. She had to make her escape before she made an absolute fool of herself.

"Four o'clock," she tossed over her shoulder as she raced for the door. "Max will give you directions."

And then she ran for her life.

RILEY MCKENDRICK whistled low. Tall, willowy, with sleek golden brown hair that brushed her shoulders like a caress. He'd been expecting a frumpy writer who spent her life in fantasyland, not a flesh-

and-blood woman who looked as if she'd like to take a juicy bite out of life. "Thanks a lot, Max," he muttered after Cat Zaslow disappeared down the hallway. "You might've mentioned she was a knockout."

Max stared at him as if he was speaking Greek. "Cat? A knockout? Never noticed."

"Time to get your glasses checked," Riley said with a laugh. "That is one helluva woman."

"Cat's not a woman," Max said, in what had to be the single dumbest statement of the year. "She's a client."

Riley shook his head, trying to banish the memory of the way her hips had swayed beneath her short black wool skirt. "You sure she has five kids?"

"She has five kids."

"How many husbands?"

"She's a widow." Max seemed puzzled. "You think she's good-looking?"

"You don't?" Riley countered.

"I never thought about it." Max was quiet for a moment. "Since when do you like skinny women?"

"I don't," Riley said. He liked his women soft, with big breasts and sweet dispositions. Cat Zaslow had a tongue like a double-edged razor blade and her breasts—

Riley stopped, galvanized by the thought of her breasts. High and round, surprisingly full for so slender a woman. He wondered if she'd been wearing a bra or one of those lacy contraptions they called a teddy. He already knew she had the legs for a teddy, wickedly long with thighs made for welcoming a man between them.

His blood shifted south and he forced the image from his mind.

"I dated her housekeeper for a few weeks," Max said. "Damn near gave me a nervous breakdown. She has a child herself." He made to drag a hand through his perfect hair then apparently thought better of it. "Diapers, barking dogs, McDonald's Happy Meals—hell. Cat lives at the edge of disaster. Gimme Lutèce any day."

"So what was her husband like?"

"I hear he was a nice guy."

"You never met him?"

"Cat started writing after David died."

Riley started to ask another question then caught himself. *None of your business, cowboy. She loved him enough to have five kids with him. That's all you need to know.*

Max looked at him with open curiosity. "You're not interested in her as a woman, are you?"

He thought about the long, lovely length of her legs, that beautiful face.... Then he thought about reality. "Five kids, a housekeeper, the housekeeper's kid and an in-home zoo?" He threw back his head and laughed out loud. "Not me, Max. Not in this lifetime."

CAT PUSHED OPEN the heavy glass doors at 575 Madison and stepped out into the brilliant late-autumn sunshine. She stood there, motionless, on the sidewalk and waited for the chilly wind whipping down the street to snap her back to normal. Whatever normal was. She wasn't sure she remembered. It had been a long time since she'd felt this way, a very long time since lust had reared its lovely head and beckoned her toward—

"Hey, lady." One of New York City's finest stopped next to her. "You okay?"

She blinked, then managed to nod at the policeman.

"Why don't I hail a cab for you?" the cop offered, raising a burly arm in the air. "You don't look too good to me."

"No," she said, regaining her powers of speech. "I—I have a car." She glanced toward the corner and saw the familiar Chevy waiting for her. "But thank you."

She drew a steadying breath into her lungs, then marched off toward the vehicle. The driver saw her coming and leapt out to open the door. Alec Marton owned the one-and-only car service in her small Connecticut town. The Chevy had served as wedding car, delivery room and taxi cab for most of the citizens of Danville at one time or another.

"You don't look so good," Alec said as she climbed into the front seat next to him. "Maybe you should lie down in the back."

She shook her head. "I'm fine, Alec." She managed a smile. "You know me. Not only can't I drive in the city, I can't even think."

He looked no more convinced than the policeman had, and no wonder. She wasn't fine. The truth was she felt as if the real Cat Zaslow had been taken over by aliens... sixteen-year-old aliens, at that. She was aglow with excitement, alive with possibilities, and all for a man she didn't know and was reasonably certain she wouldn't like if she did.

Her knees had gone weak when his eyes met hers and it was a wonder she hadn't swooned at his cowboy-booted feet.

She'd lost her mind, that's what. All Riley McKendrick did was walk into Max's office and Cat's brain cells had decided to go on vacation. How humiliating. She had five wonderful children, a beautiful home, good friends and a terrific career. She didn't need a man.

Truth was, her infrequent experiments in dating all had been less than successful. Men were either intimidated by her success, her kids or the fact that she liked her life exactly the way it was and made no bones about it.

"You just haven't met the right man," Gracie liked to say whenever she got the chance.

"Yes, I have," Cat always said. David Zaslow was a tough act to follow. Any man looking to fill his shoes would have a lot to live up to.

He could do it, Cat. That cowboy could be the one.

She shook her head, ignoring Alec's curious glance in the rearview mirror. A clock-watcher. That gorgeous hunk of man was a clock-watcher. What a waste of natural resources.

Alec maneuvered the Chevy into traffic. "Just getting out in time," he said as they headed crosstown. "Gonna be a zoo in another hour, everyone trying to get out early for Thanksgiving."

She met his eyes in the mirror. "Alec, do you think I'm disorganized?"

"Sure," he said, "but I'd never hold it against you. You got a career and five kids. Who wouldn't be behind the eight ball now and again?"

She sighed loudly.

"Not my business," Alec said, "but you asked."

"You and Sarah have three kids. How do you manage?"

"Sarah's got everyone on a schedule," Alec said not without a touch of pride. "Even put it on computer."

Cat suppressed a shudder. "Really?"

Alec nodded. "You bet. Even Annie."

Her eyes widened. "Annie's four years old."

"Never too soon to start. That's what Sarah says. How else you gonna keep their lessons and doctor appointments and everything straight?"

"Isn't that why God made refrigerator magnets?" Was it possible that the rest of the world operated with the efficiency of a Swiss watch while she was a sundial on a cloudy day?

Which, of course, brought her right back to Riley McKendrick, who made a living putting people's lives in order.

Had she lost her mind or just the part of it that governed the libido? It wasn't like there'd been any chemistry between them. Everybody knew one-way chemistry was a physical impossibility. He probably hadn't even realized she was a woman. So what if she'd noticed he was tall, dark and handsome with a voice that could undress a woman without even trying. He couldn't help the effect he'd had on her, any more than she could help the heated fantasies dancing behind her eyeballs.

She heard Max's voice, crystal clear, inside her head. *An hour with Riley McKendrick will change your life forever.*

Max couldn't be right. She didn't want her life changed. She liked her life the way it was. She had a home, she had a family, she had memories of a man she'd loved once and would never forget. So what if romance was a thing of the past. She could live without romance.

At least she'd thought she could—until today.

Riley McKendrick was everything she didn't want in a man and she was afraid he was exactly what she needed.

She closed her eyes and leaned her forehead against the car window. "Oh, Max," she murmured. "What have you done to me?"

Chapter Two

HE WASN'T GOING.

That's what Riley told himself the next morning as he strode through the lobby of the Plaza Hotel.

"We brought your car around front, Mr. McKendrick," the doorman said. "The Massachusetts road map is in the glove box as you requested."

Riley nodded his thanks and pressed a ten-dollar bill into the man's outstretched palm. They were efficient at the Plaza, efficient and polite. Too bad the place had all the warmth of Versailles after the revolution.

The doorman tipped his cap. "Have a happy Thanksgiving, sir."

Riley muttered something suitable in return. Truth was he didn't much give a damn about Thanksgiving or Christmas or Groundhog Day. As far as he was concerned, holidays were nothing more than unnecessary interruptions in the normal pattern of life. Thanksgiving was a perfect example. At least if you were going to have a day off, make it a Monday or Friday so you reaped maximum benefit with minimum disruption.

He'd spent yesterday bumming around Manhattan, trying to figure out why any sane man would choose to live in the middle of chaos. Millions of people crammed onto an island smaller than half of the ranches he'd worked on while growing up, all of them searching for something that was just out of reach.

He still wasn't sure why he'd said yes to Cat Zaslow's dinner invitation. She was hardheaded and outspoken, exactly the kind of woman he went out of his way to avoid. The kind of woman who thought her way was the only way. If he'd been stupid enough to get involved, she would've fought his organizational efforts every damn step of the way and they'd probably end up staring at each other over a pair of loaded rifles.

No, he thought as he headed north toward the thruway, he didn't need any part of it. Let Max worry about her kids and her deadlines.

As for Riley, he had a whole month stretched out in front of him with nothing to do but enjoy himself. With a little luck he'd reach Boston by dinnertime, where he knew a soft-spoken brunette who understood that some men were meant to be alone.

MAYBE HE WOULDN'T show up.

Cat swiped at a carrot with the vegetable peeler the next morning and considered the notion.

Maybe he'd wake up, realize she hadn't meant to invite him for dinner and go off to watch the Macy's Thanksgiving Day parade.

The idea of Riley McKendrick standing curbside with a score of six-year-olds made her laugh out loud.

No, the cowboy wasn't the parade type. More than likely he'd spent the night with a buxom blonde whose IQ equalled the price of a cup of coffee. One of those flirty types whose sole purpose in life was to make a man feel more . . . manly.

"Ouch!" She popped her forefinger into her mouth as Gracie poked her head into the kitchen.

"You okay?"

"Fine," Cat said around her finger. "Household utensils should come with warning labels."

"You're out of practice, that's all. Just take your time."

"Easy for you to say." She reached for the Band-Aids in the jar over the sink. "Are you sure you really want the weekend off, Gracie?"

"Either that or combat pay," said Gracie. "Twenty-four hours from now, Dawn and I will be frolicking with Mickey and Minnie and Aladdin." Dawn was Gracie's eighteen-month-old daughter who had a serious Disney habit.

"Traitor," said Cat.

"Slave driver," said Gracie cheerfully. They both knew Cat was a pushover when it came to things like that.

"How are we doing on chairs?" Cat asked, gesturing over her shoulder toward the dining room.

"I borrowed two from next door. That should do it."

"Did I tell you one of Max's business acquaintances might be coming for dinner?"

"Only half a dozen times."

"Not that it matters all that much. I don't really think he's going to show up," Cat said with studied nonchalance. "I can't imagine why he would. It's not like you can't find a perfectly good turkey dinner in Manhattan."

"Uh-oh," said Gracie. "Does this mean what I think it means?"

Cat wound the Band-Aid around her finger and tossed the wrapper into the trash. "I'm just wondering if we should set a place for Mr. McKendrick or not."

"I suppose we should," said Gracie. "Unless you plan to make him eat on the porch with the cats."

Cat looked up at the bright orange clock. "What time is the Wassersteins' pilgrim party?"

"In ten minutes, and don't change the subject."

"Are the kids ready?"

"Clean, dressed and in the minivan."

"You probably should get going, then. They started without us last year and Jack threw a gourd at Becky Morgan. I had to speak at the Danville Women's Club to make up for it."

"This clock-watcher of yours must really be something," said Gracie as she started for the door. "You're actually blushing. Wouldn't it be funny if he was Mr. Right?"

"Mr. Right," Cat muttered as her friend disappeared. Who wouldn't be flushed, standing next to a hot oven? It had nothing to do with the subject matter.

Gracie wouldn't have made that statement about Mr. Right if she'd met McKendrick. The man had Loner tattooed on his forehead in neon letters an inch high. The man might be gorgeous, but he had all the warmth of a filing cabinet.

And the saddest green eyes....

She shook her head, trying to dispel the memory. That was just her overactive writer's imagination talking, twisting reality around until it was barely recognizable. Riley McKendrick had probably never known a lonely day in his entire misbegotten life. No doubt women threw themselves at his cowboy boots with mad, passionate abandon every day of the week. In fact, Cat had no doubt he was with one of his harem women right now, lying back in bed while the tramp pranced around in some flimsy negligee straight out of a *Victoria's Secret* catalog.

A vision of her own flannel pajamas danced before her eyes and she sighed.

She was glad that she'd seen the last of Riley McKendrick. And with a little luck, sooner or later she'd stop thinking about him, as well.

"COFFEE, SIR?"

Riley looked up at the waitress. Tall, willowy, glossy golden brown hair that caressed her shoulders. A face so perfect it made your head spin like too much icy vodka on a hot summer's night.

"Sir? Do you want more coffee?"

He blinked and a short woman with curly gray hair came into focus. "Thanks," he said, as she bent close to refill the cup.

"Anything else?"

He shook his head. "Just the check."

Make that a reality check. He'd spent the entire drive up to Danville trying not to think about the yellow flecks in Cat's soft blue eyes. He was determined not to think about the long, shapely legs left bare by her short black skirt. And there was no way in hell he was going to think about the fact that he'd driven all the way up to northern Connecticut to tell her he wasn't staying for dinner.

So why'd you say yes in the first place, McKendrick?

It wasn't as if he hadn't known exactly where Max was going with the questions about his Thanksgiving Day plans. But there had been something about the look in Cat's eyes that made it impossible. An invitation? A challenge, maybe? He wasn't sure. All he knew was that he felt the pull of something stronger than his misgivings.

It wasn't like him to be a sucker for sentiment, swayed by the look in a woman's eyes. For all he knew she could've been stifling a sneeze or thinking about rush-hour traffic or trying to figure out if he was really a cowboy or just dressed like one.

Damn. Riley knew trouble when he saw it, and Cat Zaslow had Trouble written across her pretty forehead in capital letters.

He gulped down some coffee, then glanced at the clock hanging over the cash register near the door. Three minutes to noon. According to the map Max had given him, he was 8.7 miles away from her house. He'd stop by, offer his apologies, then by twelve-fifteen he'd be back on the road to Boston where he'd spend the night with a woman who had as little interest in holidays and family celebrations as he had.

A woman who wasn't Cat.

He knew all about high-maintenance types like Catherine O'Leary Zaslow. The kind who came with lots of expectations, not to mention children, pets and a house with a white picket fence. Everything he'd gone out of his way to avoid since he packed and left Nevada behind a lifetime ago.

It wasn't that he didn't believe in all of those things. He did—for other people. He'd learned early on that the things other people took for granted weren't in the cards for him, and he'd made his peace with it. You learned how to stand on your own real fast when you grew up bouncing from foster home to foster home.

He'd been on the wrong line when life had handed out lucky breaks. All he'd had going for him was his size and he'd managed to parlay athletic ability into scholarships that had funded his education. Too bad there'd been nobody around to celebrate when his dreams began to come true.

People talked about family. They talked about sacrifice and love. But Riley knew that love was the first thing to disappear when the sacrifices became too much to bear. He'd been five years old when he found that out.

And he wasn't about to forget it.

CAT LEAPT from the bathtub, sending a spray of Mr. Bubble across the room.

"Gracie!" She wrapped a bright yellow bath sheet around her body as she she raced downstairs, then through the hallway toward the kitchen. "Please be home, Gracie! We forgot the cranberries!"

No such luck. Gracie was still at the Wassersteins' pilgrim party over at Danville Park.

The smell of turkey wafted from the oven while assorted pots and casseroles were lined up on the countertops, awaiting their turn. Too bad cranberry sauce wasn't hiding in one of them.

Scooter, her ten-year-old golden retriever, bounded into the room, followed by three of their multitude of cats.

"We've got trouble, guys," she said, scratching the dog behind the ear. Gracie was out with the minivan. Cat's station wagon was in the shop. And only a monster would call Alec Marton for a cab on Thanksgiving afternoon.

She glanced up at the clock over the sink. Not quite ten after twelve. If Gracie would just hurry home, there might still be time to jump into the car and head for the minimart before the guests started arriving.

She wrapped the towel more tightly around her torso and started back toward the staircase. Anyone could forget cranberry sauce, she reasoned as she left a trail of bubbles behind her. It's not as if it was a crime against the nation, even if certain people like Riley McKendrick would probably take it as a sign of her total lack of character.

She was halfway up the stairs when the rumble of a car engine caught her attention. Turning, she raced back down the stairs, darted around two of the newest litter of kittens, and barely avoided a collision with Kevin's skateboard.

She swung open the front door. "Gracie! Don't turn off the engine, I—"

It wasn't Gracie.

It was Riley McKendrick and he was striding up the path and heading straight for her. He wore gray flannel slacks that hugged his form, a cream-colored sweater and that sexy-as-hell leather jacket.

Cat hadn't been raised in New York City for nothing. She knew exactly what to do in a situation like this. She slammed the door in his face.

He rang the doorbell. She looked down at the bright yellow bath towel and the amount of skin it left uncovered, and she felt her cheeks redden.

"Go away!" she called out. "You're three hours early." She admired punctuality as much as the next woman but this was an affront to human decency.

He banged on the door. Scooter started to bark, which woke up Bingo and Tommy, two of Scooter's offspring. They started to bark, as well, followed by Mitzi the beagle's preternatural howling.

She opened the door a crack and glared at McKendrick. "I thought you clock-watchers knew how to tell time." He was every bit as gorgeous as she remembered. Why couldn't he look the way he was supposed to look? Pale, wan and not the slightest bit interested in seeing her *en déshabillé.* She hesitated. The thought that he might not be interested bothered her even more.

"I'm on my way to Boston. I stopped by to tell you I won't be coming to dinner after all."

His green-eyed gaze swept over her from head to toe, lingering nowhere. Missing nothing. Her heartbeat lurched wildly. She wasn't certain if she should slap his face or fling herself into his arms. Both ideas had merit.

"A bit out of your way, wouldn't you say?" She opted for a more neutral approach. "You could've called."

"Don't have your number."

"You could have asked Max."

"Yeah," he said, "I could've, but Max wasn't home."

There it was again, that look of sadness, of loneliness. *Don't look at me that way, cowboy. I'm not going to beg you to stay for dinner. Not this time.*

RILEY FOUND HIMSELF vaguely irritated when Cat didn't try to convince him to stay for dinner.

"Enjoy your turkey," he said. Not a great exit line, but serviceable. Turning, he started down the porch steps.

"Cranberries!"

He stopped. "What?"

She made a funny little clutching motion with the towel, one that made the shadowy valley between her breasts look even more intriguing. He wondered if she had any idea what effect she was having on him. Probably not. If she did, he had no doubt she'd bolt the door and bar the windows.

She looked up at him and offered him a very female smile. He'd already realized she wasn't flirtatious by nature, so the smile carried considerable punch. "Are you in a hurry to get to Boston?"

"Why?"

"I—uh, Gracie forgot her wallet."

"You said something about cranberries."

"Cranberries?" Her eyes went wide and innocent. "I don't know what you're talking about. I'm worried about Gracie."

"Gracie?"

"My housekeeper. What if the police stop her and she doesn't have her driver's license? She'll end up in jail."

"Last I heard they don't put you in jail for forgetting your license."

"I don't need a lecture, Mr. McKendrick. I need a lift to the minimart. If it's too much trouble, just tell me."

"Your housekeeper's at the minimart?"

"Well, actually she's at the Wassersteins' pilgrim party but—"

"So why not call the Wassermans?"

"Wasser*steins,* and that's impossible. Dianne always takes them to the park over by the lake and—"

"Don't explain," he said. "Whatever you do, don't explain."

"You'll drive me?"

"Let's go," he said.

"I can't go like this."

"*I* don't mind if *you* don't."

"Believe it or not, I don't usually go to the store in my bath towel."

He leaned against the porch railing and crossed his arms over his chest. "Make it fast."

She swung open the door the rest of the way. "You don't have to wait out there."

Don't do it, McKendrick. Step through that door and it's all over. Every self-preservation instinct was screaming for him to put as much distance between himself and Cat Zaslow as he possibly could. But damn it, she was naked under that bright yellow bath towel and there were only so many things a red-blooded man could resist.

The way her skin took the light. The way she'd taste sweet and fresh. For a moment they stood close enough that he could smell the scent of soap on her smooth skin and he imagined having her on the floor...right next to the scruffy Barney doll with the grinning purple face.

"Get dressed," he growled. "I want to get back on the road." *Or take a cold shower.*

"There's coffee in the kitchen," she said over her shoulder as she started up the stairs, her long legs sleek and bare and inviting. "Help yourself."

Tempting, he thought as she disappeared from view. *Very tempting.*

HE DROVE a sleek black sports car, the kind of car married men dreamed about. Low, powerful, terminally sexy. No wife worth her salt would let her man drive around in a lethal weapon like this.

It put Cat in a bad mood the moment she fastened her seat belt.

"What's the matter?" he asked as they roared off toward the Danville Minimart. "Forget the turkey?"

"Very funny." He didn't know how close he was to the truth. "I was just thinking that this is the kind of car my son Kevin would call a 'babe magnet.'"

"I'll let you know," he said. "I just picked it up yesterday."

"New car?"

"It's rented."

"What kind of car do you own?"

"I don't." He shot her a sidelong glance. Wouldn't you know, harsh sunlight would be kind to him? Was there no justice in this world?

She swiveled around in her chair to face him. "You don't own a car?"

"Nope."

"Why? Is it some kind of efficiency thing?"

"You could say that."

"I'm curious," she persisted. "The only people I know who don't own cars live in Manhattan, and you don't live in Manhattan, do you?"

"Max was right," McKendrick said. "You do ask a hell of a lot of questions."

"Then you won't take this personally. Where *do* you live?"

He rolled to a stop and turned to look at her. "Nowhere."

"You must live somewhere."

"Nowhere in particular," he repeated.

"Where do you get your mail?" *Don't play coy with me, cowboy. I can badger a witness with the best of them.*

"A service in Kansas City forwards it to me."

"So then you live in Kansas City."

"I didn't say that."

"But that's where you said you get your mail."

"Because it's convenient," he said. "Kansas City's in the middle of the country. It's a good place to begin."

"You have one of those mailbox services?"

"Bingo."

"And I suppose you think that's more efficient?"

He grinned. "Now you're getting it, Zaslow."

The whole idea gave her the creeps. "Where do you keep your clothes? As far as I know they haven't invented a rent-a-closet yet."

He gestured toward the back of the car. "In the trunk."

"I'm being serious, McKendrick. Your clothes, your books, your papers—you have to stow them someplace."

"I don't own any more than I can carry."

She leaned back against the seat and stared at him. "I've heard of people like you but I never thought I'd actually meet one."

"Life doesn't have to be complicated," he said, meeting her eyes. "I travel light."

She glanced at the huge leather tote bag on her lap. "I can't even travel light to the minimart."

"It's not for everyone."

She nodded, thinking of her kids, her house, her pets and of how empty her life would be without them. The last things on earth she ever thought she'd have and they meant everything to her. "Of course you really do have a home," she said, trying to make sense of the whole thing, "even if you don't live there now. Your family... where you grew up—"

"No."

"No?"

The sports car surged forward. McKendrick's attention was focused on the road. He'd made it perfectly obvious the conversation had come to an end, but Cat couldn't let it alone.

She was certain he was exaggerating. There had to be someone out there. An ex-wife. Children. A second cousin twice removed who sent him a Christmas card every year and birthday presents that made him wince. It was bad enough that he lived out of his suitcase, but at least that was his choice. Nobody chose to be alone in the world, to be without people who loved you. People you loved in return.

Not even men as tough as Riley McKendrick.

David hadn't been tough at all. When she met her late husband he'd been a widower with four small kids, a regular kind of guy you wouldn't look at twice on the street. She'd been sitting at a crowded lunch counter, nursing a diet soda and a tuna sandwich, when David walked in and sat down next to her. He'd asked her to pass the salt. She'd asked him for the pepper. They'd talked, then laughed and made a date for dinner later that night.

She'd been a reporter at *Newsweek*, committed to her career, determined to rise to the top. Marriage wasn't on her horizon. Children were creatures who belonged to other people. She knew what she wanted and how to get it, and all of her plans went flying out the window when she fell in love with a man who only had a year to live. There'd been something about him, some indefinable quality that had touched Cat's heart, and changed her life forever. And it had nothing to do with pity and everything to do with love.

It still hurt to think that David hadn't lived to meet Sarah, their daughter who was born six months after his death.

It seemed like yesterday. "You don't have to do this," the attorney had said after the reading of the will. "You're having your own baby. We'll find foster homes for the rest of them."

"We're a family," she'd stated in no uncertain terms, even though she was scared to death. "We're going to stay a family." She hadn't fallen in love only with David; she'd fallen in love with Michael, Kevin, Ben and Jack, as well.

And she'd never once regretted her decision. Raising those kids was the toughest thing she'd ever done—and the most rewarding—and every night she offered up a prayer of thanks that unexpected blessings often turned out to be the finest blessings of all.

Something she knew in her heart Riley McKendrick could never understand.

Chapter Three

GET OUT, a voice warned him again as he watched Cat sprint toward the door of the minimart. *Get out while you still can.*

He knew how to handle sexual chemistry. You acted on attraction or you didn't, but either way it wasn't a life-altering force that moved through your world like a tornado across the plains.

This was different. All she had to do was turn those big blue eyes on him and he was lost. Done for. No wonder she wrote murder mysteries for a living. The woman must have left a trail of dead men behind her a mile long.

He watched as she disappeared inside the store. Max didn't think she was beautiful and he supposed that technically Max was right. Her mouth was too wide and mobile for classic beauty, her jawline too strong and stubborn. Still, in combination with her fierce intelligence, the effect was stunning.

You've known women who were more beautiful, he thought, and it was true. He'd also known women who knew how to flatter a man, how to make him feel like he was better than he was. Cat Zaslow didn't flatter, she didn't fawn, she sure as hell didn't flirt, but he was drawn to her by a force more powerful than anything he'd ever encountered.

"Five kids," he muttered, tapping his finger against the steering wheel. A score of dogs and cats underfoot. Hell, the woman had a housekeeper, and between the two of them they couldn't remember the cranberries for Thanksgiving dinner. Not that she'd admitted forgetting them, but he wasn't born yesterday.

She didn't look happy when she climbed back into the car. There was a furrow between her brows and a murderous glint in her blue eyes. And as far as he could tell, she didn't have cranberries.

"So, did you leave the wallet for your housekeeper?" he asked, all mock innocence.

She favored him with a fierce look. "Don't say a word," she said through gritted teeth. "Not one single word."

"We could check out the supermarket," he said, shifting into first. "Maybe your housekeeper's there."

"I'm warning you, McKendrick—"

"There's always a farm stand."

"Why would I look for Gracie at a farm stand?"

"Admit it, Zaslow. You forgot the cranberries."

"I did not."

"We'll go to a supermarket and get the cranberries."

"The supermarkets are closed," she muttered.

"What was that?" He couldn't wipe the smile off his face.

"Damn it! So I forgot the cranberries. Is it a crime against the nation?" She stared, grim-faced, out the window at the passing scenery. "Besides, what's it to you? You'll be in Boston where I'm sure there'll be a surfeit of cranberries, and you can stuff your fat face to your heart's content."

You're sunk, McKendrick. It's too late now....

"About Boston," he said. "There's been a change of plans...."

"THERE'S NOTHING SADDER than a ravaged turkey." Cat shook her head hours later as she surveyed the remains of the feast. "Thirty pounds, and I don't think we'll get two sandwiches out of those leftovers."

"And that's if we're lucky," said Gracie, housekeeper and friend. "That's what you get for asking twenty-one people to Thanksgiving dinner."

"What can I tell you? Everyone in town knows I'm a sucker for the holidays." She gestured toward the front of the house. "Did the kids clear the small tables in the foyer?"

"Done," said Gracie. "Kevin griped that it was girl's work but he did it."

"Kevin and I are going to have another talk about division of labor tonight. He's becoming a twelve-year-old sexist."

"Hormones," said Gracie sagely. "He'll get over it."

"He's male," Cat said. "He'll never get over it. It's only going to get worse. Before you know it, he'll be shaving and channel-surfing with the remote control." With three other sons and a little daughter marching inexorably toward puberty, Cat sometimes wondered if she'd make it to thirty-five with her sanity. "Where are they now?"

"Where else? Tossing around a football in the front yard."

Cat opened the refrigerator door and removed a bowl of freshly whipped cream. "I think we pulled it off. Nobody seemed to notice we forgot the cranberry sauce."

"They were too busy arguing politics with your new cowboy friend."

McKendrick. She'd wondered how long it would take Gracie to zero in on him. "He's not my friend."

Gracie leaned against the sink and shot Cat a quizzical look. "Why'd you invite him to dinner?"

Cat toyed with the whipped cream. "He looked lonely."

"You could see *lonely* through all of that gorgeousness?"

"I don't know what I saw. As soon as I heard he had nowhere to go today, I found myself asking him to dinner."

"Way to go, girl. He's the best stray you've brought home in ages."

"Don't let those outdoorsy looks of his fool you, Gracie. McKendrick's one of those clock-watching pencil-pushing types who lives to organize." She shuddered. "Max wants to hire him to put me on the straight and narrow."

"The cowboy could put me on the straight and narrow anytime."

Cat took a vicious swipe at the cream. "I thought you went for the intellectual type." She looked up at Gracie. "Like Max."

Gracie's cheeks reddened. "Max Bernstein is a jerk. He hasn't an ounce of romance in his soul." Gracie and Max had dated a few times last summer, but their attraction of opposites hadn't made for an easy alliance. "Besides, after meeting the Marlboro Man out there, I've decided to go for brawn instead of brain."

"Enjoy," said Cat, scooping a dollop of cream onto a slice of pumpkin pie. "If you ask me, muscles are highly overrated."

"I'll let you know when I've had a chance to investigate."

Cat tossed a wadded-up paper napkin at her friend. "You're incorrigible."

"No," said Gracie. "I'm hopeful. You never know when good fortune is going to smile down on you."

Apparently Gracie had a peculiar notion of what constitutes good fortune. Sharing the dinner table with Riley McKendrick had been about as relaxing as sharing a bathtub with a rattlesnake. Every time she'd looked up, he'd been watching her with that damnable twinkle that made his green eyes sparkle.

The cranberries, she thought. That was why he'd decided to stay for dinner after all. He was biding his time, waiting for the right moment to pounce. He hadn't said anything outright, but it was just a matter of time. Sooner or later the right moment would arrive and he could announce her idiocy to the world. She knew the wait must be driving his clock-watching little cowboy heart crazy.

"Cowboy," she muttered, opening the container of ice cream. "A likely story." He had the looks and the drawl and the boots, but she refused to believe he had the attitude that went with them.

She could just imagine McKendrick trying to foist his time-management nonsense on an unsuspecting bunch of *real* cowboys. They'd have him riding his calendar out of town before he knew what hit him.

The idea tickled her fancy and she grinned as she topped three pieces of pumpkin pie with three scoops of cream. Cranberries notwithstanding, parts of the afternoon had been surprisingly pleasant.

Gracie and the kids were home when she and McKendrick returned, and the cowboy had joined in a makeshift basketball game that had left her sons openmouthed with admiration. Sometimes she felt sorry for them that they had no male role model to look up to, someone who understood the mystery of sports and testosterone, but short of teaching them how to shave, she felt she was doing a good job.

Still, there was something oddly poignant about watching them in the yard, her precious sons and the cowboy, and that warm feeling had lingered right up until McKendrick came back into the house and started criticizing the traffic pattern.

But she'd got her own back. She'd seated him at the far end of the main table between Mary Mc-Gregor, who never shut up, and Cindy Hughes, who'd never met a man she didn't like.

If he had been entertaining any schemes to get his grubby hands on her house, Mary and Cindy had seen to it that he never had the chance. In fact, Cindy had been making it crystal clear all afternoon that she wouldn't have minded skipping the pumpkin pie and having McKendrick à la mode for dessert.

Cat placed everything on a huge tray then headed for the dining room.

Cindy was leaning as close to McKendrick as the law would allow, and Cat found herself wondering if breast implants were tax deductible. Not that it was any of her concern. She certainly didn't have any designs on him herself, even if he was easily the most beautiful hunk of man she'd ever seen in her entire life.

You can have him, Cindy. He's beautiful but he'll probably alphabetize your bras by cup size.

Max made room for the tray on the sideboard. He was grinning like the proverbial cat that ate the canary.

"What's up?" she asked, noting that all eyes were on her.

Max's grin widened. "There's big bucks riding on this, Cat. Did you actually forget the cranberry sauce or were you making a neoclassicist culinary statement?"

"Come on, Cat!" Her next-door neighbor John chimed in. "I've got a five-dollar bet riding on it."

"Five dollars?" Kate Lawson, town librarian, laughed. "This is a sure thing. I'll up the ante to ten."

"Not even Cat could forget cranberry sauce on Thanksgiving Day," said Cindy in her sweetest voice. "Cat, I wouldn't insult you by making a bet."

She glanced toward McKendrick who watched her with wide, innocent eyes. If he'd said one word to Cindy about the cranberries, then murder by drumstick would be too good for him.

"How much do you want to bet?" she challenged him. "Ten dollars? Fifty? Don't be shy, Mr. McKendrick. Speak right up. Everyone else is."

McKendrick aimed those green eyes right at her but said nothing.

"Your reputation precedes you, Cat," called out another of the guests. "Most of us were here last year when you showed up dressed as Princess Jasmine for the town's centennial bash."

"It was late October," Cat protested. "I thought it was a Halloween party."

"Come on, Riley," said Mary McGregor. "Are you on Cat's side or the side of the missing cranberries?"

Gracie picked that moment to stroll into the room. "I can't believe you told them about the cranberries," she said to Cat. "I figured once we made it to dessert, we'd be safe."

Everyone present broke into laughter and Cat watched, infuriated, as McKendrick and Max exchanged high fives.

"Very funny, all of you. I hope you had a good laugh at my expense."

"Admit it," said Max, getting that look in his eye that she knew too well. "You and Gracie are hanging on by a thread."

"Don't drag me into this, Maxwell Bernstein!" Gracie's tone was the same one she used on the kids when they wouldn't turn out the lights. "I'm just an employee here."

"Gracie!" Cat was appalled by her friend's treachery.

"You know what I'm talking about," Gracie said, meeting Cat's eyes. "It's your house, Cat. I just follow orders."

"Gracie's right." Riley McKendrick's voice cut through the laughter and bickering. "You own the house. You set the rules. The buck stops with you."

"I don't know what's happening here," Cat said. "We're talking cranberries, not war crimes."

"The cranberries are just a symptom," Max said solemnly.

"Oh, for God's sake," Gracie muttered. "Why don't you stick a sock in it, Max?"

"My thoughts exactly. Why is it the people with the least experience are the ones most eager to offer advice?" Cat glanced toward McKendrick who was watching her with undisguised interest. "Are you married, Mr. McKendrick?"

His thick dark brows slid toward the bridge of his nose in a scowl. "No."

"Do you have any kids?"

"No, but—"

"I rest my case." She folded her arms across her chest and smiled. "How would you know what it takes to run a home? This isn't a corporation. Real people live here, or haven't you noticed?"

Scooter chose that moment to bound through the dining room with Sarah's favorite Barbie doll clamped between his slobbery jaws and Sarah in close pursuit.

"I noticed," said McKendrick as everyone in the room once again erupted into laughter.

"Six kids, Mr. McKendrick. Six cats, four kittens, three dogs and a litter of puppies. We have enough variables to throw IBM's finest computer into a terminal tailspin. Who has the time to work out a new routine? We barely have time to breathe."

McKendrick leaned back in his chair, a dangerous glint in his eyes. "You creative types—all you do is complain about how busy you are. If you'd apply some sound business techniques to the house, you'd—"

"I'll tell you what you can do with your sound business techniques." Cat's son Jack appeared in the doorway, and she took a deep breath and struggled to rein in her temper. "We both know you'd rather be anywhere than here. Why did you accept my invitation?

"Why did you invite me when you didn't want to?" he countered.

"Max said you were going to be alone for Thanksgiving."

"And you have this thing about taking in strays."

She glanced down at the kittens nipping at her ankles. "You could say that."

"I'm not big on family celebrations." The glint in his eyes turned to ice. "And I don't put a lot of store in holidays."

"Which is probably why you were going to be by yourself on Thanksgiving." There it was again, that look of loneliness she'd noticed yesterday, the same look that had tugged at her heartstrings. *Uh-uh, pal. I'm not falling for that a second time.* He could look lonelier than the Maytag repairman for all she cared. She wasn't buying it. "If you think dinner was a prelude to a business contract, you're dead wrong. You have nothing I need. Absolutely nothing."

He shoved back his chair and stood up, all six-feet-plus of rippling, ticked-off male pulchritude towering over the assembled group. "You're a coward, Zaslow. You don't have the guts to change your ways."

"And you're a blowhard, McKendrick. All talk and no action."

"You want action?" He strode off with Cat right behind him. "You need a demolition crew in here, not a housekeeper."

"The foyer?" she said, skidding to a stop behind him. "What's wrong with the foyer?" She'd never paid much attention to the foyer before except to race through it on her way out the door.

Okay, so it wasn't *House Beautiful*. Two card tables were pushed together with folding chairs arranged around them. Chunks of turkey and stuffing littered the floor. Big deal. It was Thanksgiving. You had to expect chaos on family holidays.

"It was the only place we could put the kids," she said by way of explanation, *not* apology. "What should I do, have them eat outside?" Then she noticed the pile of galoshes stacked near the front door, right beside a tangle of tube socks and a pink ballet slipper. A basketball was balanced on the bottom step and enough Aladdin figurines to populate a condo were strewn across the desk. Red and yellow plastic blocks, a skateboard and a well-pummeled bright purple Barney doll were scattered like breadcrumbs across the tile floor that had been shiny and pristine just hours before.

As if that weren't bad enough, she watched in horror as he reached for the door to the coat closet. Adrenaline flooded her body as he closed his hand around the knob.

"Open that door," Cat warned, "and it'll be the last thing you ever do." She wondered what would happen if she leapt for his throat and tried to wrestle him to the ground.

"What the hell do you have in there, dead bodies?"

"Dead time-management experts, and there's room for one more."

"I'll bet there isn't room for a dead gnat in this closet, Zaslow."

"I suppose you think I should be thankful you'd even consider whipping my humble abode into shape. I can just imagine the sob story Max laid on you." She brushed her hair off her face with a quick, angry gesture. "Frazzled widow with five kids, living on the ragged edge of disaster, waiting for Mr. Wonderful to ride in on a white horse and save them all."

"Sorry to disappoint you, Zaslow, but the only reason I said yes was because Max called in a marker. I usually don't waste my time on small domestic jobs."

"Small domestic jobs?" She almost crowed with delight. "There *are* no small domestic jobs, McKendrick. Only small experts who can't stand the heat."

"I whipped the White House staff into shape in two weeks, Zaslow. There's nothing you can throw at me that could be any worse."

You haven't seen the inside of that closet yet, cowboy. "You're a typical man, McKendrick. Real life sends you running for cover."

"I'm not running."

"You want to," she said. "You know you've met your match and it's scaring you to death."

He moved toward her, all menace and male indignation. "Forty-eight hours," he said, his voice as close to a growl as a human being's could be. "That's all I need."

"You'd never last that long."

"Try me."

Oh, cowboy.... The breath left her body in a loud whoosh as a vivid series of erotic vignettes danced before her eyes, all of which featured McKendrick in various stages of undress. She must be losing her mind. Good grief, she didn't even *like* him.

Did she?

"Max told me what you charge," she said, struggling to regain her composure. "If you ask me, you're overpaid."

"No charge," he shot back. "All I want is forty-eight hours."

"What's in it for you?"

"Satisfaction." He grinned. "I want to see you eat your words."

"Then you're going to have a long wait, because I'd rather eat ground worms." She poked him in the stomach with her forefinger. Or tried to. The man had abs like steel beams. "You can have your forty-eight hours, McKendrick, but when they're over, I expect an apology."

He glanced at his watch. "The forty-eight hours begin now?"

"They begin now." Smiling, she reached for the closet doorknob. Victory would be swift.

And very, very sweet.

Chapter Four

AROUND EIGHT O'CLOCK the guests began to say good-night. Riley shook hands with a lot of friendly people who laughed even as they wished him luck.

"Fortitude, old man," said one of Cat's neighbors by way of goodbye. "It's always darkest before the dawn."

"What the hell does that mean?" Riley turned toward Max as the man hurried out the front door. "Isn't that what they say before you go off to war?"

At eight o'clock he didn't know what that meant, but by nine-thirty he understood.

Riley might have whipped the White House staff into shape but he'd never been faced with six kids all under the age of thirteen, a housekeeper whose idea of organization involved empty cereal boxes and lots of new Tupperware and a woman who made her living murdering people for fun and profit.

It was enough to make a man yearn for political egos and governmental interference.

"Problems?" Cat asked sweetly as she passed through the living room en route to the kitchen, carrying a tray of dirty glasses.

He gave her his best you've-got-to-be-kidding look. "Everything's under control. I'm surveying the scene."

"Sure you are," she said, then laughed her way into the kitchen.

Go ahead, he thought. Laugh. She didn't know how funny it was. When it came to home and family, Riley hadn't a clue. He understood productivity and the bottom line; he understood efficiency and economy of motion, two concepts that hadn't found their way to Cat Zaslow's Connecticut farmhouse. What was it about some people that made them buck like an unbroken mare at the thought of organization?

Take the traffic pattern. It had taken him all of thirty seconds to see how bad it was, but Cat and company seemed oblivious to the drawbacks. You couldn't get from point A to point B without side trips to X, Y and Z. Hell, they probably wasted two workdays a year just walking around the dog bed parked in the entrance to the living room.

Cat had said you couldn't organize kids, but it seemed to Riley you could at least organize their belongings. Give him five minutes and he could draw up a diagram of an efficient way to handle kids' toys, rubber boots and sleepy cats without so much as breaking a sweat.

And the coat closet. You didn't need a degree in industrial design to know what was going on in there. Some people claimed Jimmy Hoffa was buried beneath the goalpost at Giants Stadium. Riley wouldn't be surprised to find that the teamsters boss was buried in Cat's closet somewhere behind the winter coats.

There wasn't much in this world that fazed him, but when she'd opened the closet door and a huge orange tomcat exploded into the foyer, dragging a pair of panty hose and a red-and-white woolen scarf behind him, he'd considered cutting his losses and admitting defeat. The last time he'd seen anything like that closet it had had a sign marked Bomb Site posted in front of it.

But what really scared him was the fact that he was the only one who seemed to notice.

These people lived in a house that resembled a landlocked *Titanic,* but they all seemed happy. Sure, he'd heard the usual squabbling among the kids but he'd also sensed something deeper, a connection from which they drew strength. Family bonds were a mystery to Riley. He'd lost his parents before his second birthday and his grandmother before his third. Eighteen different foster families in a dozen years had taught him how to adapt to situations. He learned quickly how to control what could be controlled in life and he overcame the rest by the sheer power of his will.

Blood ties were the only unbreakable bonds left in the world. You didn't walk away from your own flesh and blood. Biology wouldn't let you. Cat Zaslow's kids had no idea how lucky they were. They'd lost their father but they still had the woman who'd given birth to them and that was what made the difference.

He'd noticed the way she looked at her children, her blue eyes aglow with love, and he'd wondered if anyone had ever looked at him that way... or if anyone ever would.

He moved through the living room to the family room. Two of Cat's sons were sprawled on the overstuffed brown couch, watching *Aladdin*. They didn't pay him any mind, but that didn't surprise Riley. At their age most adults were pretty much invisible. A litter of popcorn, candy wrappers and crayons lay scattered on the floor around them. The end table groaned beneath a tower of schoolbooks while the piano near the window played host to three houseplants struggling for life.

Hadn't these people ever heard of desks? Bookshelves? Shovels?

He avoided the kitchen for the time being, mainly because Cat and Gracie were in there, and made his way through the hall to her office at the rear of the house. At least this room had shelves and a desk. But had more filing cabinets, mountains of paper and electronic equipment than you'd find in FBI headquarters.

A boy of seven or eight years of age peered up at Riley from behind a stack of bright red corduroy cushions piled up under the window.

"My mom doesn't like anyone in her office."

Riley crouched down next to him. "You're Jack, aren't you?"

The boy took a good look at him then threw back his head and yelled, "Mo-o-om!"

Riley winced. The kid made up in volume what he lacked in size. "What's that all about?"

The kid also shared Cat's talent for dirty looks. "This is my mom's office. You can't come in."

"You're in here."

"That's different. I'm allowed."

Cat appeared in the doorway. "What are you doing in here?" she demanded.

To Riley's amazement, she was looking directly at him. "What do you think I'm doing?"

"Trespassing."

The little boy looked up at her. "What's trespassing, Mom?"

Riley'd never seen her smile like that before, kind of warm and womanly and very appealing. "Trespassing means going where you don't belong, Jack."

"Don't look at me," Riley said. "A hundred-dollar bet gives me the right."

"You're pushing your luck, cowboy," she said in a pleasant tone of voice. "This office is off-limits to you."

"I told you," said Jack, looking as smug as his mother. "My mom only lets me sit in here. Sarah's a girl and she can't even come in here."

"That's right," said Cat, ruffling the child's glossy black hair. "Jack's going to be a writer when he grows up. He likes to sit at my desk."

"Not if he can't find it."

The look she shot him would have qualified as a deadly weapon in at least seventeen states.

"Why don't you get ready for bed," she suggested to the child, "and I'll come tuck you in when you're done."

"But, Mom, I—"

"Go ahead." She pressed a kiss to the top of his head. "I want to talk to Mr. McKendrick."

"Better scatter breadcrumbs," Riley called after the boy. He'd need them.

IT WAS BAD ENOUGH having the cowboy in her house.

Seeing him in her office was more than she could take.

"Out." She pointed toward the door. "Right now. This is private property."

"This is an office."

"It's *my* office and I want you out of here."

He bent down and inspected the row of sun-bleached Smurfs lined up across the windowsill. "I've got to start somewhere."

"Not here, cowboy. This room is off-limits." She tried her best to ignore the cobwebs dancing inches above his head.

He gestured toward the piles of paper, books and magazines stacked up on every available surface.

"When was the last time you actually saw your desk?"

"August 12, 1991."

"You need help, Zaslow." He'd said the same words to her before but this time the sound of his voice sent a ripple of pleasure up her spine. Apparently male beauty could make a fool of even the most unlikely of women.

"Can't wait to get your hands on my filing system, can you, McKendrick?"

His grin was wondrously wicked. "Among other things."

She opened her mouth to say something, but the words didn't come. Quick-witted Cat Zaslow, the woman who made a living with words, was speechless.

Too bad Riley wasn't. "The bedrooms are on the second floor, aren't they?"

"Yes, but—" He turned and strode from the room. "McKendrick!" She started after him. "Just where do you think you're going?"

"Upstairs." He didn't break stride.

"Oh, no, you're not." She threw herself in front of him, a perfect imitation of a human roadblock.

"That's where the bedrooms are, isn't it?"

"My bedroom, the kids' bedrooms, Gracie's bedroom, but not—and I repeat, *not*—your bedroom."

"You said stay out of your office. You didn't mention the bedroom. I'm six-four, Zaslow. I haven't slept on a couch since I was seventeen."

"I don't care if you sleep on the floor, as long as you don't do it here." Damn the man. Damn the effect he had on her equilibrium. "I'm not running a hotel here, McKendrick. You can find your own accommodations."

He was less than two feet away from her, so close that she could feel the heat of his body, catch the faint scent of soap on his skin. She wanted to hate him, but the emotions blossoming inside her chest were something very different. Something exciting and scary and wonderful. He was pigheaded and exasperating, but she liked the way the house felt with him in it. As if she'd been waiting a long time for him to come along and complete the circle.

"There's a Holiday Inn not far from the airport in Hartford," she said. "I'll draw you a map."

"Afraid of something, Zaslow?"

"Maybe *you* should be afraid, McKendrick. I'm the one who kills people for a living."

"Good place to do it. You could hide a score of corpses in this place and no one would ever find them."

"So why do you want to stay here?"

"Call me crazy," he said. "You don't have to like me, Zaslow, you just have to listen to me."

The truth is I more than like you, cowboy, and it's scaring the daylights out of me.

SHE HAD ONE OF THOSE incredibly mobile faces that mirrored every thought, every conflicting emotion.

"All right," she said after a long moment. "You can stay in the guest room."

"You have a guest room?"

"Of course I have a guest room."

"You didn't mention it before."

A smile tilted the corners of her mouth. "I wasn't going to let you stay in it before."

"So what changed your mind?" She was a mystery to him, a beautiful, chaotic mystery, and suddenly he needed to understand what made her tick.

"I don't know," she said, then laughed softly. "A hunch, maybe. Maybe I just felt sor—" She stopped. "Why don't you get your stuff out of the car while I find some clean sheets."

Minutes later, he climbed the stairs to the second floor. His duffel was tossed over his shoulder and he lugged a briefcase and a notebook computer under his arm. The landing opened onto a long, narrow hallway that was dimly lit by a single brass lamp atop a pine table. He noticed a back staircase that probably led down to the kitchen. The doors to most of the bedrooms were closed. Small pools of light filtered into the hallway and he caught bursts of music and childish laughter. It struck him that this was more than a house. This was Cat's home. Her family's home.

And he didn't belong.

"In here, McKendrick."

He followed the sound of her voice to the second room past the staircase. The door was ajar. He was a man who felt at ease in palaces and presidential suites, but at that moment he felt singularly out of place.

Cat was seated on the bed, her long slender legs tucked up beneath her. Her son—Jack, was it?—was propped up against the headboard, his dark hair tousled and spiky. His features were rounder than Cat's, his skin ruddier. Actually, he didn't look a hell of a lot like his mother except for the straightforward expression in his dark eyes.

She offered Riley a smile that he felt all the way down to the bootheels. "Come on in, McKendrick. Jack has a question he'd like to ask you, if you don't mind."

Riley crossed the threshold into the boy's room. He caught the faint smell of bubble gum, dog biscuits and modeling clay in the air. "Hey, Jack," he said, leaning against the chest of drawers to the right of the door. "Ask away."

Jack mumbled something too low for Riley to hear, then buried his face in his pillow.

"He's somethimes shy," Cat said, ruffling the boy's dark hair. "Just give him a moment or two."

Jack peeked up at him. Riley winked. The boy giggled, then buried his face back in the pillow.

"Come on, Jack," Cat said, laying her hand on her son's shoulder. "It's time for lights out. Do you want to ask Mr. McKendrick your question tonight or can it wait until breakfast?"

"Tonight!" The boy sat up straight and met Riley's eyes. "Are you *really* a cowboy?"

"Sure am," Riley said, hiking up his pants leg so Jack could see his well-worn leather boots. "Born and raised in western Nevada."

The boy's dark eyes shone with wonder. "Did you have your own horse?"

Riley met Cat's eyes and grinned. "I had lots of horses but I guess my favorite was a mare named Fred."

"A *mare* named Fred?" Cat asked.

Jack frowned. "What's a mare?"

"A mare is a girl horse," Riley said.

"You can't name a girl Fred," Jack told him sternly. "Girls have girl names."

"That's what Fred said, too, but nobody listened to her."

Jack had a score of questions, but his mother had other ideas. "Those questions can wait until tomorrow, sweetie. It's time you got some sleep."

Jack ignored his mother. "You'll be here tomorrow?" he asked Riley.

"I'll be here."

Cat brushed a lock of hair from the boy's forehead with a tender gesture, then frowned. "Oh, Jack..." Her voice trailed off and she placed the palm of her hand flat against his forehead. "I hope you're not getting the flu."

"He looks fine to me," said Riley.

She shook her head. "I know the signs. There's a twenty-four hour bug going around town. Gracie had it last week. I was wondering when it would hit someone else."

"You can tell all that by touching his forehead?"

"I'm his mother," she said by way of explanation. "Of course I can."

Another example of all Riley would never understand about the mysteries of family life.

"You're good with kids," Cat said a few minutes later after she'd settled the boy down for the night.

"All I did was answer his question."

"You'd be surprised how few adults pay attention."

"He seems like a good kid."

"They all are. I've been lucky."

There wasn't much he could say to that. The woman lived in the middle of insanity and she felt lucky. And what scared him the most was that he understood why. All evening he'd been trying to quantify the way he was feeling, to find a name for it, some way to identify and catalog the odd rush of sensation he experienced every time he looked at her, but the words were just beyond reach.

He hoped they stayed there.

"This isn't the most masculine room in town," Cat said, as she showed him to a room at the opposite end of the hallway, "but we weren't expecting a cowboy."

"Long as it's got a bed," Riley said with confidence. "Flowered wallpaper doesn't bother me."

"Well," said Cat, cautiously, "it's a bit more than flowers on the wallpaper."

She flung open the door and switched on the light.

"Hell, no!" Riley stepped back. He stared at the profusion of deep pink roses on the bedspread, the walls, at the windows, strewn across the chaise longue and massed in pots on every available surface. "No way."

"I decorated this during my Laura Ashley phase," she said. "I admit I might have gone a tad overboard."

"A tad?"

She lifted her chin and he admired the stubborn set of her jaw. "I never claimed to have good taste. When I like something, I like it all the way."

He peered cautiously into the room. "Let me guess. You like roses."

"Very perceptive," she said, that stubborn jaw softening.

He stepped into the room and tossed his bags down on the bed. "Good thing I don't have allergies. This room is enough to put you in the hospital."

"You'll find both the closet and the bathroom through that door," she said, pointing.

"More roses?" he asked, hoping against hope.

A wicked smile played at the corners of her mouth. "Don't worry, McKendrick. I don't think Laura

Ashley wallpaper has a negative effect on a man's testosterone level.''

"Feel like putting that in writing?"

Their eyes met, and to Riley's surprise they both started to laugh. She had a great laugh—not one of those polite exhalations of breath, but a full-bodied, lusty laugh that made him wonder if she laughed like that in bed.

"It's this or the family room sofa," she said. "Your choice."

He unzipped his duffel. "I'll manage."

She backed toward the door. "I'll get you an extra blanket."

"Don't bother."

"It's no bother. This is an old house and it gets very cold at night."

"I'm hot-blooded," he said. "The cold doesn't bother me."

"Lucky you," she said after a moment. "If you need anything, I'm next door."

"I'll remember that." His blood shifted. He wouldn't be able to forget that if he tried.

She made to leave then turned back toward him. "We get up early around here. I hope the noise doesn't—"

"It won't. I get up at five."

Her eyes widened. "Every day?"

"I run."

"You really *are* organized, aren't you?"

"You've got to practice what you preach."

"You might have met your match in the Zaslow household."

"I don't think so."

"You're outnumbered," she pointed out.

"By this time tomorrow that won't matter."

"You think a lot of yourself, don't you, cowboy?"

"I know what I can do."

"We're a rowdy bunch."

"I've seen worse."

She grinned. "By this time tomorrow that won't matter."

"You'll thank me, Zaslow. In two days I'll have your life on the right track, and you'll wonder how you ever managed without me."

She knew a challenge when she heard one. Her eyes flashed fire but the fire was tempered by a sense of humor that was obviously as much a part of her as her long legs and high cheekbones. "Cowboy, I'll—"

"Mommy!"

They both started at the sound of the little girl's voice from the hallway behind Cat.

Cat swung Sarah up into her arms. "What's the matter, honey? Bad dream?"

The child shook her head. Her eyes, as blue as Cat's, were fixed on Riley. "Go home," she said, then buried her face in Cat's shoulder.

"That isn't nice, Sarah." Cat's voice was firm. "Mr. McKendrick is our guest. What did I tell you about how we're supposed to treat guests?"

The little girl mumbled something but Riley couldn't understand a word of it.

"She said, 'Be polite,'" Cat explained, reading his mind.

Riley wanted to tell the child not to worry about it, but he knew he was out of his depth.

Cat kissed her daughter's chubby hand. "Don't you have something to say to Mr. McKendrick?"

The child burrowed her face deeper into Cat's shoulder.

"Sarah." Cat's voice was firm but still loving. He wondered how she managed to do that. It was a sound he'd longed for as a child. It must come with childbirth or something.

Sarah turned her head slightly until he could just make out her delicate features. "I'm sorry. You don't have to go home."

"Thank you," he managed. The lump in his throat made it hard to say much more.

Cat smiled at him, and for the first time in his life he wanted the one thing he knew he could never have.

A home.

A family.

A woman like Catherine O'Leary Zaslow.

Chapter Five

"GRACIE!" Cat stepped in front of her friend and folded her arms across her chest. "Please, I'm begging you. You're not going to leave me alone with him, are you? I thought we were in this together."

"I don't know about you, my friend, but Dawn and I are going to Disney World." Gracie balanced her eighteen-month-old daughter against her right hip and rummaged through the diaper bag. "I know those plane tickets are in here someplace."

"You don't keep your plane tickets in *there,* do you?" Cat was sloppy but even *she* had her limits.

"Of course I do." Gracie withdrew the ticket envelope from the zippered compartment. "Except for Dawn, the diaper bag is the one thing I know I won't forget."

Cat couldn't argue with logic like that. No mother could. "Please tell me you got your dates wrong. You leave *next* Friday, right?"

Gracie met her eyes. "Today, Cat." She waved the tickets at her friend.

"I could've sworn it was next weekend."

"Why would I go next weekend? The crowds are there this weekend."

"Gracie, people don't usually want to go to Disney World when it's crowded."

"It's Dawn's first time. I want her to have the whole Disney experience."

"I'll give you a raise," Cat pleaded, her level of desperation rising. "I'll double your vacation days."

"Throw in Alec Baldwin and you might have yourself a deal."

"Doesn't our friendship count for anything? How can you abandon me in my hour of need?"

Gracie—the wretch—laughed at her pain. "We both know what you need, Cat, and he's waiting for you in the living room even as we speak."

Violent heat flooded Cat's body. "Gracie! What kind of thing is that to say?"

"It's the truth. If I could've captured the sparks flying between the two of you, I'd put the electric company out of business."

"I take it back," Cat said. "Go to Disney World. It's obvious you need the rest."

"Opportunities like our cowboy friend don't show up every day, Cat. If you don't rope him in, someone else will."

"Someone else is welcome to him," Cat declared in no uncertain terms. "The only reason he's here is because I intend to prove a point."

Gracie—the wretch—threw back her head and laughed loud and long. "And if you believe that, honey, you're even better at fiction than I thought."

RILEY DUCKED BACK into the hallway.

"Damn," he muttered under his breath. He'd always wondered what women said about men when they were together, but he never thought he'd find out quite this way.

They'd been talking about him.

And you didn't have to have a degree in psychology to know Cat didn't think much of him. The woman had flat-out begged her housekeeper to postpone her vacation just so Cat wouldn't be left alone with him.

Last night he'd entertained a few convoluted and highly erotic fantasies about Cat and him and a hot tub. Now he felt as if he'd been pushed under a cold shower and left there to think about where he'd gone wrong.

Tough luck, McKendrick. That's what you get for forgetting why you're here.

TRAITORS, Cat thought as she watched her own children sign on with the enemy. The only one who hadn't fallen under his spell was Jack, and that was only because, as she'd suspected, he was sick in bed with the twenty-four-hour flu.

"It's not going to last," she said as the little turn-coats marched off to their respective rooms to make a day list of responsibilities.

"It'll last," said Riley, sifting through a huge mound of orange index cards.

"They're having fun now," she predicted, "but just you wait until the novelty wears off. Then you'll find out what running a household is all about."

"Sit down."

She blinked. "What?"

"Sit down," he repeated.

She sat down at the kitchen table. "Better make it fast, McKendrick. I have a book to write."

"Your book can wait."

"No," she said carefully, "my book *can't* wait. That's how I pay my bills."

He plucked a stack of unopened envelopes from the wicker basket in the middle of the table. "That's the problem, Zaslow. You *don't* pay your bills."

She felt her cheeks redden. "Of course I pay my bills." She glanced at the postmark on one of the envelopes. "Maybe I don't always pay them on time, but I do pay them."

"Do you know what you're doing to your credit rating?"

She glared at him. "Do you know what my bank balance is?" Writing murder mysteries had proved to be extremely lucrative. "I doubt if my credit rating is in any trouble."

"Guess again, Zaslow. You have enough red flags after your name to start your own communist country."

"Very funny, cowboy, but you're not scaring me."

"Somebody should. I found three unanswered letters behind the television in the family room."

"Wonderful," she snapped. "You've proved your point. I'm a mess. Does that make you happy?"

"Happy?" He gestured broadly toward himself. "Look at me! Do I look happy?"

"Yes," she lied. "You look ecstatic. You look like you've waited all your life to find someone like me to—" Her words resonated in the air between them. She wished she could reach out and grab them, erase them from his memory bank, but it was too late. Her words were out there and even if her intent hadn't been provocative, the effect definitely was.

THE LAST TIME Riley had been at a loss for words was the time he shared a hotel employees' elevator with a topless Las Vegas showgirl named Bambi.

This was the second time.

Her expression didn't waver. She didn't blush. There was no indication that her words were anything more than a flip wisecrack meant to knock him down a peg or two. But he felt those words in the center of his chest and they seemed to be growing bigger, more important, with every second that passed.

He cleared his throat. "Make a list," he said. "Write down everything you do on an average day."

"I'm a mother," she said. "I have no average days."

"Humor me." His tone was one step above a growl. "Write down every damn thing you do from the time you open your eyes in the morning until you close 'em again at night.''

Her expression grew darker. ''Not everything.''

''Yes,'' he said grimly. ''Everything.''

She pushed the paper and pen away from her. ''Not in this lifetime.''

''All right,'' he relented. ''Forget the personal stuff.'' Women got a little touchy when it came to bathrooms.

''Thank you,'' she said. She pulled the paper and pen back toward her and began to write.

And write.

And write.

He paced the kitchen. He poured himself a cup of black coffee, drank it, then paced some more. Finally he couldn't restrain himself. ''What in hell are you doing?'' he bellowed. ''The secretary of state doesn't have a day like that.''

He watched, fascinated, as she looked up at him, then looked through him as if he weren't standing there in front of her. She gave her head a quick shake as if to clear away the cobwebs.

''Sorry,'' she said. ''A great plot idea occurred to me and I didn't want to let it slip by.''

''I thought you were writing up your daily schedule.''

''I was, but as soon as I wrote 'Load the dishwasher,' I flashed on a brilliant idea where the villain stashes the bloody murder weapon in the dishwasher with the Thanksgiving dinner dishes and washes away the evidence.''

He wasn't entirely sure he liked the way her mind worked.

"You're awfully quiet," she said with a grin. "Do I make you nervous?"

"I went to Harvard, Zaslow. I know the difference between fact and fiction."

The grin widened. "Are you *sure* you do?"

Truth was, she unnerved the hell out of him, sitting there all innocent and beautiful, bathed in the morning sunshine that spilled through the kitchen windows. "How'd you get started writing murder mysteries anyway?"

"I found a dead body near my rosebushes."

"Right," he said, not believing her for a minute, "and a six-foot rabbit on the porch."

"You asked, McKendrick."

Maybe she was telling the truth. "So what were you, a homicide detective?"

"I answered phones and typed envelopes by day and wrote free-lance by night."

"Before you got married?"

"No." A shadow flickered across her face. "After David died. I'd been working as a staff reporter at *Newsweek* when we met, but there was no way I could juggle that and motherhood."

"From *Newsweek* to typing envelopes?"

"Money was tight and I'm not afraid of hard work."

"So where does the body come in?"

"We were still living on the Lower East Side of Manhattan in David's old apartment. I was pushing Sarah in her stroller and I saw something funny behind Mrs. Mazzelli's rosebushes."

"*Mr.* Mazzelli?"

"Bingo, cowboy. And he was clutching the little woman's cat's-eye glasses in his hand."

"You look downright nostalgic."

"I am," she said. "It was serendipity."

A beautiful woman who waxed poetic over a corpse. "So what happened after you found the body?"

"I called the police, I hung around, I asked questions. Nobody paid much attention to the little housewife with the new baby and the four rowdy little boys. Eight weeks later I sent *Roses Are for Killing* on to Max who managed to sell it for more money than I'd ever seen in one place in my life. And the rest, as they say, is history."

"Have you found any more corpses in the rosebushes?"

"No, but I believe we make our own luck."

His eyebrow lifted. "Meaning what?"

"Meaning I'd sleep with my light on if I were you."

He wasn't sure whether to laugh or check his insurance policy. "Admit it, Zaslow, you're not your average mother of five."

"And you're not exactly my idea of the quintessential time-management expert." She made a big production out of looking him over, head to toe. She also made it obvious that her inspection was meant to get on his nerves. It didn't. He liked it. "You should have a sunken chest, a high-pitched voice and a pocket protector."

"I don't."

She swallowed. "I've noticed."

There it was again. That indefinable tug in the center of his gut. That voice in his ear that kept saying, *This is the one.*

Her gaze was steady as she looked up at him. His grasp on reality was anything but. Her blue eyes seemed smoky, darker than they had a moment ago. He moved closer. His blood pounded in his ears. Her lips parted a fraction. His hunger was a living, breathing force.

Kiss her. That's what this is all about. Kiss her and get on with it.

HE WAS GOING to kiss her.

Cat knew it in her head, in her heart, in the way her blood moved through her body like a river seeking its source.

And the amazing thing was, she was going to let him.

She was under an enchantment, that's what it was, some kind of erotic magical spell that made normally sane women do things their mothers had warned them against years ago.

Like kissing a stranger.

And he was a stranger. Just because Max had thrown them together was no reason to think otherwise. She didn't know much of anything about Riley McKendrick. Oh, she knew the basics—Nevada-born, Harvard educated—but she didn't know one single thing of importance about the man who was preparing to take her in his arms.

Does it matter, Cat? You know everything you'll ever need to know about him.

He held out his hand to her and she placed her own hand in his. A shock of recognition sizzled through her body, the certainty that something much more powerful than she could ever understand had brought her to this moment in time.

She stood up. He drew her into his arms. She'd wondered if she would ever know this feeling again, this powerful surge of light and heat that made everything else fade to nothingness.

Now she knew. It had been waiting deep inside her, waiting for the right man and the right moment to bring it back to painful, glorious life.

He cupped her face with his massive hands and her eyes fluttered closed. She was a strong and successful woman who prided herself on her independence, but as he brought his mouth down to hers, she wondered if she'd ever truly known about the wonders the world had to offer.

Wonders as simple as a man's mouth open and hot against yours, wonders as wild and intoxicating as the touch of his tongue against your lips, seeking, demanding, urging you to open for him, forcing you to acknowledge that what was happening between you was as fierce and demanding as a force of nature—and even more untamed.

Her hands came up between them and she placed her palms against his chest. It wasn't enough. She wanted to rip past the layers of clothing until it was skin to skin, heat to heat, hunger to hunger. She wanted—

The kids! The footsteps thundering through the hall were coming closer.

She pushed Riley away, feeling guilty as sin but alive. Alive to the moment and the man and the wonder of it all, and she wished she could feel that way for the rest of her life.

BEING A MAN had its drawbacks, one of which was making itself obvious as Riley struggled back to a mere mortal plane of existence. He quickly went to the refrigerator and occupied himself with checking for orange juice or some other damn thing.

"We got the lists, Mr. McKendrick," said Kevin, bounding into the room with his siblings close behind, "but my sister can't write."

"Great," said Riley with as much enthusiasm as he could muster under the circumstances.

Sarah appeared at his side. "I can so write," she said. "Mommy taught me to write my name."

"You'll have to show me," he said, pretending great interest in the contents of Cat's refrigerator.

"What are you doing in there?" Ben popped up on his other side. "You're not supposed to keep the door open that long."

"You're right," he said, straightening up. "Bad example."

Like being caught making out with the kid's mother right there in broad daylight in the middle of the kitchen. If a man was looking for trouble, that was one damn good way to find it.

Cat was seated at the table. Looking at her, you'd never know she'd been anything but domestic in that kitchen. Sarah climbed up on her lap and pushed a sheet of bright yellow paper into her mother's hands. "Read my list, Mommy," she demanded. She was Cat all over again and he had to smile as he looked at her.

Cat hugged her daughter as she read the list aloud. "Feed the fish. Put away my toys. Watch 'Barney.'" She gave Sarah a kiss atop her head. "This is a great list, honey. You did a good job."

The little girl beamed with excitement. "I wrote it myself, Mommy. I thought up all the words and Kevin just put them on the paper."

The boys snickered but quickly stopped beneath their mother's sharp-eyed glance. "Your sister put a lot of thought into her list, boys. I hope you did the same.''

"So now what?" Kevin asked, staring up at Riley. "What'll we do next?"

He looked at Cat and their eyes locked. One look from her was worth an entire night in another woman's arms.

Too bad it wasn't enough.

Chapter Six

MAYBE IF HE HADN'T kissed her, she might have had a chance, but the moment his lips met hers, Cat knew she was lost.

Totally.

Irrevocably.

Permanently.

He'd kissed her the way women dreamed of being kissed, an erotic blend of tenderness and heat, of fierce need and sweet surrender that had toppled her defenses. She'd felt that kiss deep in her soul, in her heart, in every cell and fiber of her body. And she still felt it now, hours later, as she sat at her desk and stared at the mountain of unanswered correspondence waiting for her to organize it.

She'd wanted him more in that moment than she'd ever wanted anything or anybody in her entire life. Nothing else had mattered, not reason, not sanity, not the fact that they were quite probably the most mismatched couple in the United States and destined to remain so.

She sat there in her office, oblivious to the steady hum of her computer, and considered the situation. The man had ice water in his veins. The kiss had been his idea, but if it had meant one blasted thing to him, you'd never know it by the way he'd been acting ever since. A split second before the kids burst into the kitchen, they'd broken apart, and instantly it was as if the kiss had never happened. Cat had looked deeply into his green eyes, searching for a clue, a sign, anything that would indicate he'd felt a fraction of the wonder she'd found in his arms but there was nothing.

The rat.

Missy and Taj, two of her house cats, leapt up onto the desk, sending letters and magazines flying every which way. Scooter, who'd been sleeping at her feet on a bed of manuscript pages, grumbled loudly then lumbered off to find another place to nap. She hoped it was on top of McKendrick's pillow. Scooter drooled. It would serve him right.

The louse.

She ripped open a few sweepstakes offers from Publishers Clearing House and managed to waste a good half hour affixing gold seals and labels to various locations on the entry forms, all in the name of efficiency. It occurred to her that she could be putting her time to better use, but she pushed that thought from her mind. Somebody had to win these things, a fact even the anal-retentive, clock-watching Riley McKendrick should understand.

The monster.

Even her own children were turning against her. The only one who was still normal was poor Jack, and that was only because he was in bed sick. By tomorrow, Riley would have the kid asking for a horizontal file for his birthday. She'd seen the way the other little traitors hopped to it when the cowboy barked out an order. Wasn't this how fascism got its start?

The whole thing was disgusting. With McKendrick's help they'd color-coded clothes and toys and schoolbooks, and even followed him down to the basement to tackle the dozens of unmarked boxes that had followed them from their old house, and the house before that. The same boxes Cat had assumed would follow her one day to the old-age home.

Well, not if Riley McKendrick had anything to do with it. Wasn't it enough he was turning her present inside out—did he have to stick his nose into her future, as well? She'd grown attached to the idea of having those mystery boxes with her to warm her in her old age.

She pushed back her desk chair and rose to her feet. She couldn't just sit there while he turned her children into little robots with Filofaxes tucked into their lunchboxes. Her nerves were on edge, she felt like she was coming down with something and the fact that he was pretending that kiss never happened was suddenly more than she could take. If you were going to kiss someone the way he'd kissed her, the least you could do was own up to it.

With righteous fury in her breast, she marched through the hallway and downstairs to the basement where the situation was even worse than she'd thought. Kevin, Michael, Ben and even Sarah were sorting through boxes of old comic books, doll clothes and toys. They even looked like they were enjoying themselves.

Were these the same kids who swore that even used chewing gum might be a collector's item someday? The pile of discards was astonishing. Cat spied one of her old Barbie dolls on the top of the pile and made a mental note to retrieve it later that night under the cover of darkness. Some things, after all, were sacred.

"Hi, Mom," said Kevin, looking up from his task. "Gonna have a lot for recycling next week."

She nodded. Tomorrow she'd care about recycling. Right now she only cared about justice. "Where's Riley?"

"I dunno," her son said. "I thought he was with you."

She turned on her heel and marched back upstairs, aware of her children's curious whispers.

"Where are you, McKendrick?" she muttered, peering into the living room, the kitchen, the dining room. A wonderfully delicious thought occurred to her. Maybe he was sprawled across the bed in the guest room, reading *Playboy* and drinking beer, while the rest of them sorted, color-coded and alphabetized.

She took the stairs two at a time, heart pounding with anticipation. She'd catch him in the act—that's what she'd do—and she'd throw all of his annoying platitudes about schedules and discipline right back in his smug and gorgeous kisser. The thought filled her with glee as she tore down the hallway toward his room.

She flung open the door to the guest room, ready, willing and able to face down her adversary, but her adversary was nowhere in sight.

Maybe he was in one of the kids' rooms, decorating their toys with those idiotic colored dots, the organizing tool that was supposed to make it easy to answer the eternal question, "Which one of you left the roller skate on the staircase?"

She peeked into their rooms, but there was no sign of McKendrick. She was about to head downstairs when she heard a sound from the one place she hadn't thought to check.

Her room.

Righteous fury turned quickly into shock. McKendrick was not only in her room, he was in her lingerie drawer and she'd caught him with the evidence in his hands.

RILEY SUPPOSED it looked pretty bad, what with him standing there with Cat's lacy black bra in his hands and her underwear drawer wide open.

"It's not what you think," he said, his words sounding lame even to him.

"Put my underwear down!" Her tone was lethal. "Now!"

"You don't understand. I—"

"I understand, all right. I understand you're a filthy skunk with a big problem."

"The dog did it."

"You can do better than that, cowboy."

"Damn right," he shot back, "but I'm telling you the truth. I caught one of your dogs playing with it in the kitchen."

"You did not."

"Remember the hall closet," Riley said. "Does it really seem that impossible to you?"

Her eyes flashed fire. "I don't care how or where you found that, but stop doing what you're doing— right now!"

"Stop doing what?"

"That." She pointed toward his hands. "Do you have to hold it that way?"

The bra cups rested in the palm of his hand. "What's wrong with the way I'm holding it?"

Her cheeks reddened and she reached for the undergarment. "Just hand it over and be quiet."

He glanced down at the profusion of lace, silk and cotton jumbled together in the drawer. "You'd be able to stuff more junk in there if you folded things."

"Mind your own business."

"This is my business, Zaslow, or have you forgotten the bet?"

"Touch one thing in that drawer and you're a dead man."

He kneed the drawer shut. "So what're you doing in here? Checking up on me? Afraid I'm a cross-dresser and I've got my eye on your teddies?"

"I—" She stopped abruptly, bra dangling from her fingers like a lacy flag of surrender.

"Don't get shy on me now, Zaslow. Tell me what's on your mind."

"You." She swallowed. "I want to talk about—I mean, we need to talk about what happened in the kitchen."

"The kiss?"

She nodded. "Yes. I want to know why you did it."

"Pretty obvious, wouldn't you say?"

She gestured toward the lingerie drawer. "Pretty obvious, too, wouldn't you say? I still want an answer."

"Why do men climb mountains?" he countered.

"I don't know," she snapped. "Why do they?"

"Because the mountain is there for the taking."

"I suppose you make a habit of seducing women by the Cuisinart every day of the week."

"Trust me, lady. You'd know it if I was seducing you."

"Think a lot of yourself, don't you, cowboy?"

"When it comes to seduction, I do."

"Seduction's politically incorrect."

"Not when it's done right."

CAT'S KNEES BEGAN to tremble. The man was lethal. Good thing he wasn't trying to seduce her. She didn't think her nerves could stand the real thing. "Seduction is an outdated notion, another example of male domination."

"The hell it is." He moved closer. "Mutual seduction is about as good as life gets."

"Well, there you have it, cowboy," she said with false bravado. "You weren't trying to seduce me, and I wasn't looking to be seduced. Case closed."

He took another step closer. Her skin registered his heat. "There's one way to prove this, Zaslow."

Her heart caught in her throat and she met his eyes. It was there again, that look of sadness, of vulnerability, that had touched her so the first time she saw him. And once again it threatened to be her undoing.

"I can't do this." She moved away.

Moving away from him was the hardest thing she'd ever done.

His expression darkened and she stood still, scarcely breathing, while she waited for him to say something—anything—to ease the tension.

"You're right," he said at last. "You can't do this."

You weren't supposed to just give up. He should have swept her into his arms, kissed away her fears, promised her a future together that neither believed could ever be. "It's not that I don't want to—" Her eyes stung with sudden tears.

"You don't have to explain anything to me, Cat."

"I'm not a casual woman when it comes to things like this," she said, struggling to find the words to define something she didn't understand herself. "I have a family now . . . the kids and—"

"And I'm not a marrying man."

"That's right," she whispered. "And you're not a marrying man." Whatever connection there was between them, it was too intense, too fiery, to be satisfied by a kiss. Or even by an affair. She wanted the whole package, the forever package, and anything less would only break her heart.

HE SHOULD HAVE seen it coming. She had a great career, a family she obviously loved more than anything, and she wasn't about to throw any of it aside for a quick roll in the hay with a man who'd be long gone by the time the sun came up the morning after.

He knew he could overcome her resistance, turn up the charm, call on the old weapons of seduction and take her to bed.

And he also knew it would be the biggest mistake of his life.

Somewhere deep inside, in a place he didn't want to admit even existed, he sensed that she was the one, the woman fate intended for him.

And the hell of it was he could only break her heart.

She needed a man who could be there for the long haul. A man who would love her children the way she loved them, the way ties of blood alone made it possible to love. Family life was a mystery to him, something he could only view from outside the warm circle of love that seemed to surround Cat and her children.

He thought all this, but all he said was, "The bet is canceled."

She swallowed. "I think that's for the best."

"Give me five minutes and I'll be out of your way."

"SO SOON?" *Let him go, Cat. You know this is best for both of you.* "I mean, you might as well stay for supper." She forced a smile. "Leftover turkey. How can you refuse?"

"If I leave now, I can be in Boston in time for dinner."

He turned to leave the room as a wave of dizziness swept over her with surprising force. Food, she thought, struggling to pull in a deep breath. She hadn't eaten much today. Maybe she should grab a sandwich and—

On second thought, food wasn't such a great idea. Her stomach did a backflip and she grasped the edge of the dresser.

"Zaslow?" She heard McKendrick's voice in the doorway as if through a fog of sound. "You okay?"

"F-fine," she managed, keeping her face averted. "Go get your dinner in Boston."

He placed his hands on her shoulders and forced her to turn around. "You look like hell."

There were three of him, all staring down at her with puzzled expressions on their faces. "B-bet you say that to all the girls."

"You're sick."

"... not." The room was spinning madly around the McKendrick triplets, big wide loops like an amusement-park ride designed to turn adult stomachs into blenders.

"It's the flu."

"... never get sick ... I'm the mother around here...."

And then she did what she'd been wanting to do from the first moment she saw him in Max's office the day before Thanksgiving.

She swooned at his feet.

Chapter Seven

"WHERE'S MOMMY?" Sarah asked for the tenth time in as many minutes.

"She's sick, stupid," Kevin said, tossing a comic book at his little sister.

"Jack did it," said Ben.

"Did not," said Jack, who was well enough to come downstairs for dinner.

"You're all a bunch of babies," said Michael. "I didn't have to go to bed when I got sick."

"Am not a baby," Jack cried. "*You're* a baby."

"You are."

"No! *You* are!"

Michael opened his mouth to speak, but Riley's roar stopped him cold. "One more word and the lot of you are going to bed without dinner."

"You can't do that," said Kevin. "You're not our boss."

"Yeah?" asked Riley. "Your mother put me in charge while she's sick, and I'm not taking any guff from any one of you." He put a plate of leftovers down in front of the kid. "Now eat."

You're lucky, Zaslow, he thought, taking his seat at the head of the table. The flu was a walk in the park compared with the hell he'd been through since Cat took to her bed a few hours ago. He didn't have the energy to eat his turkey sandwich. How did women manage this, day after day? He glanced around the table at her offspring. He only counted five of them but he was pretty damn sure they had clones hiding in the closets, waiting to leap out and wreak havoc on the household.

Rock music screeched from the CD player in the living room. The TV blared in the family room. Something flew across the table.

"What was that?" he asked the guiltiest-looking kid.

"What was what?" asked Kevin, squirming in his seat.

Sarah's little lips pursed. "Mashed potatoes," she said, pointing at Ben. "He did it!"

"You little squealer." Ben lobbed another round of mashed potatoes at his sister who broke into a wail loud enough to wake the dead.

Before Riley could act, Sarah scooped up a glob of butternut squash and flung it in Ben's general direction.

Too bad her aim wasn't very good.

The squash landed with a splat on his denim work shirt.

The silence in the kitchen was deafening. The five little hell-raisers stared at him as if they expected him to breathe fire. That would be one way to get these kids in line, but the truth was he felt like yelling,

"Food fight!" and grabbing the mashed potatoes himself.

Instead, he turned to the oldest kid. "Do you know how to work the washing machine?" Kevin nodded. Riley ripped off his shirt and tossed it to him. "See what you can do with this."

The kid dashed off to the laundry room.

"Are you gonna yell at us?" Michael asked.

Riley met his eyes. "Should I?"

The four of them looked at each other, then Ben swallowed hard. "We're not supposed to throw food at the table."

"I figured as much."

"You gonna tell our mom?"

"What do you think I should do?"

"I don't think you should tell her," Jack piped up. "Mommy's sick."

Which was all Sarah needed to hear. She burst into big noisy sobs that made Riley wish he could vanquish flu bugs with his bare hands.

"She's crying because our father's dead," said Michael in a matter-of-fact tone of voice. "She's afraid something's gonna happen to our mom."

Riley held out his hand to the little girl and she raced over to be cuddled in his arms. A crushing pain gripped his chest and squeezed hard as she buried her head against his shoulder and held on for dear life. She was so small, so much like Cat yet different, and he realized the difference was a glimpse of the man Cat had loved enough to marry.

"She's a real crybaby," Kevin observed as he came back into the room. "We didn't cry that much when our first mom died."

"Your first mom?" Was it possible to hallucinate on turkey and stuffing?

"Our mom died when we were really little," said Jack, who still looked damned little to Riley's thirty-five-year-old eyes, "but then our dad married Cat and we were a family again."

Sarah snuffled, and Riley handed her a paper napkin with which to blow her nose. "I never had a daddy."

Michael sighed loudly. "Everybody has a daddy, Sarah."

She shook her head. "Uh-uh."

"He died before she was born," Jack whispered in Riley's ear.

Riley wanted to run. He wanted to put the little girl down, grab up his car keys and duffel bag, then climb into his rented car and head for parts unknown. This was cutting too close to the bone, too close to the young boy who'd lost his parents and forgotten how to dream.

But he had a crying child in his arms and four boys who needed someone to keep them from killing each other while their mother fought the flu. His fate was sealed.

THE PICTURE ALBUMS weren't hard to find. After the kids went to bed, Riley let himself into Cat's office, scanned the bookshelves and soon hit pay dirt. A woman like Cat Zaslow was bound to have enough photo albums to fill a library and she didn't disappoint.

Neither did the photos. There was the wedding album with Cat, in love and happy, and David Zaslow, beaming with pride and a sense of wonder. And of course there was a group portrait of the bride and groom with four little boys, wide-eyed and hanging on Cat's skirts as if they were afraid she'd disappear if they let go for even a second.

His eyes blurred as he opened a second album and saw Cat beaming up at him from the page, hands placed on her barely there stomach as she posed next to a pink-and-white cradle. And there was a photo of a very pregnant Cat standing next to a thin and tired-looking David at a first communion for one of the boys. Riley didn't want to see that picture. It made the whole thing too real, too sad, but he couldn't look away. Her smile was wide and happy but he sensed her sadness, could see it in the way her hand rested protectively on her husband's shoulder, in the shadowed expression in her eyes.

He turned the page and found a death certificate in the name of David Zaslow.

And a hospital photo of a newborn baby.

You didn't have to do it, he thought. People took the easy way out every day of the week, shedding responsibilities the way trees shed autumn leaves. There were foster homes out there waiting to take abandoned children and if the kids had to be split up... well, they were young. They'd get over it.

But Riley knew better. And apparently so had Cat. Kids didn't get over it. It was there deep inside your gut, every day of your life, reminding you that you weren't like other kids. That no matter what else you did with your life, you'd never be good enough to belong to something as simple—and mysterious—as a family.

BY THE MIDDLE of the next afternoon, Cat was back on her feet, a little wobbly but basically none the worse for the wear. She had a dim memory of Riley McKendrick carrying her upstairs... of large and gentle hands fumbling with the buttons of her shirt... and then nothing.

She took a shower, tried to make some sense of her hair, then went downstairs. She supposed it didn't much matter what she looked like or how much of her he'd seen. No doubt he'd be out the door the moment he saw she'd recovered.

She found him in the kitchen, staring out the window as he nursed a cup of coffee. *Damn you, Riley McKendrick,* she thought. *Why couldn't you be a marrying man?* She felt as if she'd been looking at him standing there in her kitchen, for as long as she could remember. As if he belonged there.

She knew it didn't make sense, that you couldn't possibly feel this way about someone you barely knew, but there it was anyway. This wild, irrational feeling that the best thing that ever happened to you was about to slip through your fingers and there wasn't one single thing you could do about it.

Not that she wanted to, she reminded herself. The last thing she needed was an alpha male in residence, poking his head where it didn't belong, trying to make her see the error of her ways.

He turned as she walked into the room. "An eighteen-hour virus?" His voice sounded oddly husky and his eyes glittered with a glassy sheen. Somehow, she knew tears of joy weren't responsible. "Didn't think I'd see you down here so soon."

"A special deal for mothers," she said, trying to keep her tone light. "Who has time for the entire twenty-four?" His skin looked a touch green. Temporary parenthood, she wondered, or the Danville flu? "Did the kids behave?"

"Once we established the ground rules, everything went great."

A suspicious dried blob on the kitchen floor caught her eye. "Mashed potatoes?"

"We had an accident."

She took a closer look. "And squash. Are you sure there wasn't a food fight?"

He ignored the question and posed one of his own. "When is Gracie coming home?"

"Tonight."

"And you're feeling okay?"

"If you're trying to find out if you can leave, Mc-Kendrick, the answer is yes. You can—" She peered at him closely. "Did you just wheeze?"

"Get real, Zaslow. I don't wheeze."

"You did it again."

"You're hearing things."

This time he didn't wheeze. He sneezed.

"I knew it," she said. "You're sick."

"The hell I am."

"The hell you're not." She reached up and pressed her palm to his forehead. "You're burning up."

"I'll grab some aspirin in Boston."

"You won't make it to Boston with a fever like that."

"I'll take my chances."

"What about the other people on the road? Think they feel like taking chances, too?"

He swayed on his feet but was too stubborn to fall down. "Don't try and stop me, Zaslow. I'm out of here."

She leapt in front of him. "Believe me, cowboy, I want you out of here as much as you do, but you're sick and I'm the reason why. And if you think I'm going to be responsible for the highway patrol finding you in a ditch somewhere, you've got another think coming."

He sneezed again and she thought she heard him groan. "I outweigh you by a good sixty pounds—"

"Seventy."

"Whatever. You don't really think you can stop me, do you?"

"Yeah," she said, feeling her jaw tighten with resolve. "Actually I do."

RILEY WAS REASONABLY SURE he was dying. His head hurt, his eyes watered, his throat felt like a golf ball was lodged inside it. He wanted to crawl into a dark cave and stay there until he either died or recovered, and at the moment the former seemed a hell of a lot more likely than the latter. Somewhere in the recesses of his fevered brain was the memory of Cat's slender body as he'd stripped her of her clothes and bundled her into a nightgown, but he was too damn sick to savor it.

The last time he'd found himself in bed at three o'clock in the afternoon, he'd been in Sweden with a long-legged blonde who didn't believe in forever-after any more than he did.

Told you so, McKendrick. You should've made a break for it while you still had the chance.

Soon as he'd heard Cat puttering around, he should've grabbed his duffel and car keys and left temptation in the dust.

Because this was the ultimate temptation.

Real life. A real family.

A woman who could make him believe in happy endings.

It's the fever talking, McKendrick. You're dreaming. You came into this world alone and that's how it was meant to be.

But he'd had a glimpse of something else, of possibilities, and those possibilities scared him more than skydiving without a parachute.

He sensed someone standing by the bed and he opened one eye.

Sarah stood near his head, carrying a half-filled glass of orange juice. "Mommy says you should drink this."

He leaned up on one elbow and squinted at the little girl. "You carried that all the way up here by yourself?"

She nodded, obviously proud of her accomplishment. "I poured the juice but it was too full, so I had to drink some of it."

"That's real nice of you, Sarah." She handed him the glass and he drained it in one gulp. "Thank you."

He leaned back against the pillow, wondering if you could be sick as a dog and macho at the same time, then decided he felt too lousy to care. The little girl wouldn't care if he looked pathetic. Sarah didn't move a muscle. He closed his eyes, counted to twenty, then cautiously lifted one lid a fraction of an inch.

"I see you," said Sarah. "I knew you weren't sleeping."

"No," he said, "I wasn't sleeping but I'm real tired."

"When I'm tired, Mommy reads me a story and I fall asleep. I could read you a story."

Bedtime stories, he thought with a lump in his throat that had nothing to do with the flu. Who did Cat Zaslow think she was, Ma Walton or something? Nobody read bedtime stories to their kids anymore. They sat them down in front of the television or shoved a Nintendo control in their hot little hands. This whole thing was getting more dangerous by the second.

Before he had a chance to say thanks but no thanks, the little girl sat herself down on the foot of the bed. "I can't read yet," she said primly, "but I 'member what I hear. Do you have a best story?"

He shook his head. He didn't trust his voice.

"Okay," she said with a smile just like her mother's. "Then I'll tell you my best story. Once upon a time there was a man that lived all by himself in the woods. The man didn't have anybody to love him, not even a dog." Her big blue eyes widened. "That's a sad story, isn't it?"

"Yeah," he managed. "Very sad."

"Anyway, the man was all by himself until one day he heard a lady singing in the woods and he—"

THE ONSLAUGHT WENT ON all day. First it was Sarah and her happily-ever-after stories. Then it was Ben with updates on local football games. Jack found his way upstairs with a bowl of chicken soup and crackers. Kevin brought a dish of vanilla ice cream and the

Hartford Courant, and Michael set up a radio on the nightstand so Riley could listen to one of those "old peoples' stations" that played ancient music from the seventies and eighties.

To Riley's surprise, he found he liked the kids' visits, liked them almost as much as he liked the kids themselves. They were smart and funny but more important than that, they seemed to care about each other and the people around them. And Riley had a feeling he knew exactly where they'd learned it.

From Cat.

The one person who never so much as popped her head inside the door to see how he was doing.

Big deal, McKendrick. By this time next week you'll have forgotten she even existed.

He wasn't about roots or settling down or getting mixed-up with a widow with five kids, all of whom had somehow managed to worm their way into his heart.

But hell. He'd get over it. He'd never met a person he couldn't walk away from.

He dozed a little in the early evening then awoke to the sound of voices and laughter downstairs. He lay still, listening. Apparently Gracie and Dawn had returned from Disney World, bearing gifts and stories and hugs for everyone. And an unexpected traveling companion. A familiar male voice rose above the din.

Max?

He sat up straight. No doubt about it. He'd know Max's voice anywhere.

Maxwell Bernstein, confirmed bachelor and lover of freedom, was down there talking about Disney World as if he'd done a power breakfast with Mickey. Unbelievable. The Max he knew would rather be staked to an anthill.

Was the whole damn world going crazy on him?

"YOU'RE ENGAGED!" Cat burst into tears as she hugged Gracie then Max. "I can't believe this!" The clues had been right there in front of her eyes all the time and even then she hadn't seen it coming.

Gracie's eyes glowed with that radiance reserved for lovers and madwomen. "He rented a Learjet and flew down to Disney World to propose," she said. "Can you imagine? There I was, standing on line for Pirates of the Caribbean and this wonderful man swooped down on me with three dozen red roses and this." Gracie extended her left hand where a brand-new diamond ring glittered.

"Wow!" Cat shot Max a look. "Now I know what you do with all the money you've made off me."

Max looked sheepish, proud and disbelieving. "I saw Riley's car in the driveway. Go get him. We'll call in for pizza and celebrate."

"I'm not getting him," said Cat.

"I knew that stupid bet would backfire," said Max.

"The bet didn't backfire. It's just over."

"You should've just let me hire him to help you out. That would've solved everything."

She thought of how right it had felt to be in his arms and heat flooded her cheeks.

"That wouldn't solve anything, Maxie. Look at her!" Gracie beamed at Cat, eager to believe in hearts and flowers and all things romantic. "I knew you two were soulmates when you had that fight about the hall closet. Riley was the first man I've ever seen who could stand up to you."

"Stand up to me? I'm very easy to get along with." She glared at her friends. "I saw that look."

"You're a formidable woman," Max said with an amazing display of diplomacy. Love apparently did work wonders. "But the one thing you're not is easy to get along with."

"That's why Riley McKendrick is so perfect for her," Gracie said as if Cat weren't standing right there. "He can put her in her place."

"Sorry to disappoint you," Cat said, unable to control her temper, "but he didn't put me in my place. I put him in *his* place."

Max glowered at her. "You didn't poison him or anything, did you?"

"For heaven's sake, Max! I write about murders, I don't commit them. He's upstairs with the flu."

"Oh, the poor man," Gracie cooed. "How terrible for him."

"The kids have been catering to him like he was a deposed king," Cat said in a surly tone of voice. She heard the back door swing open then slam shut. "He's probably sent one of them out for champagne."

"I'm going up there to talk to him," Max said, starting toward the staircase. "All you two need is a push in the right direction."

"Max!" Cat grabbed him by the back of his jacket. "Talk to McKendrick and you die."

"Don't pay any attention to her, Maxie," Gracie said. "One day they'll thank us."

Max broke free and bounded up the stairs with Cat and Gracie and baby Dawn in hot pursuit.

"Mom!" Jack yelled from downstairs.

"Not now, Jack!"

"Mo-o-om! It's important."

"In a minute," she hollered back, wondering if she could make a running leap and stop Max before he reached the guest room door.

Who would've figured her agent was a closet sprinter?

"Wake up, McKendrick!" Max roared as he raced down the hallway, just beyond Cat's reach. "I'm here to show you the error of your ways."

"I'm going to kill you, Max," Cat muttered. "So help me, I'm—"

"Mommy!" Sarah burst from her room and threw herself in Cat's arms. "Riley's gone and he didn't even say goodbye!"

Chapter Eight

"ARE YOU SURE you don't want to come with us?" Gracie asked Cat the next afternoon. "We're driving out to the Christmas-tree farm."

Cat made a Scrooge-like face. "I can't think about Christmas when we're still eating Thanksgiving leftovers."

"You should come with us," Gracie urged. "You can't sit around moping all day."

"I'm not moping."

"You miss him, don't you?"

"Absolutely not!"

"You can tell me the truth, honey. Love is nothing to be ashamed of."

"Go chop down a Christmas tree, Gracie, and leave me alone." She intended to take a long hot bubble bath and try to forget the world existed.

"Riley will come back," Gracie said, ignoring her warning scowl. "He's crazy about you." She spread her arms wide. "He's crazy about all of us."

The minivan's horn bleated.

"Your boyfriend's waiting," Cat said, glancing around at the three huge bouquets Max had had delivered to Gracie that morning. "Maybe he needs to rob another florist."

"Oh, Cat..."

"Don't mind me," Cat said. "I'm not feeling terribly romantic today. You and Max go and have a good time. If he can survive an afternoon with six kids, marriage should be a piece of cake."

"It's good practice." Gracie dimpled. "We intend to have five brothers and sisters for Dawn as fast as we can."

Cat thought of double the chaos and shuddered. "Please tell me you'll find your own house to live in."

"Call Riley," Gracie said, edging toward the door. "What can it hurt?"

"I can't call him," Cat said as the door closed behind her friend. The man had no office, no home, nothing but a series of e-mail addresses and cellular phone numbers. Besides which, she'd rather die than let the rotten coward know her heart was breaking.

She watched from the window as the minivan backed down the driveway. Normally she loved the rare times when she had the house to herself—probably *because* it happened so rarely. Today she felt as if the silence were mocking her, reminding her of how empty the house was without the people she loved in it.

You wouldn't think a weekend could change a person's life. A handful of days and your whole world was turned upside down and there was nothing you could do to make it right again.

Whatever had happened between her and Riley McKendrick had been an aberration, some strange chemical reaction that defied reason. And it had ended as abruptly as it had begun, without even the chance to say goodbye.

To her dismay, the kids felt it, too. They'd moped around all day, acting like they actually wanted to clean their rooms and fold their underwear. She'd blessed Gracie and Max into eternity when they suggested driving out to the Christmas-tree farm.

It wasn't love, she thought as she turned away from the window. Just the thought of the word was laughable. She refused to believe an entire family could fall in love with someone just like that. Maybe Riley was some kind of cowboy wizard who'd cast a spell on the lot of them, making them believe they couldn't be happy again unless he was part of their family.

What a fool she'd been to be swayed by the loneliness she'd seen in his eyes. What an idiot to think for one second that a man like McKendrick could ever be happy in the middle of her big, boisterous family. He was a loner. He traveled through life with as little baggage as possible. Men like Riley usually ran at the first sign of big-time commitment.

Which, all things considered, was exactly what he did when he disappeared down the back stairs and vanished without a trace.

The thing to do was stop thinking about him. Hadn't he said it himself, that he wasn't a marrying man and never would be? Only a madwoman would willingly give her heart to a man like that. And no mother worth her salt would risk her children's hearts.

Better to drown her sorrows in a bathtub than spend another second thinking about what might have been.

"ARE YOU *SURE*, SIR?" The florist looked askance at the tally. "You've bought every rose in the store."

"And all of the daisies, gardenias and tulips," Riley said, handing over his credit card. "Do you have any orchids or some of those big fluffy yellow things?"

"No orchids, sir, and we're out of mums." The florist ran the card through the cash register. "Now where shall we send these?"

"Nowhere," said Riley. "I'm taking them."

"Sir, you can't possibly take all of these flowers. You'd need a van."

"I have a van," said Riley. And it was already half filled with flowers for the woman he loved.

CAT HAD JUST SETTLED down beneath the bubbles when she heard a car crunching up the driveway. Actually it sounded bigger than a car, more like a van or a truck. Gracie and company should have been happily chopping down Christmas trees by now, doing their utmost to wreak havoc on the environment.

FedEx, she assumed. Maybe UPS. Well, whatever they were delivering, it could wait. Her bubble bath couldn't. Some things in this world were sacred and, for Cat, Mr. Bubble was one of them.

Besides, was there a better place to brood about the fact that Riley McKendrick was an arrogant, obnoxious stinker of a man who didn't even have the guts to admit he didn't want to spend the rest of his life alone.

"Wimp," she said out loud. Bathroom acoustics were wonderful for singing old Beach Boys songs and talking to yourself. "Coward."

"What was that?"

She jumped at the sound of a voice. The acoustics were great but they weren't that great. They couldn't make you hear things that weren't there. She slid back down into the bubbles as a red rose whizzed through the door and landed on the edge of the tub.

Cat stared at it the way she stared at spiders that had the nerve to invade her domain.

"Gracie?" she called out. "I don't think this is very funny. If you—"

Another rose flew through the door followed by a lush white gardenia, two cherry-red tulips, and a trio of daisies that landed on top of her head.

"I'm trying to take a bath in here! You can just take your boyfriend's flowers and—"

"And what?"

McKendrick. It was really him. But she couldn't see him for the masses of flowers that filled the doorway. American Beauty red, pale pink, Texas yellow roses. And masses of daisies. How could he have known daisies were her favorite flower? Gardenias with their beautiful, haunting scent. Tulips out of season—

Good grief. She was naked.

"Go away!" The bubbles were bursting, the towels were out of reach and he showed no sign of paying one bit of attention to her demand.

"Not this time," he said, peering around the huge armful of blossoms. "I did that once and it was the biggest mistake of my life."

"I'm in the bathtub, you fool!"

He didn't hesitate. He didn't bat an eye. He just kept on walking right toward the tub. "Don't I have the right to privacy in my own house?" *You don't want privacy, Zaslow. You know you don't want anything but him....*

"We'll talk privacy later," he said in the sexy drawl that inched her body temperature up a degree. "Right now I want to talk marriage."

She gasped, then started to laugh as he tossed yellow tulips and red roses, daisies and gardenias into the tub. And then she stopped breathing when he plucked a white gardenia from the bubbles and placed it in the cleavage between her breasts. "Have you lost your mind?"

"No," he said. "I just found it."

"You can't walk out on a person one day, then walk back into her life the next."

"I didn't walk out, Zaslow, I ran. I've never been in love before and it scared the hell out of me."

"Oh, cowboy..."

And that's when Riley knew he'd finally come home.

It was all there in that one word, everything he wanted to know, everything he needed to hear. The power and the wonder of love, the miracle of family life, right there for the asking.

He dropped to one knee next to the tub and took her wet hand in his. "Damn it, Zaslow, it all comes down to this. I don't want to live my life without you in it."

She met his eyes. He did his best not to peer beneath the vanishing bubbles. "You said you traveled light, cowboy, and I'm the mother of five."

"I know," he said, grinning as she rearranged rose petals around some very interesting terrain. "I got lucky."

"Family life isn't for cowards. I love you, Riley McKendrick, but I want forever from you or I don't want anything at all."

Flowers and pretty words didn't mean a damn in the scheme of things. He couldn't play it safe, he couldn't hold back. He had to love her the way she needed to be loved, the way she deserved to be loved, or he didn't really love her at all.

Her beautiful blue eyes were wet with tears. "Five kids, a menagerie of pets and a lifetime commitment. Most men would run for their lives."

"No more running," he said. "No more traveling light. I want it all, Zaslow—everything you are, everything you ever will be. Kids, pets, housekeeper, Max, that damn fruity guest room, the way you keep your filing in a laundry basket and your laundry in the filing cabinet—"

"Yes."

It took a second for the word to register. "Yes?"

"Yes!"

He stripped off his leather jacket and tossed it to the floor.

"Riley," Cat said with a soft laugh, "what are you doing?"

He started to undo the buttons on his shirt.

"You aren't—I mean, you can't..."

"Sure I can."

"What if the kids come home?"

"They won't. They'll be out for hours."

"You can't be sure of that."

"I spoke to Gracie. I'm sure."

"Of all the sneaky—"

He kissed her.

She sighed. "Of all the wonderful—"

He kissed her again.

"Oh, cowboy," she breathed as he climbed into the tub with her, clothes and all. "What took you so long?"

GUS IS BACK

♡

Lass Small

Chapter One

AT TWENTY-SEVEN YEARS of age, Cara Porter was a divorced woman. She was tall enough to be an adult. She was slender and agile. Her hair was brown, her large eyes were blue and her bone structure was rather delicate.

In the earpiece of the phone held to Cara's ear, the voice said, "It's time to celebrate our tenth year as high-school graduates. You'll help, of course."

It wasn't even a question. Cara Porter had been directed, yet again. How come people walked all over her this way? It was because she was spineless. She ran with the crowd and did what was expected of her.

And more. There were those who wiggled out of their responsibilities, which predictably frustrated chairpeople of committees. But someone always thought of Cara to fill the gap. "Call Cara," and "Cara doesn't have any responsibilities," and "Cara needs the distraction," and "It'll make her feel included."

From the receiver held to Cara's ear, Sidra's voice was a bit more abrasive as she repeated, "You'll help, of course." Again, she was not questioning, she was telling Cara to do as she was told.

Frowning at a painting, on the wall, done by some remote ancestor, Cara replied, "Mmm." Now that was surprising to Cara. She hadn't said "Yes," or "You can count on me." She'd said, "Mmm." She was being vague in her reply? She was being non-committal. That was strange.

Sidra never recognized revolt. She accepted the sound as an assenting response.

The thought of the word "revolt" caused Cara to consider the possibility that she was revolting? No. Well, was she in revolt? Rebellion? Cara? Of course not. She then became aware Sidra was speaking and listened.

Sidra was saying, "...up to you to contact all those on the list. You have the time."

Cara instantly replied, *"No!"* That was abrupt and clear. She was not going to find all those elusive people who did not want to be contacted or who didn't particularly care about seeing each other simply because they'd graduated from high school the same year. In that little town, they saw each other most of the time. It was no big deal.

After Cara's "No," there was a very silent pause. Sidra inquired, "What did you say?" She was testing whether Cara had the stamina to repeat her negative word.

And Cara found herself glibly replying, "For a change, let them contact us. They know we're here. They can count, or they could ten years ago. They all realize it's ten years since we graduated. Let them contact us. Saves postage, time and temper.''

''Cara.'' Sidra said only the name, but it was said with such enduring patience that it was clear she should have more scope for her drama than the small town of Williamsfield, out there, on past Uvalde in West TEXAS.

Cara had the gall to ignore the patience of Job, female version, as she said ''What.'' And this time it was her word that was not a question.

Sidra sighed directly into Cara's earpiece and explained precisely, ''It is only proper that we contact all the graduates of our high-school class, so they will know that we will have a celebration here in Williamsfield to mark our tenth year as graduates.''

''Won't it be in Uvalde again?''

With extreme stability, carefully held, Sidra responded with slow determination, ''It will be here.''

''At Barney's Grill?''

''Yes-s-s,'' Sidra responded with a snake's hissing warning. ''Since the opera house burned down and the Methodists decline meetings in their church when beer is served, it will be at Barney's.''

Without any inflection at all, Cara replied, ''Whoop-de-doo.''

Sidra inquired through her teeth, ''Will another time be more convenient to discuss this?''

''Probably not.''

Bearing down, Sidra retorted in a mannerly way, ''I have a list of the graduates with their last known

addresses. Come by when it's convenient . . . today."
And Sidra gently put her phone into place . . . more
gently than she'd said that last word.

As Cara hung up less gently, she was really p-p-
perturbed. With their last *known* addresses? Yeah.

Here Cara was, not quite twenty-eight, no longer
married, no job and the patsy of all the do-gooders
who wanted free help. She had not one feeble excuse
not to help, no matter what all time it took. What
else did she have to do?

Nothing.

Cara found herself wondering if Gus would come.
It would be interesting to see a different face for just
the change.

Sourly sitting there in her faded jeans and white
turtleneck, Cara Porter felt the strange symptoms of
rebellion. What she needed was backbone, if she was
going to stay in such a little town. Stay? When had
she ever considered leaving?

It was a good, neat town. It had been settled by
Germans from over the seas in the very early 1800s
and named for the man whose land was purchased
for their town. The new citizens had started out
identifying it by saying, "William's field, out west of
here." Soon, nobody remembered the town's real
name. The chance designation had stuck.

Gus Freeman was one of William Freeman's de-
scendants. Gus. Gus Freeman.

Where had his people been and what had happened to them so that they had labeled themselves as free men? And Gus really was free.

When had Cara ever thought about Gus? Rather often lately.

Would he come to the reunion? How could he? He'd dropped out the first year of high school. In all those school years, with some grades repeated, he had mostly been absent.

The teachers had been so encouraging when Gus was at school. They had quietly seen to it that he was included and knew what had taken place while he was gone. They'd called it reviewing, but it was done after Gus had been gone for a while. No one was fooled, but the other kids had also benefited from the reviews.

Cara remembered a jacket of her brother's on Gus. It had been one given to the school for the poor. She'd seen her teacher filch it from the pack of clothing. And Gus had worn the jacket. Cara remembered Gus had felt good in such a jacket.

It was only then she recalled he'd mostly been tacky. It had been an era of careless dress. However, Gus had actually been ragged . . . and limping or healing.

Once there had been claw marks on Gus's face, and Cara had asked him if the scratches hurt. He'd grinned at her lopsidedly and said "Naw."

Why else would his grin have been lopsided? He didn't admit to being hurt.

He had taken no part in any of the school activities. He'd been so tired he'd go to sleep in class. His stepfather had hunted at night, and he'd worked Gus to a standstill.

The guys in school had liked Gus. They'd been curious about things he'd trapped and found. She hadn't been able to listen without seeming to want male attention, so she had not.

In middle school, the teacher who had taken the jacket for Gus had brought a valentine to Cara. She'd asked that Cara sign it to Gus just as *Your Friend,* no name.

Cara hadn't wanted to agree to doing it. A valentine? It was too serious. And the teacher had coaxed. "He never gets any cards and he knows the teachers' handwritings. You don't have to sign your name."

Cara then remembered the following Christmas, at school, and drawing names so that all the kids would get at least one gift. Among the gifts Cara had received were two guinea pigs from Gus. He'd drawn her name?

While the family cats had been very animated by the idea of having the guinea pigs around, Cara's mother had gotten red-faced and appalled! The creatures were given to a friend who'd raised the prolific animals and sold them to a lab for a nice little income. The fact that Cara could have had an income from the sale of the proliferating guinea pigs hadn't altered her mother's revulsion.

Gus's family had caught animals for their fur, or to sell or to eat. The family had lived in a shack on the outskirts of town, and the place hadn't been neat. There was no grass, only weeds and vehicle ruts. But Cara's brother, Ben, had said the cages were clean. It was Gus who cleaned the cages.

Then with some surprise, Cara remembered her brother telling of seeing a bobcat in one of the cages out there at Gus's. That caged bobcat was what had put the marks on Gus's face. But Cara remembered other injuries which she had wondered about.

In those days, no one interfered, not really, not in another family. If they thought a child was being abused, they would pass the question around. Was something wrong in that household? They'd pay attention. Looking the stepfather in the eye, there were men and older women who would mention how banged up Gus was.

The stepfather always had a reason. It had been a hoe, a kick from a horse, a bite from a coyote or something else. There was always an excuse. He'd complain that Gus wasn't careful.

Now Gus lived farther out west at some long distance. Cara hadn't seen him in an age.

She got up from the chair by the phone and stretched like a lazy cat. She went outside. The big house was two-storied with railed porches upstairs and down. The house sat on a corner of the block. The yard covered three picket-fenced lots, and the area was shaded by big trees. There was one oak, and the rest were mostly pecan trees her great-grandfather had planted.

Cara walked down the several blocks to her brother's office. Ben Porter was a lawyer. He'd handled her divorce from Fred. And her maiden name had been restored.

Ben was tall and slender. His hair and eyebrows were blond and his eyes were the Porter blue.

While most people in Williamsfield wore casual clothing, Ben was one who dressed in suit, shirt and tie. With shoes and socks, of course. He looked good.

Cara asked Ben, "What's Gus Freeman's address?"

Ben only blinked once before he replied, "I have it here somewhere. He wrote asking—some question—last fall. I think I gave you his regards at that time."

"Gus? I don't remember you saying anything about Gus."

"That was when you were just past getting the divorce from Peanut."

Cara corrected the labeling of her ex-husband, "Fred." Ben had never much cared for Fred.

Ben replied a nothing, "Yeah."

"What's Gus's address?"

"Why?"

With adult patience, she responded, "I'm the committee to contact people for our tenth high-school reunion?'' That was the TEXAS questioning statement.

"Gus wasn't a graduate."

She lied with a completely honest expression, "With as few people as we have, we gather in everybody who even went briefly to the school."

Ben narrowed his eyes. "That right?"

"Yes." Another lie in her boggling collection. Most of them were for courtesy, but there were those which were smudged and iffy. Like her being responsible for the people coming to the reunion. Well, now she'd have to do it. Damn it, anyway.

So Ben found Gus's address, and he appeared to study it for a minute longer than it would take to be sure he had the right paper. He looked at his sister and said, "If I give you this, you be careful of Gus, do you hear me?"

"He's no different from anybody else."

Ben smiled just a tad and said, "Okay."

What did Ben mean by that? Cara didn't ask. She put Gus's address in her pocket and walked away without further comment.

Ben thoughtfully watched after her.

So then Cara found herself at Sidra's house.

Sidra came to the front screen door and questioned, "Yes?" And she looked down her nose at such an innocent Cara.

Kindly, Cara reminded the idiot, "I came for the list. You know, the one of the high-school graduates?" And she put in gently, "For the reunion."

Sidra stared and her eyes flared, but there wasn't one thing she could do without losing a volunteer, as asinine as this one was. For an organizer, the volunteer material to work with in a small town was severely limited. Sidra opened the screen reluctantly and invited the nuisance inside.

Cara smiled, "Couldn't replace me?"

"Hush." The word was impossibly said in four voice levels.

Cara blinked admiringly, her eyes sparkling. But she didn't say a word. She did stay hushed.

Silently, Sidra handed Cara the list from her desk and just stood there.

Cara smiled sweetly and said, "Do forgive me if I just run along?"

Sidra gave one careful nod and narrowed her eyes at Cara.

First Ben and now Sidra. What did narrowed eyes mean?

So Cara took the list home. The house had been her parents'. They'd died in that horrific storm in 1992 when all of TEXAS was afloat with rampaging waters. Her daddy was a man who felt he could do and survive anything, but a gully washer had proven him wrong . . . and his wife was with him.

They'd always done everything together.

After the worst of the grieving was past, Ben had said Cara might just as well have the family house. With her impending divorce, Cara had had nowhere else to go, and she'd declined Ben's offer to move in with him and Maddie.

With neither parents nor husband, Cara had felt like a double orphan. Ben's wife, Maddie, had been hostile for almost a whole year. Oddly, it had been Sidra who'd mentioned that Maddie was jealous of Cara taking over the family house. Then Cara gave Maddie the heirloom dining-room set and the big bed and chests from the parents' bedroom, and the tension between them had eased.

Cara didn't unfold the paper with Gus's address and smooth it out to look at it until she was home again.

The writing was not Ben's. But it was a man's. It was bold and strong. It was Gus's handwriting? It said, *If you have anything to tell me, write or call me here!*

What would Ben have to tell Gus? What would be so important for Gus that he'd write such a note to Ben?

Considering those thoughts, Cara sat on her grandmother's little armless rocker and looked out the window into the spring sunshine. On the corner side of the yard, bluebonnets grew. They were a mass of blue and pinky-purple "bonnets" with five-finger green leaves. It had been a chore to coax the precious weeds to stay there and be prolific.

The first TEXAS Porter ancestors hadn't been around when the state was founded. They'd arrived just after the fact. And since they hadn't really participated in the struggle, they didn't have any relics from the time of TEXAS's independence. It was a little embarrassing. But it had been a big thing to plant a display of the state flower over one side of their yard for the sesquicentennial.

Her daddy had been diligent in getting the bluebonnets planted and encouraging them with dried buffalo droppings. Tom Porter had gotten the fertilizer from a man named Mueller who had at first raised the buffs as a sentimental hobby. But with time and strong sentiment proliferating over the state, the herd had become self-sustaining.

Even TEXANS paid to be photographed beside real buffalo. So did Yankees who came to spend the cold months in TEXAS and who were then called Snowbirds. They were now winter TEXANS.

The beasts had also been used in background films for TV and for movie films. Raising the buffs had proven quite profitable for the Muellers.

Cara now had to pay for the privilege of using the buffs' contribution to the ecology. Digested grass was—digested grass. But it had been Cara's hardnosed daddy who had insisted on the selected fertilizer. Buffalo were in TEXAS before longhorn cattle. That fact was one of the few things everyone agreed about.

TEXANS didn't need any real reason to disagree. That's what happened when people lived out there, so far away from other people. Before radio came along, arguing was the only public entertainment.

People were known for their ability to argue. That was probably why Tom Porter's son, Ben, made such a good lawyer.

As Cara lay in her chair looking out the window into the side yard, she thought perhaps TEXANS took a little pride in being peculiar. That was probably why the state's name was always said and written in caps.

Cara finally admitted to herself that when it came right down to it, she was really only interested in ... Gus. Good heavens. Really, now. Why a person she hadn't seen in just ages and knew absolutely nothing about, at all? Such distraction was ridiculous. It really was! Really silly.

It was so odd to be thinking about Gus when she was committed to writing all those other people. There had been seventy-six people in their graduating class. One was her ex-husband Fred. She was going to write all those people...and Fred...to remind them to get together and celebrate, just because she was so bored that she was curious about Gus Freeman?

Well, it was obvious she ought to study her life and get it organized. She needed to do something with her mind to elevate her potential and be of some help to the world or even for a portion of the world. It was quite probable that she wasn't going to change anything really staggeringly worldwide.

Since she would never have children of her own, she should do something for other people. She should do more to help than just writing to people about attending a tenth anniversary for graduating from high school.

So what interested her? What besides Gus Freeman, who was probably married with ten kids, with a different woman for each of the ten?

How many women Gus Freeman had had was none of her business.

One thing about that small a town, somebody knew where each missing person was and the new address. Only one needed to be hunted down. And even that one had just been traced... by her.

It was after breakfast the next day when Cara piled her brown hair atop her head. She put on a minimum of makeup. Then she pulled on vertical blue-and-white striped cotton pants with a blue turtle-neck top. She slid her feet into white canvas shoes and went to Ben's office.

She greeted Ben and smiled at his executive assistant, who was his secretary. Cara tapped the reunion letter out on Ben's computer. That done, she punched directions for the copy machine to reproduce it seventy-five times... with one extra.

She folded the letters, included one of the stamped, addressed reply cards supplied by Sidra and slid them in the addressed envelopes. Then she stamped them all. Gus's letter was the extra one.

Ben said, "You owe me for the stamps."

"Send Sidra a bill."

In disgust, Ben complained, "She'll tell me it's my civic duty to help out."

Like a parrot, Cara responded, "It's your civic duty to help out."

Ben frowned in irritation. "I said *she* would say that."

Kindly, Cara supplied the explanation, "I'm saving you a burst blood vessel?" It was the TEXAS questioning, do-you-understand statement. She shared the rest of the wisdom. "You can handle that sort of comment from your baby sister."

With some stark drollness, Ben observed, "I think our parents killed themselves to get away from us."

Soberly, Cara replied, "I've considered it, but they didn't. They enjoyed each other too much."

Very quietly, looking at the floor, he said, "I know."

She took an unsteady breath and asked, "Is Gus married?"

"No."

"He has a woman? Isn't he married to her?"

"No. Pela had no place. She moved in for a while. She left the boys with him and took off with the land inspector."

"When was that?"

"A couple of years ago. The reason I have his address is because we keep in touch. I represented him in court. He wanted sole custody of the boys."

"I see."

Ben said, "I doubt it."

"Why do you say that?"

Ben shrugged and put his hands out from his sides. "You look at everything from your limited point of view. You don't understand other people."

She became indignant. "Just what—"

And Ben grinned. "I was wondering when you'd snap back. You've been so placid and sweet since Mother and Daddy died that I thought I'd lost you, too."

"I'm myself again. I wasn't nice to Sidra."

"She called."

In disgust, Cara asked, "Now what?"

Ben gestured. "She told me you're coming out of it. You're being as difficult as you used to be before you married Fred."

"I've *never* been difficult!"

And Ben laughed.

Cara watched him laugh, then she said, "It's strange to consider it. If our parents hadn't died, I would still be married to Fred. I didn't know the lack in our marriage until I was grieving for Mama and Daddy and remembered all the things they had shared."

"Maddie and I have the same kind of sharing they had."

Cara observed her brother. "How lucky you are. I didn't realize you and Maddie had that good a marriage."

Ben regarded his younger sister very seriously. "None is perfect. We have one that's better than average. Maddie loves me. She's jealous *for* me. I don't need any confirmation I'm a Porter. She felt I needed proof in the furniture she wanted. I would have left it at the house for you. You already know that. But Maddie wanted it for me. I took it to satisfy her."

Cara reassured Ben, "I've known all along she did it for you."

Ben looked at his sister. "I'm glad you and Maddie are friends again."

Cara said, "She was lucky to get you."

"Nope. I'm the lucky one."

"I ... envy you."

"That's just for now. You'll find him."

"Him?" Cara frowned and was puzzled.

Ben explained, "The one who'll be right for you."

Bitterly, she turned away, but she asked, "What man would marry a sterile woman?"

He didn't hesitate. He immediately said, "A good man."

She countered seriously, "I think the world is sparse in its supply of 'good' men."

Ben straightened and slid his hands into his trouser pockets as he turned to the window overlooking the quiet, side street. His words were gentle. "It depends on what your requirements are."

She, too, looked out his window at the seldom-used street. "Perhaps."

"Come to supper tonight."

Her thoughts distracted, she barely shook her head. "I have some things to do. Thank Maddie for inviting me."

"What will you be doing?"

She replied seriously, looking at her brother. "Thinking."

"Don't be too hard on yourself. You're a good woman."

She kissed her brother's cheek with a quick, soft touch, gathered up the stack of envelopes and said, "I'll drop these off at the post office."

Ben replied, "I'll be talking to you."

Cara paused. "Do you think he'd be embarrassed to get an invitation?"

"You could ask him to escort you."

"Yeah." She tucked the box under her arm as she exited the building. It wasn't until she was outside that she remembered she hadn't mentioned Gus's name, and neither had Ben. How had Ben known to whom she'd referred?

Well, Gus was the only name they'd talked about. No. They'd mentioned Fred.

She wondered if Fred would come to the reunion. With that many people—almost eighty—if only fifty came, with some husbands and wives, it would still be a crush of people in Barney's Grill. She wouldn't need to even exchange nods with Fred. It would not be a problem.

How strange to consider it awkward to speak to a man who had been her husband and shared her bed.

Life changes. People change. She was an adult and could handle anything. Of course.

Yet again, she wished her parents were still around. It was almost two years, now. When would her grief ease? She had so many things to share with them. The thoughts and comments just stacked up as if waiting for her parents to come back home.

Talking to Ben wasn't a release. He was a problem-solver rather than a listener. What she needed was an adult ear—to listen while she sorted things out.

She was an adult. She was almost twenty-eight years old. It was a formidable age. An adult. Yeah. Why did she still feel so young? So untried. So... unsure. Maybe when she was thirty that feeling of adulthood wouldn't be so elusive.

Should she leave Williamsfield? Go to a city? Find a place where there were strangers who didn't know her? Maybe there she could appear as if she was— adult.

Cara waved a hand at Phoebe, who was across the street. Phoebe Morgan Filmore called back to Cara, but a big truck went past and Cara pretended not to hear. She wasn't in the mood for Phoebe's cheerful chatter.

Main Street was also part of the state highway, which had been bent to go through the town. Their state representative was a blustery loudmouth who didn't do much, but he had done that.

Cara went on toward the little post office. She returned waves and called replies, but she didn't pause to visit. She carried the box of reminders to the post office and gave them to Juanita.

"What's this?" Juanita asked with a frown. "You going into business or something?"

Cara replied, "It's for the tenth anniversary of our high-school graduation."

"My God, you twenty-eight already?"

And Cara replied coolly, "Not quite, and don't be nasty."

Juanita was rude enough to laugh. "Ah, Cara, you're so funny!" She didn't need a reply, but continued, "Who's coming? Any single men? Or are they all married? You looking for a man, now, since you run around loose again?"

"Nuh-uh." And Cara lifted a hand in farewell and walked out of the post office.

Juanita hollered, "Hey! Want the box back?"

But Cara pretended she hadn't heard the question.

As she sought the quiet of a side street, Cara considered her conduct. Her mother would have had a fit over a child of hers being that unmannerly. Even her daddy would have chided her. His eyes squinting as he studied her, he'd have said, "Hey, punkin, what is it that's troubling you?"

So Cara knew she was troubled. Restless.

Why?

Cara really didn't want to face the question all by herself. Not yet. She went to the drugstore, which still had a soda fountain. She said an automatic, "Hello, Mr. Schuller."

"Yes, Cara Porter. And how is the family?"

Mr. Schuller was losing it. One always watched what he put into the malts. Ben was especially good at that. He told Mr. Schuller he wanted to learn to make malts so that he could get a job there when he graduated. Ben understood people.

Mr. Schuller said, "You want the malt?"

"Not today. I came by for gossip."

Since his memories were oddly retrieved from incidents back in time, and he recalled only bits and pieces, it was always interesting to hear what he remembered.

Mr. Schuller looked seriously at Cara and said, "Gus is back."

Chapter Two

GUS? CARA WAS STARTLED to find that Mr. Schuller's and her own thoughts were locked together. It was unsettling to have a man in his mental fog be parallel to her own thinking. What did that say about Cara Porter's mind? With rampant disbelief, she asked, "You saw Gus?"

"He still has those claw marks."

That comment really rattled Cara. Mr. Schuller remembered Gus having been clawed fifteen years ago, and he knew it well enough to compare the marks in seeing Gus again? "Gus was here?"

Mr. Schuller looked at Cara soberly. "He's in the back room."

Cara sat still and stared, but she pushed it. "When did you see him?"

Mr. Schuller took a breath as he looked at the door to the back room for some time. Then he turned his head to look out the clean glass at the highway-main street. Finally he turned his faded blue eyes to Cara and asked, "Going to the prom? It's spring."

One must keep such a person in touch. She was honest. "We're having a class reunion. Know anyone who needs a place to stay?" Now, why had she asked that of Mr. Schuller? God only knew what might catch in his flawed mind and who all might turn up at her door.

Ben would handle it. She'd just send the people on to Ben.

It was only then that Cara realized she shifted all her problems over onto Ben. He was a married man. He had children. He had a business. He was busy. He didn't need to be her constant consultant. She had to find somebody else.

Not herself? Why couldn't she solve her own problems? She didn't need to constantly turn to some other person. Some man. She could stand on her own two feet. From here on out, she'd make her own decisions.

She focused on what Mr. Schuller was doing and said hastily, "Mr. Schuller. Let me make that malt."

He was startled. He held the tongs' burden of shredded lettuce just above the malt shaker and asked, "You want to be hired, too?"

"Sure." She got down from the stool and went around the counter.

Mr. Schuller said, "Wash your hands."

Well, that was a good thing for him to remember. She washed her hands.

THE REPLY CARDS CAME in with most of the proper "yes" or "no" boxes checked. Some of the cards neglected to indicate either. What a great mental group those now-mature adults had been all along.

Some carried notes. One said, "Hey! We'll get to *visit!*" That one was from her next-door neighbor, Cynthia Melrose Thornburg. She'd always been cheerfully strange.

Cara called Sidra each day and gave the acceptance count. She had to write another note to those who hadn't indicated whether or not they were coming to the celebration—and enclose another reply card.

There was no reply card from Gus.

Each day Cara watched for the mail. She told herself she was just curious who all would be there. But actually, she didn't even notice who, she noticed only the total and that Gus had not replied.

When his card finally came, he'd written on it in a very male scrawl that was surprisingly clear, "We'll need two bedrooms in your house."

Before Cara assimilated the message, her brain had matched up the handwriting with the written address that Ben had given her. It did match. Exactly.

She thought: her house? Why... her house.

Two bedrooms? Why...two bedrooms. He would hardly bring two little children all that way. Women?

Cara wandered around, picking things up off tables and replacing them precisely; and she reviewed those two questions. Her house? Two bedrooms?

She found herself wondering if Mr. Schuller was as flipped out as everyone claimed. She remembered mentioning extra room at her house for the reunion.

How could she turn Gus away? She was bound by her word to Mr. Schuller.

Cara smiled a little. Who would believe Mr. Schuller's denial he knew about any such thing?

She laughed silently at the ceiling as she stretched. She was stuck with Gus as her guest at her house. What a burden! She laughed out loud.

Then she frowned. Why the other bedroom? Was he bringing some hussy along? Surely not. Of course, he'd had Pela. But if he had another woman, why two bedrooms?

Cara sat down and wrote a note to Gus welcoming him courteously to be her guest. She said she'd put aside two rooms as he'd indicated.

She didn't question him. She was a lady. A rather peeved lady, but one nonetheless.

She walked down to the post office and mailed her reply. She acknowledged the people who called to her and went on.

She returned home, went upstairs and looked at the extra bedrooms. They were large and comfortable. The furniture was covered with sheets to protect them from dust.

One room had a connecting door to her room. She'd leave it open. She laughed softly in amused delight. How shocked Gus would be in the middle of the night when she opened the door and came to his bed.

He'd be terrified. He'd say, "No! Not that!"

And she'd reply, "You have to pay your room and board some way. I've chosen this way. Don't resist, relax. I'll handle everything."

Actually, Cara had never been very interested in sex. Her only experience had been with Fred, and it had been disappointing. The people on TV pretended it was something really special. It was a lie.

But books did that, too, and made it sound as if having sex with a person of the opposite gender was wonderful. Why all the fuss? In the times Fred and she had coupled, she'd thought, "This time, it'll be that way."

Once it had come close. He'd finished and gone to sleep. She was left restless.

She looked at the connecting door and thought Gus would probably barricade it.

Disgruntled, she went to the telephone and called her Aunt Agnes. Although she was Cara's aunt, she was only ten years older. Cara had to wait forever as the phone rang, because her aunt was a writer, and she would get so involved with her plotting that she wouldn't even hear the phone.

The answering machine finally kicked in after fifteen rings, and her aunt's voice said, "Leave your name and number." And she hung up.

After the buzz, Cara said, "I need a chaperone for our high-school class's tenth reunion. Would you please come? Come early so we can visit first."

Then Cara sat there holding the phone and wished there was a way to erase the message. She was, for

Pete's sake, almost twenty-eight years old and a divorced woman. Why would she need a chaperone? She hung up quietly.

She'd cope.

All her life, she'd coped.

No. She'd avoided coping. She'd simply gone along with whatever she was supposed to do. And any problem was turned over to her parents, to Fred and now to Ben.

She was woman, she could roar and all that old song's words. She didn't remember all of the song's cheeky declarations of independence. She really only remembered the roaring part. But that gave her the upright stance, head flung back in challenge and the attitude of control.

Attitude had actually been the important buzzword. It still was. Of course, it would always be important. It would be renamed, but it was still how someone felt about anything.

Cara Porter was in control of her own life.

She called her Aunt Agnes's answering machine back and said, "Erase the other message, dear heart, I can handle this by myself." She hung up and tilted her head around, lifting her eyebrows minutely—a woman in control.

So THE VERY NEXT morning, Cara's Aunt Agnes drove up into the big yard. She stopped under the spring-leafed trees. Agnes got out of her little preserved V.W. It was painted such a soft powder blue that no man would drive it.

Cara greeted her aunt with, "You're still running around in that?"

Her aunt turned and looked at Cara with lifted eyebrows, questioning such a statement.

"The car."

"Yes. It's quite good driving."

"And it attracts attention?"

Her aunt smiled a cat smile.

Cara told the sky, "And I invited her here to chaperone me?"

The sky was silent.

So was her aunt as she unloaded a middle-size case and a garment bag. "I brought you a gown."

Cara's aunt had dyed her hair a bronze that was remarkable. It made her eyes seem yellow. She could carry it off. She was slender and vital. Her light tan pants fit well and showed her subtly rounded bottom and the length of her legs.

Cara eyed the rakish spaghetti straps of the blouse as they went over her aunt's bare shoulders. The straps were supposed to support the rest of the black silk blouse, but appeared inadequate even for that light weight.

Agnes had a scarf around her shoulders that would only intrigue any male eyes to wait for the wind to shift the soft silk.

Cara observed, "I suppose it's the title of Aunt which always misleads me."

Her aunt replied, "You've called the right person. You may refer to me as Agnes? Or you may say Aunt Agnes. Who is the wolf who is to be around you and who scares you enough to call in the marines?"

"You don't look anything like a marine."

"You haven't seen the off-duty female ones." Agnes smiled at her niece. "Will I see Ben while I'm here?"

"Of course."

Agnes carried her things inside, up the stairs and started for the attic rooms.

Cara said, "No. You ought to be down on this floor."

"Why?"

"A chaperone wouldn't be a whole floor away."

"Honey, you're almost twenty-eight. By that time, I'd sampled at least six men?" That was the TEXAS questioning statement. "This was some time back, you understand, before the diseases were so deadly. But if a man is coming here to see you, let's give him some elbow room."

"You're shocking."

Agnes comforted her. "I've settled down considerably in the last ten years? You'll be stunned to witness how careful I am."

"You're careful—about you." Cara clarified the premise. She then asked her aunt, "What about me?"

"You're old enough to do your own figuring. You've been divorced. Men shouldn't be a surprise. I'm here solely for the town's curious speculation. Williamsfield is somewhat—staid."

"Not as much as you'd imagine. They get TV out here and HBO. They've been *exposed!*"

"Mercy to goodness."

"You're not wearing a bra."

Agnes pulled out the loose, top edge of her black silk "blouse" and looked. "Why, you're right!"

"While Gus is here, you must wear a bra."

"Rules?"

"I can't have Gus distracted."

Agnes lifted her chin as she said a soft *"Ahhh"* of realization. "So he is coming back?"

"How do you know about—Gus?"

"Everyone around these here parts knows about Gus. I believe nine-eighths of the population toasted God when Gus's stepfather was killed."

"Gus didn't do it."

Her Aunt Agnes replied gently, "Everyone knows that."

Cara tidied their conversation, "It's eight-ninths, not nine-eighths."

Agnes was kind. "I was indicating how more than a hundred percent celebrated that person's demise."

"How can there be more than a hundred percent?"

"Cara. Cara. You can be so abominably literal."

"I suppose. But there could have been one or two people who grieved for that—person."

Agnes said, "You probably come by compassion genetically. Your mother was a very tenderhearted, illogical woman."

"Daddy loved her."

Agnes shrugged at fate. "She was lovable, and Tom was fascinated by how kind she could be. I had hoped you'd be more like your father."

"I am like him. Mother said so."

Agnes was sure. "Ben is."

"And I."

"You're a darling."

Cara chided, "You're evasive."

"There are times when one must be evasive."

"Yes." Cara was pensive. "I've encountered those times, too. That's how come I called you. Do you remember Mr. Schuller down at the drugstore?"

"Why, yes. I saw him at your parents' funeral. He's rather lost it, as I recall. He thought I was still at college. How flattering."

"Well," Cara took back the conversation. "I was down there at the drugstore, and Mr. Schuller said he'd seen Gus."

"So."

"Gus hasn't been around here for several years. I don't know how this all came about, but I told Mr. Schuller if anyone needed a place to stay for the school reunion, they could call me. Gus wrote he needed two rooms."

"*Two* rooms?"

"Yes. That rather surprised me, too. If he's bringing a woman along—"

"A wife?"

"No. He's reasonably single. Legally single."

Agnes tilted her bronzed head back and looked at Cara over her cheekbones. "A new lover? Why two rooms?"

"I have no idea."

"Maybe it's a good thing you called me, after all." She looked at the doors of the bedrooms and said, "I'll take that one."

"Why not the one next to mine?"

"We'll give that one to Gus."

Cara was shocked. "There's a connecting door."

As Agnes moved toward her selected room, she glanced back over her bare shoulder. She lifted her brows just a tad as she said, "Lock it on his side. That'll protect him from you."

"Why, Agnes Porter!"

And Agnes smiled like a cat who has a canary feather on her whiskers.

Two days later it was still four more long days before the reunion. Four more days. Actually, the time had gone quite fast. It was just Gus's arrival that was slow.

Agnes was such a perfect guest. She'd pitched right in, and they'd both helped the cleaning couple to straighten the house.

Dust covers had been removed and carried away to be washed. The house was now pristine. A spring storm's twig debris was removed from the yard, and the bluebonnets were spectacular.

The house was ready. Food had been selected. Agnes had chosen the wines to be delivered. The flower vases were placed, ready to be filled.

All that work for one weekend. Would it be worth the effort?

And that day Cara received a note from Gus, saying, "We'll be there."

After her exuberance settled, she realized she had no inkling who the "we" were. Who else among the nonrepliers was coming with Gus? Or when. Today? Tomorrow? Saturday, the day of the reunion? Not until Saturday? Surely he'd come ahead of time.

He came that day.

Cara and Agnes were out buying the staples, checking to be sure the other ordered things would arrive on time. Agnes was in an orange top with flowered trousers and sandals. Cara had on a plain blouse and white skirt.

When Cara and her aunt returned home, they found a truck and a big horse trailer at the back of the drive that bisected the large yard. Two small children were up in one of the more impossible trees. Two horses came around the house from the bluebonnet patch in order to see who was there.

And there was Gus.

He was standing, watching her approach. He was as big as she remembered. His hair and eyebrows and lashes were white from the sun. The undersides of his hair were dark blond. His body was simply marvelously, wickedly masculine. He wasn't naked, but Cara didn't ever remember what he'd had on.

Agnes said a soft, "My goodness."

Cara was in a time warp. She stared. Her lips were parted. Her cheeks got pale. Her freckles chose that time to appear vividly. She said, "Well, hello." Her eyes were enormous.

Agnes asked, "Are you sure those children should be in that tree?"

And Gus spoke. His voice was deep and gently rough. He said, "If the tree don't want 'em, it'll shake 'em out."

That sounded logical.

Cara said, "I'm Cara Porter."

"Yeah." His smile was remarkable. It wasn't big. He still had the faint claw marks on his face. They made him look like a man who could tackle anything... and survive.

"And this is my aunt, Agnes Porter."

"Ma'am."

"How do you do? I remember you from when I lived here. You gave Cara some guinea pigs."

"Yeah. She gave 'em away."

Cara explained, "It was Mother who did that. I thought they were just darling."

He smiled.

Cara's insides shivered in a most erotic manner.

To end the long, awful suspense for Cara, Agnes asked, "Is there a Mrs. Freeman? Or a potential one?"

"Not yet." But his gaze was on Cara and he smiled again. It was like a healing sun.

But Cara's heart faltered. Not yet? Who?

The horses became bored and wandered back to the bluebonnets.

Cara exclaimed, "Oh, no!"

Gus asked quickly, "What's the matter?"

"The bluebonnets!"

"Yeah?" He was looking around, trying to figure out what was bothering her. Nobody else was there.

Staunchly, Cara said, "It's all right."

Agnes added, "The Porters carefully encourage the bluebonnets."

"Oh. You oughta come out to my place. It's loaded with 'em."

Cara nodded.

Agnes said gently, "They are rarer in town."

And the light turned on inside Gus's head. He whistled the horses back, calmed his dog and—

He had a dog there. It was big and black with curly hair, a beard and shaggy eyebrows.

Gus was attaching the horses to a couple of trees.

Courteously discarding the whole bed of bluebonnets, Cara said, "Don't tie them. We'll close the gates and they can be loose."

"I'll be back. We'll fix it." Gus winked at Cara and smiled.

He whistled differently, and the kids scrambled down from the tree. They were both boys as far as Cara could tell, and they were—different. They were obedient and quiet, but they weren't tamed.

They were just like Gus.

Gus opened the cab of the truck. Then he waited for the two kids to get in before he watched as they buckled their seat belts. He closed the door and went around the front of the truck. He grinned at Cara, lifted a hand in farewell, got into the truck...and left.

There the two women were, left with a horse trailer and two horses. The dog had gone in the truck. The two women glanced around and then considered each other.

Agnes said, "He'll be worth it."

Cara's regard for her aunt was oblique. "Worth—what?"

Agnes shrugged. "Whatever it takes."

"I'll see."

Cara's aunt advised, "Don't do too much comparing or criticizing." Then Agnes added that time-worn admonition, "You only live once."

So it was a thoughtful Cara who, with her silent aunt, went slowly across the yard and into the house. Cara betrayed herself as she asked her aunt, "Did he say when they'd be back?"

"No. He just said he'd fix it."

"What?"

"I suspect it'll be something that he feels is bothering you."

Cara frowned. "He'll transplant bluebonnets?"

Agnes looked at her dear niece. "Probably."

"Bluebonnets don't transplant at all well."

Agnes advised gently, "Don't tell him that." She looked at the other spring flowers. There were the tulips and jonquils against the barn, and along the front fence there were the fire bushes. The garden took a lot of Cara's idle time.

Since their guests were going to be in the house, Cara went to Williamsfield's florist to fetch the flowers for the empty vases. She was reluctant to take her own flowers from the yard because they looked so pretty there.

She drove back into the yard, and Gus's truck was there. He was carrying branched, naked limbs around the back of the house.

Cara's insides stilled. What was he doing? She eased the car to a stop by the barn and exited to close the car door gently.

The two kids grinned at her as they pulled smaller, branched limbs along over the neat grass.

The horses were still attached to two of the trees. They turned their heads to watch the limbs with curiosity and they noted her. They were large animals. They weren't neat.

The two kids ran back around and closed the gates. Then they went to those monster animals and untied them! The horses immediately had to see why the branches had been dragged around the house. Cara followed, equally curious, not as bold.

Gus was covering the bluebonnets!

He was laying out the branches in such a way as to thwart the horses and still give the bluebonnets sunshine.

It looked really tacky.

To the amazement of the eavesdropping Agnes, who stood behind the lace curtain at a near window, Cara said to Gus, "How clever of you."

He grinned. "I hadn't knowed you liked the weeds."

"How could a real TEXAN disparage bluebonnets?"

"We got a ton of 'em out at our place."

His grammar was atrocious. He was standing there regarding her in a relaxed, tolerant manner. He was . . . tolerant of her.

He was marvelously made. He was very comfortable in his body and with wearing those worn clothes. The two rather grubby kids were laughing and healthy.

The dog loved Gus. His horses were curious and interested. They were tolerant of the kids and the dog. Gus was gentle and kind. The kids, the dog and the horses paid attention to the man and obeyed him willingly. He expected them to do so.

Well, she could be equally tolerant of him, couldn't she? Perhaps.

She had to study him for a while to understand him. Why was he so fascinating to her? He'd always been so... different. Even at school she had slid her carefully slitted eyes over so that she could peek at him. And he'd always looked back at her as if he had radar in him and knew when someone was watching him. She'd close her eyes and open them, looking away, somewhere else.

He never had any reason to know that she had been interested, fascinated by such a strange boy.

Now he was a man, grown, and he was even more stimulating to her... curiosity. It wasn't—physical attraction, not at all. Of course not. It was just being interested in a very different kind of person.

People were all so strange. People tended to do such odd things. They were unpredictable. Look at her aunt. Who else would bronze her hair in order to make her eyes look yellow?

In another time, Agnes Porter would have probably been burned as a witch. She was fortunate to be living in this loose time, when oddity was tolerated and even encouraged!

Cara had those same genes. Just like Agnes. Just as rash and rampant. But hers were controlled. A lady was known by her conduct.

How could Gus appear to be so confident when Cara Porter was such a stiff lady? He moved his marvelous male body, and the pit of her stomach was affected. How could that be?

The answer was obvious.

So she wanted to try sex with this man? Surely not. Was she curious to see if someone else could do it better than Fred? Could it be different with another man? Why?

Was she going on a rampage, testing that theory, tasting, discarding, ruining a whole slew of susceptible men? Surely not. She had more backbone than to go around behaving so outrageo—

And Gus turned to look around his broad shoulder and smile lazily at her.

Her thoughts ran the words together, There-was-hay-up-in-the-barn-loft! The hay was left over from last year, but the doors and openings had been closed, and the hay would be clean enough to—

Who cared if it was clean?

And she stiffened. Straightened. And her glance fled from Gus. She found she was staring at his children. They most assuredly were his. They looked like him. They were young, she noticed that clearly, now, as she sought distraction from Gus. One child was about, what, five and the other must be four. Both boys.

They were in overalls and long-sleeved shirts. The clothes weren't new. Gus must still be poor. The truck was old, the horses were sleek and well cared for. Actually, so were Gus and the kids.

What would it be like to live in a shack?

Cara remembered seeing where Gus grew up. It seemed a long time ago. The shanty had been braced and cluttered and patched. She'd been embarrassed for him. It wasn't until she was older that she'd found shells really weren't much of an indication of what was inside.

Gus no longer lived in that shack. His post-office box was out toward the Big Bend country.

And her eyes again rested on the two really marvelous horses.

Gus asked, "Would you like to ride one?"

"May I?"

"Yeah. We got saddles in the trailer."

"When!"

And Gus's laugh squiggled around in odd places inside Cara's body.

He said, "Now."

Chapter Three

CARA LOOKED DOWN at her white skirt. "I'll have to change."

Gus smiled, "You could ride with that on. I'd not mind."

Knowing how far the skirt would ride up while sitting on a horse, she snipped sassily, "Don't shock the children." She was prissy, and she moved a little in a never-before-used, and unfamiliar, automatic response to his potent presence.

"You gonna insist?"

She didn't know how to continue in the flirting. Fred had never teased her. She said, "I won't be long." She turned and ran toward the house. His soft laughter followed after, catching her.

Filled with his teasing laughter, and a little giddy, she ran up the back steps and into the house. There, she went up the stairs, her steps light and her breathing high. She went quickly to her room and closed the door. What should she wear? Jodhpurs, of course, and her hat.

But as she took the hat off its round, blank-faced holder, she heard Gus's voice through her open window. He was outside, talking to the kids as he saddled the horses. His voice low and quiet, he was saying, "We'll ask her if it's okay. Otherwise, you can stay here with Blackie."

Otherwise...the kids...could stay...with the dog. The kids wanted to go along.

It was then Cara had the mental image of her in her riding gear with that ragtag threesome. They would look ridiculous in those circumstances, and so would she.

She put the jodhpurs back into her closet and took out jeans. Then Cara turned to replace the hat and out of the corner of her eye, there was Agnes in the connecting doorway.

Her aunt smiled. "You're smarter than I thought."

"I'd look silly."

"Yes."

Cara said with a small smile and a courteous lift of her brows, "When in Rome?"

"Or when a woman is courteous."

Cara touched the hat. "I love wearing that hat."

"There could be another time."

"Yes."

So Cara came down the stairs in jeans, a striped long-sleeved shirt and soft kid gloves. She had on a Stetson and western boots. Hell, everyone in TEXAS wore boots at one time or another.

As she exited the back door, she looked for Gus; and he was waiting, watching for her.

She smiled.

He just looked at her.

The horses were saddled. She asked, "Which is mine?"

And Gus said, "That one."

She went to the gelding, and he was too tall. The stirrup was too high. She reached up to the saddle—and Gus put a big hand to her bottom and gave her a boost. She was up and sitting correctly. She smiled down at Gus, and he wasn't as far down as she thought he'd be. He was a tall man. He adjusted the stirrups just right for her.

He put his hands possessively on her booted foot as he said, "Can you take Ned up with you?"

"Yes!" She grinned at the smaller urchin, but the kid backed against Gus and ducked his head shyly.

So both kids rode behind Gus. Gus came alongside Cara and told her, "They'll get used to you."

What did he mean by that? He sounded as if he was thinking of more than a few days' visit? Had they moved in on her? Their dog and horses were there.

They rode down the drive and onto the unpaved gravel street. It had once been oiled to keep down the dust. It was in a neutral time. It was neither too oily nor too dusty.

Her horse trotted and danced and shook his head and loved being out and about. He was so curious. She was kept busy keeping him under control, enough. Actually, he was simply energetic. He wasn't trying to be difficult.

With the two kids behind him, Gus kept his own horse walking and under his gentle control.

Cara had to turn her horse back and wait. She liked watching Gus coming toward her. She walked her horse alongside his and asked the kids, "What are your names?"

The younger one hid his grinning face against Gus's back, but the other said, "I'm Willy. He's Ned."

She asked the boys other questions. And she made them smile and laugh. It was Willy who replied to her. But Ned peeked at Cara, and his grin was big.

When Cara considered it later, they went quite a way, winding around through the town. Talking, remembering, walking the horses, the kids listening and looking around. The houses and yards were neat. The surprise was how many of those residents they encountered called greetings not to her but to Gus.

And Gus replied in such ease.

The Williamsfield dogs had had to find out if the strange black dog was real, and if he was challenging any of them.

He was courteous.

The stranger-dog wagged his tail and stood his ground. He allowed the bullies to run into him, and he didn't snarl or bite or chase.

Cara asked Gus, "Is he from our diplomatic corps?"

Gus replied, "Yeah."

"What's his name?"

"Blackie."

Cara nodded once. "How imaginative."

"I guess it's too late to rename him." Gus appeared to weigh the option. "He's used to being called Blackie."

"You could have named him Black Cloud."

"He's not Indian."

"What all is he?" she asked.

"He's never said."

Cara put her head back and just laughed. Even as she did so, she realized his reply wasn't that funny. She just felt lighthearted and filled with laughter. It spilled over.

When had she ever felt so joyful?

And yet again, someone called, "Hey, Gus!" It was Phil Wiggens. Then he turned to call over his shoulder into the house, "Gus is back."

Cara became aware of the number of times people had spotted Gus and yelled in asides to others, "Gus is back!"

It wasn't just male voices who called to her guest. It was shocking the pushy women who called to him and demanded his attention. One even said, "If you don't have a way to come to the reunion, I'll take you." It was Meg Dorpher Bedford.

Gus replied, "I'm quasi-legit."

His reply caused Cara to blink. Where had he learned those words to use them so perfectly?

Cara called to Meg, "He's my guest." Cara then smiled in such a charming way that if her grandmother could have heard Cara, she would have been especially pleased with her granddaughter's manners.

And Meg had the crassness to call back, "How'd you work that?"

Gus responded, "She's my hostess."

So the whole town knew right away that Gus was staying with Cara Porter. Hell, they'd known that ever since his truck was driven into her yard pulling the horse trailer when Cara wasn't even there. And it wasn't until later that day the knowledge was mentioned regarding Cara's Aunt Agnes Porter was also a guest at Cara's house.

The town was a little disappointed. The rumor then ran that when Agnes heard Cara was harboring a potent male without a chaperone, her aunt came a-running.

That was blown out of the water because Agnes had already been at Cara's when Gus arrived.

Another rumor started about the couple and kids sleeping in the same bed, but someone mentioned there were only five people in the house, and nobody had any need to double up. So that juicy rumor died a-borning.

Not even the very start of the speculation survived that the kids were actually Gus and Cara's. It just didn't make it. Cara had been in Williamsfield all her born days.

But any niece of a bronze-headed woman was suspect. Fair game.

The venturers finally returned to the Porter place and found lunch was ready. Agnes had cooked it.

The fact gave Cara some hesitancy, because she could never remember her Aunt Agnes cooking anything. Cara subtly tasted here and there among the offerings and was pleasantly astonished. She looked with new awe at her aunt.

Gus had to unsaddle the horses and wipe them down first. And the little kids did allow Cara to invite them inside. So it had been Cara who washed the little hands and faces. The kids hadn't minded, but they would go to the door and call to their dad, "You coming?"

And Gus would reply, "Pretty soon." He was deliberately slow to give the boys times to interact with the two women. The boys didn't meet very many strangers. It was good practice.

Agnes had the little ones carry plates to the dining-room table, and she asked that they test the crisp, barbecued ribs to see if they were all right.

The kids were serious. Willy was first to try things, then Ned would.

When Gus came inside, the little boys told him, "The grub's okay."

Gus grinned. Cara directed him to the downstairs lavatory and pointed out his fresh towel. He looked down at her through his sun-whitened lashes and smiled, but he didn't say anything.

She blushed for some reason as she smiled, but she ducked out of the confined space with some odd, giddy feelings in her stomach, which made her want to giggle. How strange.

It wasn't surprising that Agnes had fixed the perfect lunch. Of all the things Agnes knew, she knew males. Everything was just right.

The ribs were finger food. Crunchy on the outside and easily chewed from the bones. The sauerkraut was just exactly tart enough, the fruit was cut up and easy for little fingers or a spoon. The cornbread soaked up the butter and honey, and the milk was cold.

Filled, the little boys relaxed back on their chairs. They smiled and blinked slower and slower.

Cara noticed and said, "Their rooms are ready."

"They just need one."

It was Agnes who mentioned, "They might find a rinse-off nice."

Gus said, "I'll do that."

Cara exclaimed, "We've been so busy, I haven't shown you the rooms."

The four went off up the stairs, and Cara came back to the kitchen, almost immediately. She wore a small smile, and she hummed while she pitched in to clear the table.

So the women were putting the dishes in the dishwasher when Gus came downstairs. He swept the floor. One did that faithfully in TEXAS to discourage cockroaches and ants.

Being a savvy adult, Agnes said, "I believe I shall lie down also. You will excuse me?"

They never noticed.

Almost without deciding, the pair drifted out onto the side porch, overlooking the bluebonnet-protecting, tangled mess of branches.

Since the branches had to be big enough and thick enough to discourage horses, being on the porch was like looking over a brush barricade. With the bluebonnet patch on the corner, the brush appeared to be a bulwark against the rest of the world.

Cara found that to be pretty much the way she felt in keeping Gus to herself. Women were pushy. As they'd ridden along, all the female calls had been for Gus. Cara thought that had been scandalously intrusive conduct.

The men who called to Gus had been okay.

In the other rocker, with his boots on the pristine and freshly painted porch rail, Gus said, "Ben told me about you all's parents. That was tough. I didn't know how to say anything to you, then. I've never had anybody—that was close." He considered and went on, "Except maybe Ben."

"My brother?"

"He kept in touch."

"He told me so not long ago when I asked if he knew your address."

Gus was aware the invitation to the reunion had been solely Cara's doing. Both Ben and Sidra had said so to Gus. So he had already known she was interested. He just needed to know if her interest was boredom or curiosity or if she could be serious.

Gus told Cara, "You were always so busy. In school, I remember watching you draw your letters. And when you were in the drum-and-bugle corps, you were really something."

She wasn't sure if what he said was good or bad. "Drawing" her letters? She'd thought she'd written them quite well. And she was a good drummer. She'd practiced in the barn with the doors closed. Drums aren't subtle.

She once could do the drumming of "Wipeout." The fact she could, and he couldn't, had alienated the male drummer in the band. But the school kids would come to her practices in the barn and dance to her tempos. The girls would wiggle and writhe. No one danced with Cara. They let her be the rhythm sounds they needed.

"Do you still play the drums?"

"On occasion. I never find the time to practice."

"You did good."

"Why, thank you, Gus."

"You're a very talented woman."

"Outside of drums, I'm not at all clever."

"You wrote good words in themes. You made me see what you said."

She felt tears prickle her eyes. No one ever, in her entire life, had given her the gift of having shared something. That was probably because she always needed some sort of response from others, but those responses she'd had, hadn't included her own endeavors. Very vulnerable, she looked at Gus and said, "Thank you."

"You've given me a lot. You never knew how important you were to me. Your shy valentine was all that kept me going during a very hard time."

She was stunned! He assumed that reluctant Your Friend had been voluntary?

Only then did she realize he had spoken quite easily, just like anybody else. What sort of scam was he pulling here?

Cara looked at Gus very soberly. And he returned the same look. She didn't want him misled. She said, "You can speak quite well."

"I took the equivalency classes and passed the tests."

As she said, "Good for you," she thought he could say "equivalency" without even thinking about it. He was sly. She became cautious.

She scrambled around in her head to change the subject, and she said, "I feel as if I'm keeping the natives at bay with a brush bulwark." She gestured toward the horse-stymieing naked tree limbs over the bluebonnets.

Gus inquired with lazy humor, "Neighbor trouble?"

"Here?" She pulled back and frowned in almost amused astonishment. "We quarrel and forgive because we have so few people here in Williamsfield. We can't change friends. We become tolerant."

Gus replied, "Everywhere else, there's trouble. In families. Between neighbors, in cities, in countries between peoples and probably out there in other worlds. There've been more saucer sightings."

"Have you seen any?"

"I haven't had the time to look."

Cara considered him. He was something the saucer creatures should study. He was a survivor.

Then her mind went on thinking about Gus. He not only was a survivor, he would protect anyone he wanted to survive with him.

She wondered if his protectiveness would include a wife. Why had his woman run off with another man? How would Cara find out?

Ben. She'd ask Ben.

"Come out to the barn," Gus rose and extended a hand to help her up. "I have a surprise for you."

What? She was perfectly capable of standing up by herself. She didn't need his hand to lift her from the chair. But she took his hand and allowed him to pull her up. He lifted her as if she was weightless. He led her to the stairs and went ahead of her down the front steps; then he waited in order to walk beside her around the house to the barn.

Where had he learned manners? In these days, very few gentlemen went first down stairs so that the lady could fall on him if she tripped. There was a time when women were considered precious.

Did Gus consider her ... precious?

Well, now, she was being really silly.

He led her to the barn and slid the big door aside enough. Her stomach scary with anticipation, Cara walked into the shaded interior. She immediately saw her drums had been uncovered. He would want her to play—the drums.

While she hesitated, he went past her and sat on the chair in back of the organized percussion instruments. He grinned and said, "I'm going to show you what I've learned."

With one foot on the pedal, he began the beat. The skins were loosened and the sound was muted. *BOOM boom boom boom, BOOM boom boom boom...* He continued the beat, and with the sticks in his hands, he added little scatterings of sound from the other drums. He was not playing a piece, he was offering rhythmic sounds.

It was irresistible. She began to move her body a trifle.

He grinned. "Dance for me."

And she moved more. She'd never danced for anyone, like this. She'd played the beat for others. She'd danced to rhythms by herself. And now she danced for Gus. Her movements matching the beat, she moved with the primitive rhythm.

He watched her.

She loved it and danced more wantonly for this first actual observer. She turned and moved her shoulders and hips in the subtle invitation alluded to by such writhings.

She noticed he was breathing through his mouth and looked very serious. She understood his concentration because the beat had to be sustained perfectly. She saw it was an effort for him because he was sweating.

He was hot. But it wasn't from keeping the beat. It was from watching her. He saw that she looked back at him. Her shoulders were back so that her breasts were obvious. Her stomach was tight as her hips were thrust in turn. She was really dancing for him! She was showing off. Her body was alluring, and she meant for him to notice.

She should have been in a grass skirt or nothing at all. She wore cotton slacks, and her shirt was long sleeved and buttoned modestly. But her breasts shivered in her dance. Her hips swirled and her arms were inviting.

He watched her face and saw that her lips were soft and puffy. Her pupils were dark and large. She was intense.

Still keeping the beat, Gus rose from the chair, leaning over to make the skittering sounds harsh. Then he laid the sticks on the top drum and he went to Cara.

He took her against him and kissed her, and she allowed that hungrily. He was extremely stimulated by the fact that she not only cooperated with the kiss, she put her arms around him and clung to him, pressing against his body.

He began to tremble as he walked her backward to the burst hay bale he'd loosened just that very morning.

He eased her down against the underlying bulk of a second bale, and he moved his hips between her trousered legs as he kissed her mouth very seriously.

He was gentle and thorough. He was pressing his jeans-covered sex against hers, and she moaned in sexual heat. His weight rubbed against her as she lay under him. He moved his hands along her sides and pressed the bulges at the sides of her squashed breasts.

He kissed her deeply, and she gasped, opening her lips and curling her body to his.

He moved against her, and her thighs spread.

He shivered and panted, while she made sounds of hunger.

He sweat.

Her mouth opened, and she moved soft lips over his mouth in a caressing way. He slid a hand down her back between her and the flattening straw until he'd lifted her bottom so that his hard, jeans-covered sex was against her trousered core.

She gasped and made relishing sounds. Her fingernails scraped along the back of his shirt as she tried to get him closer. She said, "Guusss!"

And he moved, rubbing against her until the sky-rockets exploded inside her body. She stiffened and shuddered. Her eyes were tightly closed. And then her mouth relaxed and a little smile began as a tear slid out of the corner of her eye.

"Did I hurt you?" He was stunned.

She made a murmuring sound as her smile widened smugly. She sighed, "Aaahhh."

He wasn't sure. He was still hyper.

She moved languorously, and her fingers touched his shoulders and moved into his hair as she made contented sounds. She said, "That was wonder-ful. My goodness. Ahhh."

"You okay?" Gus asked. He didn't know what else to say.

She smiled and made more contented sounds.

He was amazed. He was also very unstable. He was jerk-kneed and hyper. He was pitched to the limit.

And she was a cat whose heat was smothered.

She kissed him of her own accord and about shot off the top of his head.

Then she lay back and said, "How nice." But she understood immediately that he had not achieved release. She touched his rigid member with new empathy. She said, "I'll take off my trousers."

Starkly, he replied, "I don't have any condoms."

"It doesn't matter. I'm sterile."

He promised earnestly, "I don't have any of the diseases."

"Neither have I." She unzipped, and he watched in fascination as she wiggled out of the trousers, lying flat and mostly under him. One leg was still partly covered, but she'd pulled off the other trouser leg.

Then she unzipped his pants and about ruined everything. But he made it around the edge of her panty leg, into her sheath and rode her down.

As they lay panting, trying to get their breathing systems under control, her intimate muscles squeezed him, making him groan with the pleasure.

She laughed. "You're enormous. I can still feel you inside me."

"Kiss me."

And she did that quite willingly. Her mouth was sweet and eager, and his was devouring. He said, "Love me."

She laughed a throaty laugh she'd never realized she could, and she hugged him to her.

His breathing picked up and he began to move!

She exclaimed, "Again?"

"I've waited for you forever."

"Of course." Her tone was all wrong. "You have two boys to prove that."

"That was before your divorce. Pela and I weren't married."

"You—just—lived together?"

"She had no place else to go and she hung around. She was easy with me. She was around."

"So when she ran off, she left the boys to you?"

"I'd taken care of them all along, anyway. She . . . wasn't very maternal."

"I'm divorced."

Gus smiled.

She asked, "Why did you smile just then?"

"I'd been planning on getting rid of him but—"

She was shocked. "You wanted him dead?"

"No. Just gone."

"You need to know I'm not only sterile, I'm cold."

Gus laughed until he had to separate from her and lie beside her, collapsed, but he was still laughing softly.

Cara raised up over him and said earnestly. "This was probably a fluke. I'm really cold. This is the first time it's been . . . this way."

"You have me. You'll never again be cold or unfeeling. You'll be clawing at my body and eager. I'll be telling you it's the wrong time of the month."

She thought that was hilarious. She really laughed, smothering it.

Suddenly, Gus said seriously, "Quick, get your clothes on."

"Wha—?"

"I hear the boys."

He helped her, stuffing her foot into the empty trouser leg of her pants and pulling them up.

While she was getting her shirt into her trousers and zipping up, he was tidying himself.

He stood quickly, pulled her to her feet and said, "Comb your hair with your fingers. It's full of straw."

With amusement, she had the audacity to inquire, "How'd that happen?"

He almost put her right back down again to show her. She was perfect.

But he did get his own clothing tidy and rubbed his hair roughly to get the straw out as he looked at her. He brushed the back of her shirt and trousers as he said, "Sit down and play the drums...softly."

She did obey. She was fiddling with the drums. She chewed on her love-fattened lower lip and slid her heavy lidded eyes over to watch Gus.

He warned, "Don't do that. Don't look at me thataway."

She straightened, and her love-fattened breasts were so obvious that Gus groaned as his hands curled.

He said, "Slump."

She curled her body down and pulled her shoulders forward, and he put a hand over his eyes. He said softly, "I think you ought to disappear so I can calm down."

She protested, "Having *just*..."

"It's been a long, long, long wait. You should appreciate my restraint."

"Restraint?" she gasped.

He nodded and opened his mouth to retort something outrageous, when Willy managed to slide the barn door open enough, and he and Ned came inside.

Gus said, "Howdy."

Willy said, "Aunt Agnes gave us cookies."

Gus said, "That was nice. How'd you sleep."

"The bed's big!" Ned was impressed. He was still eating a cookie, turning it to take bites all around before he devoured the middle bite.

Gus asked, "Did you straighten it after you got up?"

Willy said, "We forgot."

"Go do it."

"Yes, sir."

They left. Gus went to the door and watched them into the house. Then he carefully slid the door shut and came to Cara. He put his hands under her armpits and lifted her from the chair. He kissed her in a perfectly scandalous manner. It was wonderful.

When he raised his mouth, with the soft myriad sounds of parting tissue, she said, "There is a connecting door between our rooms."

He said *"Whump!"* and leaned over a little as if she'd hit him in the stomach.

They had barely gotten themselves presentable again, when the boys returned. Willy said, "Aunt Agnes said Uncle Ben called. You're to call him back. Who's Uncle Ben?"

Gus said, "He came to see us. Remember?"

And Willy said, "Mr. Porter is our Uncle Ben?"

Gus looked at Cara quite seriously and with some speculation. Not taking his gaze from her, he said, "We'll see."

And Cara blushed scarlet, but she had to lick a smile and tighten her mouth so as not to beam at him.

Gus's eyes were so tender.

Chapter Four

THE FOURSOME WENT BACK to the house, and Gus went to the library to call Ben.

Cara wondered if it was legal business.

Leaving the children in the kitchen with her Aunt Agnes, Cara went into the hallway and tidied the top of the glove and hat chest. Then she got a cloth and wiped the mirror carefully. She was earnest in her tidying, but she couldn't hear a thing.

Actually, she could hear the rumble of Gus's deep voice, but she couldn't distinguish his words. He laughed in a softened way. The sound shivered her skin erotically, peaking her nipples. How astonishing.

Cara heard Gus put down the phone. She took a hat from the drawer and went to the coat closet as he emerged from the library.

Gus grinned at her with undue humor and asked, "Are you free to go to your brother's for supper?"

"I'll check with Agnes."

"She's invited also." Then he added, "So are the boys."

"That was very nice of Maddie."

Gus considered before he asked, "Doesn't Maddie like Agnes?"

Evasively, Cara replied, "Maddie is somewhat ... stiff."

Gus thought of the flamboyant Agnes and mentioned, "It's nice Agnes is so normal."

Cara laughed. It burst from her. She tightened her lips to try to dam the laughter, but it burst through.

Gus stood watching, his own smile spilling from his eyes. He told her, "You're wicked."

"I am not. But thank you for the compliment."

He crowded slowly closer as she bravely stood her ground. He said, "I'll bet you roll around in the hay in the barn."

"Never." She tilted up her chin and looked superbly aloof. It would have been better if she hadn't blushed.

His smothered laugh curled her toenails and did awesome things deep inside her body. Her eyes were unfocused as she lifted her mouth for his kiss. He gave her a teeny, stingy peck. Her lower lip came out in a moist pout.

He growled, "Cut that out."

She was genuinely surprised. "What?"

"Quit looking like you want to be in my bed."

She probably turned scarlet all over as she blushed, and he loved it. So he kissed her witless.

Then he expected her to walk with him to the kitchen. She looked down at her feet to see if they could move.

Apparently he understood, because he said, "You just assume your feet remember how, and they generally do."

"How do you know that?"

"When I'd see you in the hall at school."

Her eyes widened as she stared at him.

His voice was low and growly as he told her, "And that's why men have pockets in their pants."

She blinked in figuring that one out. Her lips parted and she looked up at him very seriously instead of looking down his body.

Gus said, "Before we get too serious, we need—"

"Before!"

Gus went on, "Yeah. We need to take you out to see where we live."

"When?"

"In the morning?"

"Why wait 'til then?"

"I'm gonna share your bed tonight. So if you don't want to live out yonder, I'll have that memory. And then there's Blackie."

"Blackie?"

"Blackie sleeps with me, generally—"

"Do you mean to imply that I would be replacing a dog?"

"I have to see if you can keep me warm."

Knowing he watched avidly, she was elaborate in her response. She pulled her mouth in an exaggerated tightness, she turned her head as if in monumental control and she drew in a great breath to expel it in exquisite tolerance.

He loved it all. And he chuckled softly just for her and because he couldn't help himself. But he didn't shout the laughter he felt, to celebrate her flirting.

With his hands stuffed in his trouser pockets, they went to the kitchen and no one was there. Hearing the boys' voices, the pair looked out the windows.

There was the aloof Agnes in her multi-shades of rust, silken, soft trousers and naked-shouldered blouse, playing ball with the two little boys. Even Ned could catch the soft cloth ball. Close enough.

"Your aunt is a wonder. Look at the ball she made."

"She's—interesting."

"I know a man who ought to meet her."

Cara looked at Gus. "Who?"

"You'll see."

With some contrived irritation, Cara asked, "If you hadn't intended to tell me about him, why did you have to mention him and get my curiosity up?"

Gus explained practically, "Because you'd tell Agnes, and she'd run."

Cara considered, then she said, "Probably."

Gus told her seriously, "Let me do it my way."

"You haven't been very energetic about getting around to me."

"You weren't ready. You got the divorce because you knew you ought not be married to somebody else."

"I only recently began to think about you. How did you know so soon?"

"I've known all along. I had my finger on your pulse."

"Through Ben?"

Gus nodded a couple of tiny nods and said, "And Mr. Schuller, Meg, Sidra—"

"Mr. *Schuller?* What would he even remember?"

"He does. I was there when you told him you had spare rooms for anyone coming to the reunion. He even told you I was in the back room. I had to wave my arms and scowl at him to get him to fake a regressive attitude."

Even as Cara was assimilating his using the words "regressive attitude," she asked, "You were there?"

"Yeah."

Cara was somewhat indignant. In realization, she gasped, "Why, he *looked* at the back of the store for a long time when I asked if you really were there. Then he asked if I was going to the prom this spring."

"Yeah. I waved him off telling you."

"So his memory loss is a fake?"

"Mostly."

Cara exclaimed, "Why... the fraud!"

"Don't tell. He has a wonderful time, and it isn't all fake. He has periods of not remembering or thinking it's years ago. He quotes his wife as if she's still alive. He tells me she has lunch waiting."

"How often are you in town?"

"Every chance."

"I haven't seen you but that once."

"I know. You hardly ever go on the path across the woods. You were so surprised to see me."

"I didn't know you were anywhere around."

"I wanted to hold you and comfort you. I know how much you miss your folks."

"You helped. You didn't talk about them at all."

"I didn't know what to say."

"You talked about something concerning the ecology."

He said it very easily, "I have a degree in environmental preservation. After I got the high-school equivalency certificate, the government sent me to school. I'm paying off my school debts taking care of fragile West TEXAS lands. TEXAS is always said and wri—"

"I know. No one told me what you were doing. They just said you were way the hell out West in a nothing place."

Gus nodded a couple of times and replied, "That describes it pretty well."

"Do you get . . . lonely?"

"I'm not a gregarious man."

She blinked. That wasn't a word he'd probably know. "A loner?"

He smiled at her. "Not recently."

"Who do the kids play with?"

"We aren't that isolated. There are other people around. A variety of nationalities. There're other kids. We meet at least once a week just to hear other voices.''

She guessed, ''A companionable group of friends?''

''Not entirely. There's a sticker burr or two, but they're tolerant of me.''

And she laughed.

So THAT EVENING, they cleaned up reasonably. Taking a clue from Agnes's lovely outfit, Cara wore a long silk skirt, which appeared to be quite casual. Her blouse was long sleeved, but it was cut quite low. Her cleavage was apparent.

Gus asked softly, ''You got a safety pin?''

She found one, and he pinned the neck of her blouse together.

She watched his face as he did that, and he finally looked into her eyes.

Neither of them said anything. He'd censored her clothing, and she'd allowed it.

The safety pin amused Agnes especially, but when they arrived at Ben's, he laughed. Maddie looked at Cara as if a harlot had been detected and censored.

Ben's kids were open and friendly to the two little strangers. It didn't take long for the new friends to fit in. They had a normal time of playing, laughing and resisting each other. But the adults sorted them out—enough.

Around Gus, Maddie was just like any other woman. She was silly. Cara looked at Ben with shock, then she glared at Maddie. Gus and Ben and even Agnes appeared not to notice Maddie's appalling flirtatious behavior.

Cara found the opportunity to say to her brother with some strident indignation, "Maddie is not behaving like a married woman."

Ben said easily, "She's competitive. Once you're safely married, she'll relax."

"But doesn't it bother you that your wife is making a fool of herself with another man?"

"You need to notice that Gus is only being courteous."

That showed how adult Ben was. Maybe Cara was right in believing she hadn't made full adulthood as yet.

When only Cara and Maddie were in the kitchen, Cara said with a smile, "Gus put the safety pin on my decolletage."

Maddie retorted, "Somebody should have!"

After that, Maddie observed Gus, how he handled himself and to whom he spoke. He really talked to them all, but even as he spoke to the others, he'd look at Cara to be sure she was listening to him.

Soon, Maddie was touching and glancing at Ben. He smiled at her and was just darling without being silly about it. Cara considered the Porters were all superior people.

Well, there was Agnes, the aunt who was not usual. And there'd been her parents who had been remarkable people, most of the time.

Gus interrupted what he was saying to ask, "Cara? What's wrong?"

She lifted her glance to him in surprise, but she replied, "I was wishing our parents were here."

And Ben said, "Yes."

Then Gus told several stories that were hilarious about times he'd witnessed Tom Porter doing something typical. One concerned an old lady, and one was about Mr. Schuller. There was one that was a tender scene between Mr. Porter and Cara, and another was about one of Ben's serious rebellions.

They laughed until tears ran and their cheeks were tired. Agnes knew earlier stories.

In all the shifting around of people and kids, Cara found Maddie had taped the remembrances. Cara told her, "You're really bright." Maddie was pleased with the compliment.

It was then when Cara realized she'd been so wrapped up in her own life, that she'd neglected the overtures of friendship with Maddie. Maddie had been vying for Ben's entire attention while Cara assumed she had first claim on her brother.

She looked at Maddie and said, "Ben was lucky to find you."

And Maddie burst into tears!

It was a sloppy, sentimental time. Even as Ben comforted his wife and found her a clean handkerchief in his pocket, he smiled and smiled and smiled at—Cara. He said, "You're growing up."

Cara replied, "At last!"

Even Maddie laughed, but in a watery way.

But Gus's low laugh carried such knowledgeable pleasure and delight in Cara that her body was only aware of Gus.

When they were ready to leave Ben's house, Cara had said it was time to leave only about twenty times. After probably the twelfth time, Gus found he needed to cough hard in order to cover his hilarity.

By then, the two littlest visitors were sound asleep on a sofa.

Ben and Gus carried the boys to the truck, as Agnes and Cara helped Maddie tidy up.

When they were ready to leave, Cara hugged Maddie and said, "Thank you for a wonderful evening. May I have a copy of the tape?"

"Of course." Maddie was still in a vacuum of amazement over Cara's conduct. Ben would go to sleep that night with Maddie still exclaiming.

Aunt Agnes put her arm around Cara's shoulders as they walked out to the truck. She said, "I wondered how long it might take you. I'm proud of you."

With some insight, Cara mentioned a bit vacantly, "I never even thought about Maddie."

Agnes reminded Cara, "You gave her the furniture."

With honesty, Cara replied, "I did that for Ben. I knew Maddie was nagging him."

"Welll..."

"I've been an unthinking witch with her. I never paid much attention to her."

"You're a spoiled only child."

Cara exclaimed, "You forget Ben?"

"He was raised normally. Your father spoiled you. He thought you were a miracle."

Cara closed her eyes a little and smiled a cat's smile. "Of course."

Gus asked, "What are you two discussing, that Cara would look thataway?"

"I said she was spoiled rotten as a child."

Gus chided, "Never."

And Cara laughed.

So Agnes tilted her head back and quoted, "Precede as you expect to go on."

"I gotta start beating her right away?" He was elaborately aghast.

Ben said, "No." His voice was pleasant, but the warning was there.

"Now, Ben, you know me better'n that."

Cara spoke. "There will be a new Cara in the future. Courteous, considerate and compassionate."

Agnes mumbled, "Hallelujah, Lord."

Gus just smiled at his love.

Since the boys were asleep on the seat next to the driver, Agnes drove while Gus and Cara sat on the truck bed.

The gears were some problem for Agnes and an adventure of a kind. Gus's teeth lost some strength, but Cara didn't hear any of it.

The moon was out, the spring evening was cool, and Gus was there beside her. Cara took off her shoes and slid down to hang her feet off the back end of the truck bed.

Gus was right there. He put his arm in front of her across her body and held to the end of the truck bed. He said, "I've always been under the impression you were levelheaded and logical."

She suggested, "You'd better be more careful and do some research on me before you entrap me completely."

He frowned down at her. "I'd planned to do extensive research tonight. But your character hadn't been considered as a subject, before now."

"You—probably—ought not sleep—in my bed."

"You could be right."

She took a deep, despairing breath, and her breasts pushed against his restraining arm.

He said, "Other research might be more... pressing."

She bit his arm, enough.

He kissed her. It was just a miracle they both didn't bounce off the back of the truck when Agnes went over the bump. But Gus's hands were like iron locks on the back edge of the truck bed and on the side of the truck.

Cara mentioned, "Sitting on the edge with me this way could be dangerous."

"Honey, you've been dangerous for one reason or another all your born days."

"Nonsense."

In a town the size of Williamsfield, even a cater-cornered ride wasn't that long. Having arrived back at the Porter house, Gus and Cara carried the kids while Agnes held the doors.

When they got inside, Gus whispered to Cara, "Sit there. I'll be right back."

So Cara sat, still holding Ned. He was totally out and limp. She looked down at the sleeping child and something stirred inside her chest she hadn't known existed.

Agnes had gone up the stairs to open bedroom doors. Gus said, "They sleep naked." And he eased the lax Willy onto the bed. Then he left Agnes there with the child.

Gus went back downstairs, so it was Agnes who eased the heavily sleeping Willy out of his clothes and into bed. And it was she who stood, and something similar to Cara's experience touched in the chest of Agnes. How strange.

Staunchly, Agnes recalled that little boys don't sleep all the time, looking like angels.

She went to the top of the stairs and whispered "Good night," to Cara who led Gus with Ned, up the stairs.

The adults smiled and nodded in turn. Agnes went to her own room and gently closed the door. She was quite serious as she disrobed and prepared for bed. Earlier, Agnes had gone out to the barn to be sure the horses had water, and she'd seen the flattened hay.

She'd been in barns before. She'd been in that barn as an experimenting adolescent. She knew what caused hay to be flattened in that manner.

Agnes debated whether she was concerned or envious.

AS GUS CAME INTO Cara's room through the connecting door, she lay silently interested in how he would approach her. He came over to the bed without hesitating and slid in on that side.

He reached for her and gasped with a surprised, indrawn breath. "You're naked!"

"Well, you did say you all slept naked."

"That's mostly to help with the wash. If you move in with us, we'll probably have to have nightclothes." He sighed in a hugely burdened way.

"Some adjustments?" she inquired with courtesy.

"Yeah."

"Well, I could just stay here."

"No." It was quickly said, like slapping a hand to kill a mosquito.

She moved over just a little and slid her hand along under the top sheet until she could touch his body. He didn't have any clothing on, either. She gasped.

"Fred slept in a tux?"

Cara replied, "While he was a formal man, he did have night-clothes."

"I don't wanna think of him fooling around with you."

"He was very neat and quick."

And Gus laughed.

"In all those years," she chided, "I never knew the pleasure I shared with you today in the barn."

He said, "Good." He took her close to him and his breathing was very audible.

His body hair was a texture that was erotic to her soft skin. She wiggled a bit to feel it against her sensitive breasts, against her stomach, under her hands and with the inside of her thigh.

In a rather smug questioning, Gus inquired, "Missed having a man around?"

"You can't be so dense you don't understand that I've never known this marvelous salaciousness with sex."

"It's hard to believe, when I haven't made much effort to get you in this position."

"I like it...with you."

"Oh, Cara, how I've dreamed of you."

"I didn't. I haven't dreamed of you. I've thought about you, but I didn't yearn before this. I had no idea it could be this way. I thought all those books and films were imagination. Now I feel I've been cheated."

"Not anymore."

"But I wonder if Fred wasn't cheated, too."

"Forget him. He isn't your problem. Anyway, he's married again."

"Fred found another woman? This soon? How'd he do that?" She was astonished.

"You can ask him in four more days."

"Why, Gus, I couldn't do that. It would be rude."

"He'll ask what you're doing with me."

"I couldn't possibly tell him we were together in this bed."

Gus jerked up. "He was in *this* bed? With *you?*"

"Good heavens, no. The bed is relatively new. This room was mine all my life. Fred never slept here. We lived just down the road."

"I remember that, but I thought . . . well, never mind."

"No bed I shared with Fred was special." She then hastened to add earnestly, "He was a very pleasant person."

"I find this a weird subject at this particular time." And she smothered her laughter.

"Do you think I'm a very pleasant person?"

"I believe you're a remarkable man. People are drawn to you. You're a leader. I find you stimulate emotions inside me that no one else's presence touches. You make me feel that I need to touch you."

"Where."

"Well, I want to put my hand on you."

More urgently, even softer he asked, "Where." His voice was foggy.

"Anywhere at all." She was earnest.

"Go ahead and touch me . . . anywhere at all."

She moved her hand on his hairy chest and told him, "I already am. Haven't you noticed?"

"Lower." And he kissed her thrillingly. His mouth was sweet and searching on hers. It was gentle and coaxing. He shivered.

Her hand petted the hair around his navel.

His hand enclosed her breast and began to work it, gently squeezing and rubbing. He said in a guttural voice, "Lower."

And she encountered his eager sex. She laughed in her throat as it bobbled with her touch. She was surprised to hear that sexy sound coming from her.

Cara remembered a woman on TV laughing with the same sound. The actors were in bed. It was very dark, so dark the viewer couldn't really see anything. Was she a good actress or was she really doing something just this—personal—and had the actor's sex reacted like Gus's?

Of course not. With all those people around and watching? Nobody would be deliberately aroused.

Gus kissed her again. And his lips caressed hers softly, sweetly, relishing her. Then his mouth went to her ear, and the thrills were such that she grasped his sex quite hard!

His breath went out in a *whoosh!*

"Did I hurt you?"

"Do it again."

"You animal."

Gus was serious. "I am, you know. I'm a very basic man. I had to have you. I've dreamed of you for so long. Kiss me. Kiss me and tell me you want me. Tell me you need me."

"I would really like to do it again with you. I like the feel of you. But, Gus, today might have been a fluke. After all those years to finally... I might not ever..."

"Kiss me."

He was so gentle in such a violent manner as he kissed her and moved against her, allowing her to feel the strength of him, the texture of him and the need he had.

She felt. She was almost fainting with all the rush of desire which flooded her senses. Low in her throat, she moaned, and his responding sound was another agony.

His mouth became greedier, and his hands were harder. His breaths were harsh, and his body crowded hers.

His fingers were surprisingly gentle as he probed to see if she was ready, to feel the differences of her that were so feminine.

She curled her hips to meet his hand, and he gasped with reaction. She found her body doing things it never had, as she rubbed against him and stretched along him and wiggled against him. She was shockingly bold, but she didn't quit. Her hunger made her teasing, taunting, demanding.

She slithered on his sweaty body and she loved the feel of it. She loved how hot he was and how eagerly demanding was his sex.

The sexual smell in the bed was potent, and she breathed it as she went a little wild. She rubbed against him and her thighs opened to him. She tugged on him, wanting him.

And he complied.

He raised up, and she lay flat, reaching, grasping, guiding him to her, curling her body to him and taking him.

Gus chuffed and blew air and gasped and sank into her with a smothered groan.

The hall door opened in the other room and a naked little boy asked, "Daddy? I lost the bathroom."

There was dead silence. Then Gus's strangled voice called, "Go out in the hall. I'll be there in just a minute."

"Okay."

Braced on his elbows, Gus breathed deeply a couple of times, then he slowly, reluctantly pulled himself from Cara. He said, "Don't move one muscle. I'll be right back."

Cara lay wide-eyed and abandoned for a whole minute before the laughter came. She did everything not to laugh, but it only built and exploded in silent gasps.

Eventually, Gus returned. He came to the bed whispering, "Of all the times to— Honey? Are you crying?" He was appalled.

She shook her head with her hands over her mouth. Her eyes sparkled so with the tears of laughter that Gus thought she was upset. He asked, "What's the matter?"

And she took her hands away and said, "It's just—so—fu*nnnyyy!*"

"No." He was sure. He got back into bed and lay flat on his back.

She leaned up and over his lax body and said, "So you've lost interest?"

"A man has a tough time of it. He needs some care and consideration. Tender care. I need a woman who'll treasure me."

"Aaahhh."

He completed the lecture. "Not one who laughs because a kid interrupts me in the middle of a really spectacular—uh—coupling."

"It's ruined?" She put her hand on his less-rigid member.

He moved his eyes. She saw that because the streetlight caught a glint as he did. He said, "It might be coaxed alive again by an earnest woman who is tenderhearted."

Cara pulled back a little as she said a thoughtful, "Oh." Then she said, "Mmm." And she looked at the ceiling. "I wonder who we could get to help out."

He grabbed her, turned her over onto her back and said, "It's you, you dummy!"

"I'm not at *all* tend—"

But he kissed her and did all sorts of outrageous things to her body, to her mind and to her libido. She breathed fire and writhed and struggled to get at him, and he finally allowed her to do as she wanted.

And she did.

Their coupling was actually very quickly done. It apparently wasn't any time at all before they were sprawled out, their breaths laboring, their bodies inert, their brains ruined for all time by just the *heat* of it all.

And when he could, he asked, "Who the hell *are* you?"

With her eyes closed and through puffy lips that could no longer work, she replied in her literal way, "Cara Porter."

Chapter Five

IN THE FOUR HOURS they traveled west, the nasty, thorny, scrawny, lacy mesquite trees were even shorter. Cara had never ventured in that direction, and she was noncommittal about the trip. She watched out of the truck windows as, pulling the horse trailer, they drove on west from Williamsfield.

She mentioned, "This is the first interstate highway that's been two-lane."

"We're exclusive out thisaway. Closer. Friendlier."

Soon the trees were sparse. Even the young trees were gnarled, twisted and tough, their barks rough and hard. The leaves were small. The vacant land was taken over by sharp cacti, sparse growth and a further lack of moisture.

Cara was surprised to notice that the changing land had a beauty of its own.

Here, too, the barbed wire was strung along. TEXANS never realized there was an "r" in barbed. They called it bob wire. But it astonished Cara that anyone would bother with fencing anything. There wasn't anything out there to fence in. The deer and wild horses could easily jump over those wires.

The two little boys were loose in the confines of the space behind the solid front seat. They talked. They took turns sitting in the middle, up front. There was an extra seat belt.

In the back, they had pillows. There were picture books, stubby crayons and coloring books.

The truck radio was on, and there were occasional chatty CB communications. No problems, just contacts.

The dog had the truck bed to himself.

Cara considered the passing scenery. It was different from the Williamsfield area. She said, "It's very different from . . . San Antone."

Gus understood the pause was to move the comparison even farther east. He replied, "You get used to it. Then the eastern part of TEXAS looks sickly lush instead of this unobtrusive cleanness. This is pure land. It's staunch."

"It's fragile."

"That, too. That's why I'm out here."

She guessed, "To...learn to be fragile?" And she laughed over the impossibility of him changing.

"To defend and protect this wonderland."

"Oh-oh. You don't intend leaving when your debts are paid off?"

"It's crowded back yonder." Gus looked around at the unoccupied vista as he drove the remarkably preserved truck.

"So you're not a facade, after all. You really are a very basic man."

"Yeah." He looked at her to share the amusement that such a cultured woman was going to have to live clear out there.

She inquired, "How big is this place where you live?"

"It's big enough."

She reminded him, "I'm a city woman."

He laughed. "In *Williamsfield,* you can claim that?"

"Readily."

"Well, you did grow up on the hill, but, honey, that little old one-horse town ain't all that cosmopolitan."

"Now, how did a hick like you learn a word like that." It was one of the questioning statements, which invites a reply.

Gus responded in an instructing manner, "There's a magazine so named, which all us males go through every month? It means 'slick women' are shown."

She instructed gently, "The word means elegance, erudition, élan."

He turned his head so that his chin was above his upper right arm as he observed this creature sharing the front seat of his truck. His whitened eyelashes almost covered his eyes, and he said, "I'm erudite."

And she responded instantly, "Of course."

He looked ahead at the long, empty road and said, "Aren't you glad we've got these two busy little boys in the cab with us, or we'd be off the road by now, and I'd be undres—I'd better not even think about it."

Did she get prickly or flirty? No, she laughed.

Gus said, "The next time, we'll bring Agnes along. She was kind not to insist she come along this time."

He watched Cara shrug as she replied, "No one will ask her where we've gone. They all think she's so strange that nothing would surprise them. And they *did* see us leave. So they know we did leave of our own accord and weren't blotted away by a toss of Agnes's head."

OUT IN THE MIDDLE of nowhere, his "place" was a marvelous conglomeration of cared-for buildings. There were wire-strung metal fenceposts near the house. Nearby, the well had a wide roof covering. And shading the porch were some cherished trees. One bunch were small pin oaks. Scrawny and rough, they were hostile to one's touch.

Blackie got out and greeted the other dogs. It was a surprise to see the discipline of the animals. They stood grinning, wagging their tails and waiting for a greeting.

The greetings were accomplished with a tussle of hugs from the little boys, after which the dogs went about their business.

The house—fit. It was exactly right. It was one story, but it sprawled out. The covered porch went around the house entirely. And there was a wider second roof above the original one. It looked like a low-held umbrella. Inside the wind space between the two roofs were all kinds of birds, but they were monitored by the cats.

Even the barn had a wider, second roof. She said, "I've never seen that before."

"It's experimental. We borrowed the idea from New Guinea. We're seeing if a really impressive cyclone'll take it off. But it keeps the house wonderfully cool."

They spent parts of two days at Gus's place.

Cara saw that the people working at the station were easy together. That evening, Gus invited the people from around and about for a big, leisurely supper, and they all came.

He laughed as they got out of their pickups and looked around. Even an old Comanche Indian lady came from her deathbed to meet the woman Gus had brought home for a visit.

In a doubtful whisper, Cara asked Gus, "Her *deathbed?*"

"She's bored and willing, but God isn't paying her any mind. With you here, she'll probably last another ten years."

There was a lazy-moving, sleepy-eyed, dark-haired man with a pirate's beard. Gus whispered, "He's the one for Agnes."

Cara was impressed. "Wow!"

But Gus told her, "Don't get excited. You're mine."

His words made her eyes sparkle, and she licked at her smile.

An additional interest was an artist. Everyone knows artists are peculiar. They're a little like writers. The female, self-designated artist spent the whole time making sketches of people.

Another guest told Cara, "She's in competition to do a panel in the old, renovated post office? God knows why. We seriously doubt she could trade the use of her body to influence the judges. What man'd want that chore? But she is *in* the running. Her work is so strange. No one knows why she's going to the bother of actually sketching anyone, unless she's going to allow us to bribe her not to include us? We just pray she isn't chosen, because they might label the images on the wall as us."

The area judge couldn't remember what happened yesterday, and everyone kindly supplied names when he was telling the familiar, long-ago stories.

Fortunately, they were reasonably normal people, and everyone appeared cheerful. They all liked Gus.

Along with the visiting children, the kids were put to bed during the evening. Gus did that. And the guests stayed and stayed. It was really a very nice evening, and Cara enjoyed it all.

With the guests finally gathering their kids and taking their leave, the two were finally alone. Gus showed her to her room, kissed her at the door and then went into the room with her.

She protested in whispers, but her arms were over his shoulders, her body was pressed to his and her hands were in his hair.

He growled in a hushed whisper, "Let go'a me, you scarlet woman. I've been trying to peel you off my body since I first caught a glimpse of you earlier this week."

She sputtered a laugh.

"See? Now you're making sexy sounds to lure me."

She shook her head, gasping, because he was undressing her.

He did that quite well.

And he was even more skilled at getting his own clothes off. Her bed was conveniently close, and they slid into it with no problem.

She told him in a hushed tone, "You can quit being host and go to your own room. You don't have to be this conscientious."

"I'm grateful for a compassionate woman. You do the seducing. I'm exhausted, driving you here, entertaining you, entertaining the whole countryside, no rest—"

"How put-upon you are."

"Rub me here." He placed her hand. "I hurt so bad."

"There?"

"Yeah. Women get headaches if they aren't rubbed in a similar place." He kissed her marvelously, his own hands soothing and stimulating her.

She smoothed her hand along him. "I hadn't known that."

"Since you learned how relaxing it is, you get uppity."

She tilted her head and watched her hand and his reaction to it. "I've never needed sex. It wasn't a priority. However, I am compassionate. Let me stroke your forehead."

"My forehead is fine—keep rubbing there."

"I'm really not calming you at all. It's frustrated and anxious. I should stop."

"I'll show you how to control it. It needs direction." So he turned her flat and carefully encased it.

She said, "Well, how remarkable. It does fit."

"Naturally."

"With you, there is a question. If it hadn't been so dark at home, I probably would have demurred."

He laughed low and wickedly.

He investigated her and teased her. He made love to her in ways she hadn't ever imagined people actually doing such. He was a wonder. He was delicious in the things he did to her. Her body loved his innovations and writhed to get closer to him.

She found her breasts had become heavy and needful of his attention. Her knees rubbed restlessly and her body turned as her shoulders moved to attract him.

He was assuredly attracted. His hands shook and his hair trembled with his pounding heartbeats. His breathing was harsh and his muffled moans and gasps were thrilling to her intensely alert libido.

Their coupling was exquisite, and their ride was marvelously wild. They struggled to the ultimate gasp and held rigid, shiveringly clenched for that brief pause before they fell back, swirling through the thundering climax.

As they recovered, she mumbled, "I'm not sure this is wise. You are so debilitating."

He muttered slowly, "I've got you addicted. You'll be clawing at me for the rest of our lives."

After a silent time, she mumbled, "You may be right."

She was almost dozing when he heaved up from her bed and said, "We've made your bed look slept in, now we have to go and fix mine."

Relaxed, she stretched her naked body and turned to her side as she pushed her pillow up under her head. She said, "Run along. You can do that by yourself."

"Like hell!" He scooped her up and staggered in exaggerated stumblings as he complained, "You had breakfast again. I told you to fast. Why do you think it's called fast."

"If you will replace the first word, it is 'break', which means you break the night's 'fast' and eat."

"How'd you know that?"

She turned her head in pseudo-boredom and sighed hugely with the burden of knowledge.

Apparently just carrying her to his room was an aphrodisiac. He had to see how replete she was, and the investigation just set things off again! It was amazing.

She couldn't understand it. She gasped and whispered and denied she wanted to go through it all again, but she rubbed her body against his hot one and darned if it didn't all happen just like before.

As they were recuperating from their feverish tangle and lazily petting one another, Cara asked, "Why is it they are all just a little strange?"

Her comment appeared to surprise Gus. "Who?"

"Your guests. Remember, earlier?"

And he had the gall to reply, "My people are strange? How can Agnes Porter's niece ask such a question?"

"You speak differently out in these here parts."

He gestured with a floppy hand. "I've been careful not to give you a false impression."

She smothered laughter.

That made him sound indignant. "No. Come on, now you're *supposed* to be impressed. If I'd'a come on to you wearing a suit and acting like I'd been to Paris, you'd have frozen up."

And Cara knew he was right. "How did you realize I'd be that way?"

Yawning, he said, "I've made a lifelong study of you. I know every facet of your personality, and I can handle you."

"I've certainly noticed the handling part."

"I have to get used to you."

"Then you'll quit?"

"Yeah. In about a hundred years."

Cara had been meaning to inquire about the horses. She hadn't been long in realizing the two horses who'd visited her backyard were only a part of the place's working string. This was her first opportunity to ask, "When you came to my house, why did you have the horses with you?"

"Hmm?"

"When you came to stay with me, why did you have the horses along? They weren't ailing. Even if they were, you have a perfectly good vet not far from here. You weren't selling them, so why did you bring them to Williamsfield?"

He guessed, "An outing?"

"Guuusss."

He was perfectly logical. "So you wouldn't throw me out."

"What?"

And Gus explained as he moved his fingers gently in her hair. "Even if I'd just brought the boys along, you could have suggested we'd be more comfortable in the hotel. With the horses and Blackie in your backyard, you were trapped."

"How sneaky."

"By this time, I've given you enough time to experience the world. It's time for you to settle down and devote yourself to me."

"I've looked around," she told him. "And I see no reason or need for me here."

"You're tolerant. You ride well. You're curious, and you entertain me."

She sighed hugely, deliberately lifting her naked chest. "That again."

He drew back as if shocked, but his voice was a low, sexual growl. "You voracious woman!"

"How do you know that word. Your vocabulary is amazing. From when you arrived at my house with your 'Me Tarzan, you, Jane' limitation, you've gone ahead in great leaps with communication."

"It's the injections you've given me."

She laughed. "You have that backward."

In shock, he inquired, "We haven't been doing it right? How crass. Show me the right way."

"How interesting for you to claim ignorance. You told me just last night that all TEXAS boys were born knowing how to love a woman."

"Well, that's true. But Eastern women have tricks us Western boys don't know. Teach me." Then he added in kind elaboration, proving her qualifications, "Williamsfield is east of here."

"Are you saying Williamsfield is Eastern? The citizens will be indignant."

"They think of themselves as Western?"

"Yes. And what about here? Do you consider this the ultimate part of the West? There's all the rest of TEXAS, New Mexico, Arizona and California, on out west of here."

"At this point, there's very little real TEXAS left out thataway."

"So you don't count New Mexico and Arizona as Western?"

"Neither is named TEXAS." He shrugged as if that ended the discussion.

But she persisted. "San Antonio doesn't even realize we claim affiliation with the state. They believe the word TEXAS is synonymous with San Antonio."

"That's 'cause they got the Alamo."

"Ahhh." She made the sound of information received. She confirmed it, "Of course." However, she couldn't resist arguing, "But out here, I can see where New Mexico might think they're as Western as we are... and perhaps, just a tad more?"

"Even if they thought they were equal to TEXAS, they'd beg for an audience and listen, since they know they can never be TEXANS."

"Are you this insufferable because you're a descendent of the William Freeman who sold the land for Williamsfield?"

"Probably."

"Then, with that reply," she surmised, "you admit you could be prejudiced?"

"Now, that's doubtful."

"Why?"

He yawned hugely. "I'll hire just about anyone, and I'll marry you."

"I don't believe I've asked you."

He settled her in his arms and nuzzled her cheek. Sleepily confident, he said, "You will."

THE LITTLE BOYS came in and climbed into bed with them the next morning. Cara was embarrassed, but no one seemed to notice. She tucked the sheet around her and watched as Gus and the boys tumbled around and laughed.

Gus took the boys to a different shower down the hall, and Cara used the one between their rooms. Over cotton underthings, she pulled on slacks and shirt. She chose tennies instead of boots.

Being a TEXAN, she shook out her clothing and emptied her tennis shoes with a thump. And in the second one, there was a scorpion. She gasped and shivered even as she squashed it. Their sting could be painful.

When one is found, there is always a second one. And she searched for it, finally finding it in last night's shirt so carelessly pitched at the chair when Gus had first taken off her clothing.

The insect, too, was dispatched with her shoe. Although the supposition is there are always two scorpions, it didn't particularly comfort her to be sure she'd squashed two. What if there were four? She didn't find another.

She combed her hair and put on sunscreen and makeup. Then she sought food.

The other hands at the station had eaten and were gone. The cook was reading the paper with a cup of coffee at his elbow. The dishwasher was running. Everything was neat.

Gus and the boys were at the table, and they looked up to witness her entrance. They greeted her.

To realize everything was already past being started was a little diminishing. She responded, "Good morning."

Gus was already watching her with such a possessive smile.

The two boys laughed, their faces bright and clean as they ate from cereal bowls. They were surprisingly tidy eaters. They then carried their dishes to the sink as they left the kitchen.

"Where are they going?" she asked Gus.

He replied, "They each have a school desk with the required supplies. Both boys are blessed with being interested and they watch the lessons for the day. Those are taped for replay on the VCR."

"Why did you choose for them to learn at home?"

"That was decided before the boys came along. The bus trip took too much time. The parents around here get all the kids together every other weekend. They go over the material they've learned, they have a cookout and learn to do that and they visit. The parents visit, too."

"There are people who teach their kids at home in the cities."

"This is a local solution. Busing not only takes too much time. Too much education money goes into buses and gasoline. But the actual riding hours were what triggered this change. I approve of it. There were very few of the isolated houses that didn't have a television. We solved that. When the time comes, they'll board at school during the week and come home weekends."

"Awww."

"It'll be good for them. They'll be around other kids and learn to rub along with them. They'll make lifelong friends."

"How old will they be?"

"Oh, about fourteen or fifteen."

Cara was appalled. "I remember my grandmother quoting from the poem, 'My son John who went to sea—' And in the poem, they never heard from him again. He'd been fifteen. They didn't ever know what happened to him."

Gus assured her, "We'll keep close tabs on these."

"Fourteen is young."

"No." He shook his head. "Fifteen is the time when a boy wants to live in a hotel and visit his family on occasion."

She remembered the independent fifteen-year-old Gus, trapped with an abusive man who used him as a peon. And Gus had wanted to be free. He was. He'd made it. He'd changed his life. It'd taken time and perseverance, but he'd made it.

After breakfast, Cara changed into boots and got her hat.

They went to the corral, saddled horses, and Gus took her out and about. He showed her what they were doing to encourage new grasses. Actually, the grasses were old ones which could survive the hot, dry climate.

The original grasses were as hardy and tough as the cacti, but too many cattle had been run in that area and the place had been overgrazed. To hold the soil and some of the moisture, the ecology had to be reverted to olden ways.

"It's interesting," Gus told Cara. "A challenge. The people out here are ready to cooperate. It's logical."

So was he. Cara studied him with glances and listened to him. She looked at the land and lifted her face to the breeze.

He asked, "Do you know we're almost closer to the Pacific than to the Gulf of Mexico? It's like Hawaii. That state is five hundred miles closer to Japan than it is to our mainland? So if you're on one of the Hawaiian Islands and they sink, you swim for Japan because it's closer."

"I'm so grateful for that information."

He nodded. "You seemed the practical type."

"Being practical, you have to realize I must return home today? I'm on the reunion committee. Sidra will be having fits if I'm not there."

"There's no hurry." He smiled at her lazily.

"If we don't show up, they're going to wonder where we are."

"They'd probably guess about right." He'd led them to a place where the new old grass was flourishing. He dismounted and left the reins to trail along as the horse moved away. Gus said, "Come down and see this growth."

She said practically, "If your horse left, would I be unable to follow and convince him to return?"

"He'll come with a whistle."

"You're that sure." It was a statement.

"Yeah. Come down here. I want to initiate you into being a native."

Cautiously, she eyed him with a very tiny beginning smile. "How do you intend doing that?"

"I'm not good at oblique explanations. I'm a hands-on man."

"What about this horse?"

"He's chancy, but we'd still have the one."

"My eagerness embarrasses me. If I slide down off this animal, it will make me seem willing."

"You are."

"I know, but I could be more subtle."

"I didn't say you had to take off your own clothes and parade around nak—"

She waited, but his head was back, his mouth was open and he was breathing oddly. She looked around in some alarm. "What's wrong."

"My libido wants you to take off your clothes and parade around naked. The idea was almost too much for the rest of me."

"I probably could do that." She slid off her horse. "Do I drop the reins the way you did?"

He nodded very seriously. If she was really going to do a strip for him, how would he survive? He felt his blood pressure might go into overdrive.

However, although she was very amused, she was a little shy. She didn't undress to tease. She simply, neatly undressed! And she didn't know to tease and taunt. She just...undressed.

She ruined him.

She glanced at him. She would check to see if she had his attention. She folded *every*thing neatly.

She didn't deliberately jiggle or pose or shiver or turn to display herself.

It was just so natural and innocent that he couldn't believe her. Hadn't she ever seen any of the tapes? Apparently not.

And married as long as she was, she was an innocent. Fred was a fool! But Gus had her now. She was untouched clay. He could mold her. And his breathing was harsh.

He was very utilitarian about taking off his own clothing. It never occurred to him to do it otherwise. To him, only men were interested in women and, in turn, it never entered his mind to tease her.

Since he hadn't delayed at all, he was already naked when she was just removing her trousers. She glanced up and was surprised.

He grinned and said, "Fortunately, we don't have to use any condoms."

"Plural?" She was somewhat uncertain.

He put his arms out from his naked body and smiled at her. "Who knows?"

Sometime later, as he lay depleted and inert, she said, "It's probably just as well that I'm sterile. How would we get to a hospital?"

Barely able to speak, he replied, "It takes longer to deliver one than just in an afternoon. There's warning."

"I know that."

Then he questioned, "You gonna stay with me?"

"You'd have to marry me first."

"Okay." Then he reared up, proving he wasn't inert, and he grabbed her. "You finally *asked* me!"

"Good grief."

WHILE THEY MADE IT back to Williamsfield in time for the reunion, they were still sleeping together. They were so mellow and placid that they weren't worth the space they took up.

Fred was courteous, Sidra hostile and Maddie had become very tolerant of Cara. Everyone was glad to see Gus, but he never let go of Cara. Even when she went to the ladies' room, he stood outside the door and waited for her.

It was no great surprise the lovers were married the next week. But they were married twice.

The first time was in Williamsfield. The town was still talking about it years later. They said it was certainly the *fastest* courtship they'd *ever* witnessed! And Maddie had cried all the way through the ceremony and reception because Cara had given Ben the Porter house.

The newlyweds' second marriage was out in the outer limits, where they would live.

At one point, Cara had mentioned, "Twice?"

And Gus had replied, "Being married once doesn't work with you. I got to nail you in so as you can't wiggle outta this'un."

"I see."

That was done with Agnes there as their prime guest, along with Ben and Maddie and all the kids.

Agnes met the smoldering dark-haired man whom Gus had reserved for her. Agnes's instant interest was shared with that of her new acquaintance, whose ears perked up immediately and he lost his sleepy look.

AUGUSTUS FREEMAN WAS BORN four and a half years later. There were those who said, "Was it a surprise?" And Cara would reply, "No, not at all. It was a *shock!*"

Somehow an energetic, innovative, microscopic sperm had fought his stubborn way up one of Cara's clogged tubes—and made contact. Then he had had to struggle and encourage the egg to go back down the same impossible path. But the embedded sperm-guide was smart and recalled every wiggle and dodge. The two united units got where they were supposed to be in order to multiply and get organized into being a real baby. It was a miracle.

They called Augustus, Aw, because that's what everyone who heard about him, and what those who saw him, said. Cara added an "e" at the end of those two skimpy letters. It just seemed appropriate.

In spite of the resulting rampant confidence between the legal lovers, they never had another.

But they did live happily ever after.

1994 MISTLETOE MARRIAGES
HISTORICAL CHRISTMAS STORIES

With a twinkle of lights and a flurry of snowflakes, Harlequin Historicals presents *Mistletoe Marriages*, a collection of four of the most magical stories by your favorite historical authors. The perfect way to celebrate the season!

Brimming with romance and good cheer, these heartwarming stories will be available in November wherever Harlequin books are sold.

RENDEZVOUS by Elaine Barbieri
THE WOLF AND THE LAMB by Kathleen Eagle
CHRISTMAS IN THE VALLEY by Margaret Moore
KEEPING CHRISTMAS by Patricia Gardner Evans

Add a touch of romance to your holiday with *Mistletoe Marriages* Christmas Stories!

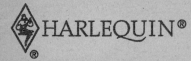

HARLEQUIN®

MMXS94

Fifty red-blooded, white-hot, true-blue hunks
from every State in the Union!

Look for MEN MADE IN AMERICA! Written by some of
our most popular authors, these stories feature fifty of
the strongest, sexiest men, each from a different state in
the union!

Two titles available every month at your favorite
retail outlet.

In September, look for:

WINTER LADY by Janet Joyce (Minnesota)
AFTER THE STORM by Rebecca Flanders (Mississippi)

In October, look for:

CHOICES by Annette Broadrick (Missouri)
PART OF THE BARGAIN by Linda Lael Miller (Montana)

You won't be able to resist MEN MADE IN AMERICA!

MIRA ™

The brightest star in women's fiction!

This October, reach for the stars and watch all your dreams come true with **MIRA BOOKS.**

HEATHER GRAHAM POZZESSERE
Slow Burn in October
An enthralling tale of murder and passion set against the dark and glittering world of Miami.

SANDRA BROWN
The Devil's Own in October
She made a deal with the devil...but she didn't bargain on losing her heart.

BARBARA BRETTON
Tomorrow & Always in November
Unlikely lovers from very different worlds...they had to cross time to find one another.

PENNY JORDAN
For Better For Worse in December
Three couples, three dreams—can they rekindle the love and passion that first brought them together?

The sky has no limit with **MIRA BOOKS**

Where do you find hot Texas nights, smooth Texas charm and dangerously sexy cowboys?

Crystal Creek reverberates with the exciting rhythm of Texas. Each story features the rugged individuals who live and love in the Lone Star state.

"...Crystal Creek wonderfully evokes the hot days and steamy nights of a small Texas community...impossible to put down until the last page is turned." —*Romantic Times*

Praise for Bethany Campbell's *The Thunder Rolls*

"Bethany Campbell takes the reader into the minds of her characters so surely...one of the best Crystal Creek books so far. It will be hard to top...."

—*Rendezvous*

"This is the *best* of the Crystal Creek series to date."
—*Affaire de Coeur*

Don't miss the next book in this exciting series. Look for
GENTLE ON MY MIND by BETHANY CAMPBELL

Available in October wherever Harlequin books are sold.

Harlequin® Historical

LOOK TO THE PAST FOR
FUTURE FUN AND EXCITEMENT!

The past the Harlequin Historical way, that is. 1994 is going to be a banner year for us, so here's a preview of what to expect:

* The continuation of our bigger book program, with titles such as *Across Time* by Nina Beaumont, *Defy the Eagle* by Lynn Bartlett and *Unicorn Bride* by Claire Delacroix.

* A 1994 March Madness promotion featuring four titles by promising new authors Gayle Wilson, Cheryl St. John, Madris Dupree and Emily French.

* Brand-new in-line series: DESTINY'S WOMEN by Merline Lovelace and HIGHLANDER by Ruth Langan; and new chapters in old favorites, such as the SPARHAWK saga by Miranda Jarrett and the WARRIOR series by Margaret Moore.

* *Promised Brides,* an exciting brand-new anthology with stories by Mary Jo Putney, Kristin James and Julie Tetel.

* Our perennial favorite, the Christmas anthology, this year featuring Patricia Gardner Evans, Kathleen Eagle, Elaine Barbieri and Margaret Moore.

Watch for these programs and titles wherever Harlequin Historicals are sold.

HARLEQUIN HISTORICALS...
A TOUCH OF MAGIC!

HHPROM094

HARLEQUIN®

Temptation®

HART GIRLS

Bestselling Temptation author Elise Title is back with a funny, sexy trilogy—THE HART GIRLS—written in the vein of her popular miniseries THE FORTUNE BOYS!

Rachel, Julie and Kate Hart are three women of the nineties with heart and spark. They're determined to win the TV ratings wars—and win the men of their dreams!

Stay tuned for:

#509 DANGEROUS AT HEART (October 1994)
#513 HEARTSTRUCK (November 1994)
#517 HEART TO HEART (December 1994)

Available wherever Harlequin books are sold.

SILHOUETTE®

Desire®

brings you 3 sexy tales of love from Lass Small...

In September 1994, look for LEMON (SD#879)—part of the Fabulous Brown Brothers series. When the Brown Brothers are good, they're very, very good. But when they're bad... they are fabulous!

Silhouette Desire also brings Lass Small's devoted fans a fun-filled Man of the Month in December 1994 and January 1995!

Be sure to meet the rugged, no-nonsense Clint Terrell as he "shacks up" with wild Wallis Witherspoon in AN OBSOLETE MAN (SD#895), Silhouette Desire's Man of the Month in December 1994.

And don't miss out on A NUISANCE (SD#901), Desire's Man of the Month title for January 1995. Confirmed bachelor Stefan Szyszko and roving reporter Carrie Pierce find their way to love in a town called Blink, Texas!